Ten

Jane Blythe

Bear Spots Publications
Melbourne Australia

Paperback
ISBN: 0-6484033-7-8
ISBN-13: 978-0-6484033-7-1

Cover designed by QDesigns

I'd like to thank everyone who played a part in bringing this story to life. Particularly my mom who is always there to share her thoughts and opinions with me. My awesome cover designer, Amy, who whips up covers for me so quickly and who patiently makes every change I ask for, and there are usually lots of them! And my lovely editor Mitzi Carroll, and proofreader Marisa Nichols, for all their encouragement and for all the hard work they put into polishing my work.

AUGUST 2ND

3:33 A.M.

Something startled her awake.

It took less than a second for her mind and body to snap to attention.

You didn't live a life like she had and not become perhaps the most paranoid person on the planet, or at least paranoid enough to expect the worst in any and all situations.

She didn't move a muscle.

If someone was in here, she didn't want them to know she was awake just yet.

There was a knife under her pillow.

She *always* slept with a knife under her pillow.

She knew that probably made her borderline crazy, but she already knew she was a paranoid nutjob when it came to safety.

With good reason.

She weighed her options. Her hand was close to the knife. Depending where the person in her room was, she might be able to grab it without them noticing. If, however, they were standing watching from in front of her, they would see any attempt she made at reaching for her weapon. Maybe waiting until they made their move before making her move would be the safer thing to do.

That someone was in the room was a given.

That they meant her harm was also a given.

All that remained to be seen was why.

For now, though, the why wasn't important. What *was* important was figuring out everything that she could before he decided he'd spent enough time waiting and did what he'd come here to do.

Focusing her senses, she tried to figure out where the man was. He wasn't close to the bed. Her door was open; she always slept with it closed. If she had to guess, he was standing in the doorway watching her.

She hated watchers.

She always thought they were more dangerous because they usually thought they had a reason for doing what they were doing. They weren't acting on instinct or in the heat of the moment. They were doing something they had probably spent a long time planning, and they wanted to savor every second.

Right now, she was wishing that she kept a gun under her pillow instead of a knife. A knife required her attacker being close enough for her to strike; a gun would have meant this was over already.

Even though this man had broken into her house in the middle of the night to harm her, she wouldn't have shot to kill. Just to incapacitate. She had killed someone before, and it still haunted her even though she knew she'd done the only thing she could to survive. She didn't want to do it again.

Her room was large, probably three times the size of the average master bedroom. The bed was on the opposite wall to the door, in between two large windows. Although the night was hot, both windows were closed. She was way too paranoid to ever go to sleep with her windows open.

It was probably nine or ten yards from the door to the bed; when he decided to move, he'd be on her in seconds. There were two chaise lounges and a coffee table between the bed and the door, he'd have to go around them, which gave her maybe an extra second.

She was going to have to time things perfectly.

One wrong move, and she'd be dead. Or wish she was.

Her life was going to come down to a matter of seconds.

No one was going to ride in on a white horse to save her. She was a widow with one son. The two of them lived alone in a huge mansion on a secluded estate. Her fifteen-year-old son's room was on a different floor, there was no way he could know what was going on. And if she screamed, she was putting him in danger.

That was something she would never do.

Her son was her life, and she wouldn't do anything to risk him getting hurt.

The person in her room moved.

She could sense it.

Feel it.

He took a step toward the bed, and then another.

Her hand reached for her weapon, her fingers curling around the handle of the knife.

She realized what was happening a split second too slowly.

She was already trying to move preemptively, but it was too late.

Pain flamed through her body like red hot lava.

Her body spasmed, and her limbs jerked uselessly instead of doing something to protect herself.

She tried to fight against it, but it was all she could do not to pass out.

The second she was incapacitated, her attacker pounced.

A strip of something soft covered her eyes and was tied behind her head. It was followed by another strip of material being shoved between her lips and tied in the same way.

By the time he yanked her arms behind her back, she was just regaining her ability to move.

She lunged forward, trying to grab her knife.

It was so close, and yet, so far away.

She wasn't coordinated enough yet to do anything productive, and the man easily kept control of her and bound her wrists and ankles, then lifted her and flung her over his shoulder.

She was being kidnapped.

Why?

Why couldn't he just kill her?

As long as he left her son alone, she was fine with him killing her.

If she didn't have a child, she'd have taken her own life years ago.

But she *did* have a son, and he still needed her, so she would do everything in her power to make sure that she wasn't ripped away from him.

It wasn't completely hopeless yet.

She still had a few tricks up her sleeve.

It was too bad she no longer had the security system. It was one she'd designed and built herself and it would have alerted her the second that the house had been breached.

But things had been quiet for so long.

She had grown complacent.

She'd thought she didn't need the fancy system anymore and gone with something more low-key, more normal.

Now she was paying the price.

She let herself go limp, letting her abductor take her full body weight. She wanted him to think that she was either unconscious or so terrified that she'd drifted into shock.

Unfortunately for this guy, this wasn't her first rodeo, and she didn't do shock like regular people.

She wasn't like regular people.

She never had been, and given everything she'd gone through in her life and everything she'd lost, she knew what she was doing. She knew how to fight back. She knew how to not give up, and if this guy hadn't done his homework and learned that about her, then he was in for a shock of his own.

The man carried her downstairs and out the front door, then tossed her into the back of a van.

The second he closed the doors, she worked free the small razor blade she kept in the band of her watch. Thankfully, he had tied her wrists together with fabric and not rope or plastic zip ties, and she cut through it in seconds. She ripped off the gag and the blindfold then reached into her pajama pocket. She carried around a disposable cell phone with her everywhere she went. Including in the pocket of her pajamas when she slept.

You could never be too careful.

There was only one number she wanted to call, and it wasn't 911.

Her best friend lived with his wife in a small cottage behind the main house. He was a retired cop and one of the very few people she actually trusted.

She dialed, and her friend answered on the second ring.

"Hello?" His voice was groggy with sleep.

"Someone broke into the house," she whispered without preamble.

"What?" He instantly snapped into awake mode, and she could already hear him getting out of bed. He would get here as quickly as he could, but there was no way he would make it in time. The cottage was a quarter of a mile from the main house, and by the time he threw on some clothes and jumped in his car and drove here, they would be down the driveway and out onto the street going who knows where.

She was about to tell him everything she knew, so he'd be able to figure out whom he was looking for, when the van suddenly swerved to the side.

Did he know she was on the phone?

She was trying to be quiet, but he was in the front of the van. It wouldn't be hard for him to hear her.

The van swerved again, and the phone flew out of her hand. She pressed herself against the side and tried to hold on.

When the crash came, she was tossed violently about.

Something sharp pierced her leg.

Then her head slammed against the floor.

Pain spiraled around inside her body then grabbed hold of her and threw her into unconsciousness.

* * * * *

4:00 A.M.

"Hmm. Wyatt? What's going on?"

Skylar Wyatt barely paused in throwing on the first clothes he could find. "Tessa just called me," he said over his shoulder as he shrugged into a pair of jeans.

"What does she want?" Casey struggled with the sheet, which had tangled around them while they'd been asleep, and sat up, leaning over to switch on the lamp on the nightstand. "Is she sick? Is something wrong with PJ?"

"She said someone broke into the house. Then there was the sound of screeching tires and a thump, and then the line went dead," he told his wife as he shoved his feet into a pair of sneakers.

"What?" Casey's dark eyes grew wide, and she scrambled out of the bed. "What do you want me to do?"

"Call 911, get a gun from the safe, and lock the doors behind me," Wyatt ordered as he retrieved another gun from the drawer of his nightstand.

"I should come with you," Casey said, already looking around for clothes.

"No. I don't know how many men were there; I don't know whether they're armed, and I don't know whether they have just Tessa, or Tess and PJ." He wasn't risking his wife's life. She was staying here whether she liked it or not.

"Wyatt," Casey started to argue, but he silenced her with a kiss.

"Stay here, Casey," he said again and then ran from the room. He took the stairs three at a time and barely paused to grab his keys before unlocking and flinging the front door open.

He could run the quarter mile to the main house, or he could drive.

On the phone he'd heard tires squealing. That meant whomever had broken into Tessa's house already had her outside and into a car. If he ran, he'd be too late.

Even driving, he might not make it in time.

It had already been at least a minute, probably closer to two since the call to Tessa had been disconnected.

On autopilot, Wyatt jumped into his car and floored the gas.

It had been fifteen years since he'd felt this rush of fear and adrenalin.

After the death of his partner, he'd left the police force. He just hadn't been able to face going back and working without the man he'd known since they were kids there with him. So, he had resigned, and Tessa had loaned him the money to start up his own private security firm.

Ever since, life had been a lot quieter.

He had more time to spend with his wife, their two kids— Sam, who was now twenty-eight, and Serena, who had just turned twenty-three—and their four grandchildren. He liked the relative safety of his new job, but most of the work was pretty mundane, and he couldn't deny that he had missed this feeling.

Wyatt just wished it wasn't Tessa's life hanging in the balance.

This wasn't the first time Tessa had been in danger.

It wasn't the first time he had come running to try to save her life.

He just prayed that this time there would be the same outcome.

Tessa was like a younger sister to him. They had known each other for almost twenty years. They were good friends—more like family—and he had helped her raise her son after her husband's death.

She had to be okay.

She just *had* to.

It was Tessa, after all.

She always survived.

Always.

This time wouldn't be any different.

Although a feeling in his gut told him that something *was* different this time.

All of that flew through his mind in the twenty seconds or so it took to drive up from the cottage to the main house where Tessa had grown up.

The first thing he saw as he rounded the house was a van.

It was resting against a tree two thirds of the way down the tree-lined driveway.

The front was scrunched in like an accordion.

Wyatt drove straight toward the van and jumped out the second he'd put the car in park.

Gun in hand, he approached slowly. He didn't see anyone, but it had only been a couple of minutes since Tessa's call had woken him, so if whoever was driving the van had gotten out, they hadn't gotten far.

The back doors of the van were open, but he bypassed them and headed for the driver's door.

Approaching cautiously, keeping a check on his surroundings in case the abductor was lying in wait, when he rounded the van, he found both the drivers and passenger's seats empty.

Which didn't mean the kidnapper had fled.

He could be in the back with an injured—or unconscious— Tessa as a hostage. The airbag had deployed, and he'd seen blood on the steering wheel. The kidnapper had been hurt, but obviously not badly enough that he couldn't walk. Wyatt hoped that meant Tessa had survived. He didn't want to bury another person that he loved.

It had been thirty years since his firstborn daughter had been killed. It had been fifteen since his best friend died. Both his parents had passed away in the last year.

No more death.

Wyatt stepped around the open van door, expecting—hoping, maybe—to see Tessa and the man who had broken into her house in the middle of the night and abducted her.

Instead, he saw nothing.

Nothing.

The back of the van was as empty as the front.

She was gone.

Whoever had broken in here, had gotten what he'd wanted. He had Tessa. Wyatt just wished he knew what the man wanted with her.

Not that it mattered.

Gone was gone.

The van wasn't completely empty.

There was blood.

At least two puddles of it, one larger than the other, but both indicated that the injuries that caused them had been serious.

Tessa was hurt.

Wyatt wished he knew how badly. If they weren't going to get her back alive, he had to start preparing himself for that.

He scanned the large yard. There were lots of trees because Tessa liked to feel like she was secluded in the woods. There were too many places to hide, and he had no idea which direction the kidnapper had gone. It would take him hours to search the grounds, and Tessa and her kidnapper could be long gone by then.

The best thing he could do right now was check on PJ. Tessa's fifteen-year-old son could be hurt, or dying. If he wasted time looking for Tessa when she might already be gone, her son could die. And he didn't want to bring Tess home only to have to tell her that her son was gone.

Fighting his instincts, which were to search every inch of this property until he found Tessa, he turned and headed back to the house. It was three stories, and there was a possibility that the kidnapper had come back in here, thinking he could hide out and then make a run for it when he thought no one would notice.

Wyatt didn't really think that made sense, but if the guy didn't know that Tessa had had a phone on her and that she'd tried calling for help, he might not know that the cops were on their way here. He might not know that anyone even knew that he'd been here.

Moving as quickly as was safely possible through the house, he made his way to the third floor. Tessa's bedroom was on the second, and PJ's on the third. When her son had been a baby, Tess had him in the room beside hers, but now that PJ was a teenager, he wanted his own space.

Being that they were on separate floors, there was a chance that PJ wasn't even aware that anything had happened. Tessa wouldn't have screamed for help because she wouldn't have done anything that would have put her son in jeopardy.

It depended on who the abductor was and what he wanted as to whether he'd taken Tessa and PJ or just Tess. This man obviously didn't know Tessa well enough to know that she was the most paranoid person on the planet and was always prepared for the worst.

Ready for the worst but hoping for the best, Wyatt swung the door to PJ's room open.

Then sighed in relief when he found the teenager in bed, the sound of soft snoring confirming he was alive.

PJ might be safe, but Tessa wasn't.

Who had her?

And why?

What did they want from her?

This place was secluded; it wasn't the kind of house you just stumbled upon. Someone had come here with the express purpose of snatching her and taking her away. That either boded well for Tessa and bought her enough time for them to find her alive, or it meant that she was already dead.

Wyatt wished he knew which.

Sirens filled the air, but like they had been so many times before, they were too late.

Tessa was gone.

And while he knew there was nobody more equipped to keep herself alive than Tessa, Wyatt just couldn't shake the feeling that this time was different.

This time he didn't think they were getting Tessa back alive.

* * * * *

4:49 A.M.

"This case is going to be high profile," Detective Jack Xander said to his partner as they passed through a huge wrought iron gate and turned up a long tree-lined driveway.

Through the leafy branches, a large, stone three-story mansion came into view. The house reminded him of the one that his brother Ryan's wife had lived in when she was growing up.

Only this one had a more ominous feel to it.

A *very* ominous feel to it.

The house looked like something out of a gothic horror movie. The predawn glow probably added to the fact, making it appear creepier than it otherwise would.

"Just how rich was this woman?" his partner, Xavier Montague, asked.

"Richer than Sofia's family," he replied. "Her grandparents built a fortune, their son was disinherited, and although she had a brother, she inherited everything."

"I heard she was basically a recluse," Xavier said.

He had heard the same thing.

Everyone had heard of Tessa Bell.

The woman was like some sort of weird urban legend. After living the kind of life she had, it was no wonder.

"From what I've heard, she rarely leaves this place; her fifteen-year-old son is homeschooled, and although she has some family and a few friends, she didn't like to meet new people. She runs several charities and donates millions a year to dozens more. She also manages all of her family's businesses, but she does it all from here."

"A woman that rich ... it's no surprise that someone would want to abduct her."

"You think this is a kidnapping for ransom?" Jack asked.

"I think it's a definite possibility. Think of the money that the family would pay to get her back. Talk about getting rich quick. If you could get her off the property—and this guy did—then all you have to do is email or mail in a letter, then collect, and flee the country. If you could pull it off, you'd walk away with more money than you'd ever even imagined."

"Flip side, her family has enough money to turn over every rock to find her and bring her home."

"If they can find her in time," Xavier contradicted. "Yeah, the family will probably hire their own people to work this, but when that first body part arrives in the mail, they'll be paying whatever they're asked, just for a chance at getting her back."

Jack couldn't help but shudder at the mention of dismembered body parts arriving in the mail.

It wasn't even six months since that terrifying reality had touched his family.

While it was something they all wanted to forget, the lingering psychological effects of that ordeal still touched every single member of his family.

From the way Xavier fell silent as he drove up the driveway and pulled in beside the white van that was still wedged against a large tree, Jack knew his partner was thinking the same things he was.

Determinedly shoving those thoughts away, Jack focused on this case. This wasn't about him and his family. This was about Tessa Bell and her family, and he would do everything within his power to bring her home to them.

"It's a wonder the kidnapper was able to walk away from that and get himself and another—possibly unconscious—person along with him in less than a couple of minutes," he said as he and Xavier climbed from the air-conditioned comfort of the car out into the already muggy morning.

"He mustn't have sustained any serious injuries," Xavier said as they walked toward the van.

The airbag had deployed, and there was blood on the steering wheel, but his partner was right, the kidnapper mustn't have been seriously injured if he was able to flee and take his hostage with him.

They walked around to the back of the van, and the first thing he noticed was the blood. Enough of it that it was clear that whoever was in there had been badly hurt.

"Think she's still alive?" Xavier asked quietly.

"Yes," he replied immediately. "If she were dead, he would have left her behind."

"Not necessarily. Even dead, he could still use her if all he wanted was money. If there was even a chance she was alive, then her family would do whatever he asked them to, to get her back."

Jack nodded.

Unfortunately, that made sense.

"I'm working this case with you."

They both turned as a tall man with graying blond hair, bright green eyes, and a terrified expression appeared behind them.

"Skylar Wyatt, I presume," he said. He'd met the man once or twice many years ago when he was still on the police force, before he'd retired to go into private security.

"Yes," the man said shortly, his gaze fixed on the puddles of blood in the van.

"She called you," Jack said, trying to distract him. The man had been a cop for two decades. Even if it had been fifteen years since he'd retired, he could still be a huge asset to them on this case. He knew Tessa Bell, and if anyone was going to be able to figure out who had taken her and why, it was this man.

"She did. From in there." He indicated the back of the van.

"How?" he asked. There were strips of fabric on the floor of the van, which he presumed had been used to restrain Tessa. Fabric was an interesting choice. It wouldn't have hurt her as much as rope or plastic zip ties. That hinted that the killer knew her and possibly even cared about her in some way. If she'd gone into the van restrained, how had she gotten free and made a phone call?

"If there's one thing you need to know about Tessa, it's that she's paranoid. *Very* paranoid. Or, I guess since she usually turns out to be right, it's not really paranoia. She keeps a small metal blade in the band of her watch."

He'd heard that before.

A story about how Tessa had used that same trick to try to escape from a man who wanted to kill her and her husband.

Everyone at the precinct had heard that story.

His brother and one of his best friends had even tried to implement it before when they were bargaining with a killer for the lives of their daughters.

"She keeps a disposable cell phone on her at all times too?" Xavier asked, pointing to the cell that lay in two pieces in a corner of the van.

"Yes. Always." Skylar Wyatt's gaze fixed on the phone, no doubt replaying the conversation and thinking of everything he could have or should have done differently.

"What exactly did she say?" Jack asked.

"Just that someone had broken into the house. Then I heard tires screeching and the call was disconnected."

"Do you have any idea who would want to hurt her?" Xavier asked.

Skylar Wyatt finally tore his eyes away from the van and met their gazes squarely. "You know who she is, right?"

"We know that she's a rich recluse who lost her husband fifteen years ago, and that her life has been like some old Greek tragedy. Or a soap opera," Jack added. His wife Laura had a bit of an addiction to daytime soap operas.

The man nodded. "Tessa's family was pretty mixed up. Abusive dad left when she was ten, mother was depressed and a drug and alcohol addict who tried to kill Tess when she was twelve. Life outside the home didn't turn out to be much better for Tessa, and when we first met her, she was being stalked by a serial killer she was intending to let kill her. She fell in love with my partner, and although their relationship was rocky, they loved each other, and she was devastated when Parker was killed. Ever since, she's basically locked herself away here. But she is one hundred percent devoted to her son, and there is no way she would leave PJ. This isn't some hoax ... this isn't some game ... she isn't mentally unbalanced ... she didn't do this to herself."

Based on what he'd already known about the woman whose cop husband had been killed by someone who'd been out for revenge against her, and from everything that Skylar Wyatt had just told them, Jack didn't believe that Tessa was involved in this.

Someone had come here with the express purpose of abducting her.

And succeeded.

Tessa was missing—abducted.

And the quicker they figured out the why, the quicker they would find the who, and then the where.

Skylar Wyatt was their best chance of doing that. It wouldn't be the first time they'd worked with a consultant on a case. As Jack understood, Tessa herself had worked with the cops on more than one occasion.

The only thing left in question was whether or not Skylar Wyatt could remain emotionally detached enough to actually be of use to them.

"Can you hold it together?" he asked the older man.

With clear green eyes and a steely expression, he said, "I can do whatever it takes to find Tessa and bring her home to her son."

* * * * *

5:12 A.M.

Pounding in her head roused her.

Pain clanged about behind her eyes as though someone were using them as a drum.

The pain in her skull was matched only by the pain in her leg.

Tessa felt groggy.

Unfortunately, this wasn't a new feeling to her.

She'd been knocked unconscious and, no doubt, now had a concussion.

Memories slowly trickled back into her aching head. The man in her bedroom … cutting away the strips of cloth that bound her … calling Skylar for help … the van swerving then slamming into something … excruciating pain as her unrestrained body was thrown about … then the emptiness of unconsciousness.

How long had she been out?

As bad as she felt and as nice as it would be to slide back into the blissful ignorance of unconsciousness, she couldn't.

She was already waking up, and if she was going to get home to her son, she was going to have to find strength she didn't think she had left and find a way to fight back.

She could only do that if she was awake.

So she drew in a long, deep breath, took hold of the pain and shoved it into a box, locking the box and burying it away, then slowly opened her eyes. Blood from her head wound had dribbled down her face and over her eyes. As it had dried, it had stuck her eyelashes together, so she had to pry her eyes open.

As soon as she did, light pierced her eyeballs and she groaned and quickly snapped her lids closed again.

If she couldn't use her sense of sight right now, she was going to have to let her other senses pull their weight. She had to figure out where she was if she was going to discover who took her and why.

Once she concentrated, the first thing she noticed was that her clothes were on.

Relief flooded through her and momentarily washed away the pain.

If her clothes were still on, she hadn't been raped.

With that horrible possibility out of the way—for now, at least—she focused on her surroundings.

She was lying on something soft, no doubt a bed. There was no breeze, so she was probably inside. The room smelled fresh and clean, so she didn't think she was in a basement or an attic or some old dilapidated building of some sort.

That could be good or bad.

Tessa wasn't sure yet.

She needed something concrete to go on. She liked facts. They made her feel more in control in a world that was anything but.

She was going to have to open her eyes, figure out where she was.

Slowly, she cracked them open. The light still shafted straight through her, but she was prepared this time, and it wasn't quite as bad.

She edged them open a little more, and when the pain didn't get any worse, she went for it and opened them the rest of the way.

Once she did, she saw that she was indeed lying on a bed. It was a large, four poster with heavy red and blue curtains which were currently hanging down, enclosing her inside.

She had to see what was out there.

Tessa rolled over, intending to pull the curtains back and climb out of the bed to investigate the room, but she immediately regretted the movement.

Sweat broke out on her brow, and her stomach roiled. The pain was so intense it came charging out of the box she'd tried to lock it up in and reached out its tentacles to take over every single cell of her body.

She sank back down against the mattress, but her stomach wouldn't settle.

Spinning and spinning in a series of slow and then fast revolutions that made her feel sicker by the second.

Tessa just managed to roll back over and hang her head over the edge of the bed before she threw up.

Over and over again until her stomach was empty.

She continued to dry heave for another minute before her stomach finally started to settle, and she, once against, sank back against her pillows.

How was she going to find a way out of here when she couldn't even move?

She had to pull it together.

She *had* to.

She didn't have any other options.

Skylar knew she was missing, but he didn't know who had taken her or why, so he wouldn't be able to find her.

Tessa knew he would call the police and make sure that every cop in the city was looking for her, but that didn't mean they would find her.

She could die here.

As much as that appealed to her on some level, she couldn't leave PJ. He was only fifteen, and he'd already lost his father. He needed her.

Dragging in a breath, she wiped at the sweat that dotted her brow and pushed through the pain and nausea to drag herself into a standing position.

It wasn't until her feet touched the floor that she realized just how badly hurt her leg was. It collapsed underneath her, and she crumpled to the floor. The thud that jarred through her as her body hit the floorboards served to point out to her every other injury she had yet to notice.

Her chest and her left arm stood out from amongst the myriad of bumps, bruises, and scrapes she'd received when she'd been tossed around inside the van as it swerved and crashed.

How was she going to do this?

She couldn't.

She couldn't do it.

She didn't have the strength to fight anymore.

It had been sapped from her little by little every time life had thrown another monster at her.

And now she had to fight again, but she didn't think she could.

PJ.

PJ.

PJ.

She had to keep reminding herself of what she had to live for.

If she didn't have any strength of her own, she was just going to have to draw on her son's.

The window.

If she could just get to the window, she might have a chance at figuring out where she was, and then she could go from there.

Baby steps.

That was the only way she was going to get through this.

Take things one step at a time; don't overthink things; don't try to do everything at once. Otherwise, she was just going to get overwhelmed, and that was going to leave her incapable of doing anything.

Dragging herself back to her feet, Tessa hobbled as best as she could to the window and threw back the curtains.

Then she let out a half annoyed, half scared groan.

The windows had been boarded up.

On the outside.

The only way she was going to have a hope at seeing out of

them was to break the glass and try to pry the planks of wood loose.

Something she couldn't do in her condition.

She could barely remain upright right now, and the pain continued to stab at her no matter how hard she tried to shove it away and ignore it.

The door.

The chances of it being unlocked were slim to none, but she had to try.

Using the walls and the furniture to support herself and stay upright, Tessa made her way around the room to the door.

As soon as she got to it, she froze.

Someone was out there.

Were they watching her?

Propping herself up against the wall, she scanned the room, searching for any hidden cameras or microphones. She couldn't see any, but that didn't mean they weren't there.

Footsteps.

Was that footsteps she could hear?

Tessa pressed her ear to the door to try to hear better.

Voices.

She could hear voices.

Two of them.

There were two men here. Only one man had been in her home, but he obviously had a partner. That was probably who'd brought them here, after the other man had crashed the van and she'd passed out.

The men were speaking in hushed voices. She couldn't make out the words they were saying, but it sounded like an argument.

As much as she wanted to check the door handle to see if it was locked, she knew she couldn't. There were two of them to her one, and she was injured. Although the driver of the van probably was too, which evened out the odds a tiny bit.

A gunshot suddenly reverberated through the house.

The loud bang was followed by a thud as a body hit the floor.

One of them had just killed the other.

What did that mean for her?

Who were they?

What did they want from her?

Her head hurt so badly, her leg was shaking, and fresh blood dribbled down her arm. Each breath she took was like someone was adding one brick after another on her chest.

She was hurt.

Pretty badly.

She needed to go lie down. As much as she wanted to figure out a way to get out of here and home to her son, she needed to rest.

Somehow, Tessa managed to drag herself back to the bed, where she collapsed into a fitful slumber the second she lay down.

* * * * *

5:25 A.M.

He had just taken his first human life.

He stared at the lifeless form lying on the floor in front of him.

He should feel something.

Anything.

Pain, sadness, fear, regret, anxiety—something. Anything.

This wasn't normal.

He wasn't normal.

Instead of feeling any sort of remorse for the life he'd just taken and the implications that would have on the dead man's family and friends, all he was thinking about was everything he needed to do to safely dispose of the body.

There was no way he was going to let this man ruin things for him.

At least, not any more than he had already.

21

The man was incompetent.

He really should have put more time and effort into choosing a partner, because this one had almost ruined everything. He'd specifically told him that Tessa Bell was not to be underestimated, under any circumstances. That he should be prepared for anything and not to take his eyes off her. If the man was going to leave her in the back of the van, he should have made sure that she was unconscious first.

Really, if you wanted something done right, you had to do it yourself.

Which he would be doing, from here on out.

If he was completely honest with himself, this was probably always going to be how things were going to turn out. He didn't really want a partner; he just hadn't wanted to do the abducting himself. He didn't want anyone to know who he was.

That would ruin everything.

As would the police managing to track down the man who'd grabbed Tessa from her bed and kidnapped her. It was a possibility before, but now it was pretty much a done deal. The man was in the system, and he'd been stupid enough to crash the van and injure himself, leaving blood and fluids, and who knows what else, behind.

The cops would find that man. He just couldn't risk them finding him as well.

At least, not just yet.

Right now, he wanted some time alone with Tessa.

Leaving the body for now, he went into the room next to the one he'd put Tessa in. His phone—an untraceable, disposable cell phone he'd bought just for this purpose—was on the nightstand, and he needed to use it. He had it set to link to the live streaming footage from Tessa's room, so he could watch her.

He picked up the phone and put in the password, then opened the app which brought the bedroom up on the screen. He'd put the camera inside the bed because Tessa was unconscious, and he wasn't sure how long it would take her to wake up.

She was still there.

Wearing the same blue tank top and pink sweatpants that she'd been sleeping in when his partner—*ex*-partner—had grabbed her.

She was lying sprawled half on her back and half on her side, her mass of blonde curls fanned out around her head. Her eyes were closed, and she didn't appear to be awake, but she clearly had been at some point.

The curtains around the bed were parted and the covers a little mussed. She must have woken up and searched the room, probably looking for a way out.

He had left the light on for her. Since she was already hurt, he hadn't wanted her to stumble into something in the dark when she did the inevitable walk around the room. She wouldn't find anything, of course. He had boarded up the windows, and the door was locked. He'd cleared out anything he thought she could effectively use as a weapon while still making sure he left her with enough things to be comfortable.

She might be here for a while.

Until he got what he wanted at least.

And he *always* got what he wanted.

He'd been used to getting his own way his entire life. He'd been spoiled; he knew that. And now, he would make sure that this worked out just the same way everything else in his life did.

His fingers hovered above the screen.

He wanted to touch her.

Really touch her.

But not right now.

Right now, he had to take care of the body in the hall.

Then he would come back. He'd go into her room and tend to her wounds and tell her how glad he was that she was here.

And then he'd move on with the next stage of his plan.

Well, "plan" made him sound kind of crazy. Like he was some sort of deranged serial killer out to slaughter as many people as he could for whatever warped reason he'd dreamed up. But that wasn't the way this was at all.

He was sane.

One hundred percent sane.

This wasn't some sort of crazy plan. This was just one guy getting what he wanted. Nothing more and nothing less.

He gently brushed one fingertip across the screen of his phone. "Sleep well," he whispered to Tessa.

Then he put the phone away. If he didn't, he could stand there forever just staring at her. It felt so surreal knowing she was in the next room.

He was really doing this.

For so long now he'd thought about it, dreamed about it. He played out in his head; everything he would say and do, and how perfectly it would all end.

And it would end perfectly.

Because everything else in his life did.

Well, *almost* everything.

But this would go off without a hitch. It had to. After all, he had put months of effort into working out every little detail, everything that could go wrong, every conceivable variable, until he had it all sorted. This couldn't go wrong.

Cleaning up the mess, that had to be his priority right now. The blood in the hall could wait. Getting rid of the body was paramount. Not that there would be anyone to stumble upon it here. This place was secluded, and there was no one else here but Tessa and him. But still, he couldn't just leave it lying about. It really was very unsightly; plus, it would scare Tessa if he could trust her enough to let her have free reign of the house. Locked in, of course.

Grabbing hold of the man's ankles, he dragged him down the hall, then down the stairs. The sound his head made as it clunked onto each step amused him for some reason, and he couldn't help but chuckle.

Okay, maybe he was a *little* crazy.

But it wasn't his fault.

He was a victim of circumstance and bad DNA.

Once he'd tossed the body into the trunk of his car, he went back inside and collected a few supplies.

He got into the car and started to drive. He wanted to get far enough away from the house so when the cops found the body and searched the surrounding areas, they wouldn't stumble across it, but not so far away that he was gone too long. He really did want to get back to Tessa.

When he felt like he had driven the perfect distance, he pulled over to the side of the road. It was quiet, and he didn't expect to see another car, but still, he draped a blanket over the body as he pulled it from the trunk and carried it a little way into the woods.

He didn't really care when the body was found. Within the hour or months from now; it made no difference to him. There was nothing to connect this man to him, so he wasn't afraid of the police finding him.

With the body out of view of the road, he turned to his bucket of supplies. First, he stripped the man's clothes and tossed them into a bag. He would burn them later at home. Then he unscrewed the lid of a large carton of water and went to work scrubbing and shaving every inch of the body. He didn't want to leave a single piece of himself behind.

Satisfied that the body was sufficiently cleaned, he tipped the last of the water over it and watched as the droplets ran in rivulets down the smooth skin and puddled in the grass and leaves beneath it.

He was done. It was time to get out of here. The body was sorted, and there was nothing on it that would link this man to him. The man had served his purpose. He'd brought Tessa to him, and that was all he really wanted.

Now it was just the two of them.

The way it was supposed to be.

Tessa and him.

He was so excited.

He loved this feeling. The one where you had waited so long to have something, and now that you had it, you felt a mixture of excitement and nervousness, and even a little scared because one wrong move, and you could lose it all.

He wasn't under any illusions.

He knew that all it took was one wrong move, and he would lose everything.

* * * * *

10:31 A.M.

Already, Xavier was getting a bad feeling about this case.

However this turned out, he wasn't sure they were going to be able to bring Tessa Bell home to her family.

He hoped he was wrong, and he and Jack would do everything in their power to find her, but he just had this feeling in his gut that he couldn't shake that this was going to end badly. It was making him feel edgy, antsy; he wanted to be doing something, but right now, they didn't have a lot to go on. Crime scene techs were going over the house and the van. They would interview Skylar Wyatt and the rest of Tessa's family, looking for a possible suspect, but it didn't feel like enough.

"Paige and I are going to be helping with this case." His partner's brother Ryan appeared in the doorway.

Xavier wasn't surprised.

Like Jack had said as they'd turned into the driveway of Tessa's estate, this case was high profile. Although he and Jack would be the lead detectives on the case, two other detectives had been assigned to work with them, and now Ryan and Paige as well.

"Come on, let's get started," Wyatt growled as he stalked through the door.

The man had insisted on doing the notifications to Tessa's family but had allowed him and Jack to tag along. Although technically, Skylar Wyatt couldn't actually prevent them from doing the notifications themselves, they had decided it would probably be easier for Tessa's family to hear the news from someone they knew and trusted, than two strangers.

The family had taken the news as well as could be expected. They'd been angry; they'd cried; they'd been scared. No one had been able to think of anyone who might hurt Tessa off the top of their heads, but they would interview them all in more detail over the next day or so. Xavier still believed that, for the moment, Wyatt was going to be their best source of information. He was a cop, and he was more likely to pick up on things that the rest of the family wouldn't have even noticed.

"We're ready," he told Wyatt and indicated that they should all take a seat at the table. Ryan remained by the board to jot down notes as they spoke.

"When was the last time you saw Tessa?" Jack asked.

"My wife and I had dinner with Tess and PJ last night," Wyatt replied.

"What time was that?" Xavier asked. They needed to figure out a timeline. They knew when Tessa had called Wyatt, so they knew the approximate time of the abduction, but if they could figure out when the man got into the house, it might help them figure out who he was, or could be used as evidence against someone if they got a suspect.

"We left around ten. Casey and I live on the property; we moved there after Parker died." A flash of sadness passed through Wyatt's green eyes as he mentioned his friend and partner.

Some wounds not even time could heal.

Xavier knew because he still often thought about his daughter who'd been stillborn. If she had lived, she'd have turned eighteen this year. She would have graduated high school and been ready to start college in the fall. Sometimes he wondered what she

27

would have been like. He knew she would have been smart and sweet, but would she be funny, or serious? Would she like art or sports or literature? Would she know what she wanted to do with her life already, or would college be where she found herself?

He couldn't imagine what Tessa's life had been like.

Wyatt had given them a brief rundown of her tragic childhood when they'd driven down to the station. Tessa had been through so much only to find happiness with the first person who had ever given her the love that she craved but was too afraid to seek, and then she'd lost it.

She'd been left alone to raise the son who was the absolute spitting image of his father and was no doubt a constant reminder of all that she'd lost. Xavier suspected from what Wyatt had said—and what he hadn't—that her son was pretty much the only reason Tessa got out of bed each morning.

"When you left, did you notice anything unusual?" Jack asked Wyatt.

"No. Nothing out of the ordinary."

So, the man with the van had arrived sometime between ten and three in the morning. "Does Tessa have a security system?" Xavier was sure she did; all rich people did.

"Yes, she does, but it's not a very sophisticated one." Something passed through the man's eyes again. Guilt.

"Why not?" he asked, sensing there was something to that.

"When Parker and I first met Tessa, she had an over-the-top security system. Her entire house was wired with cameras and motion and sound systems. She used the system and her fears as a way to keep people out. Parker had to work hard to break through her barriers, and even then, he only got so far. After he died, we were all afraid she was going to shut herself away again. I convinced her not to go back to the security system because I didn't want her to use it as an excuse to lock us out. If I hadn't … if I'd let her put in a system like she'd had before, that man would never have gotten in there."

"You know it doesn't work that way," Xavier admonished gently. "What you and your family did was what you believed was best for her. She needed you, and you were there for her. You kept her in the real world and didn't let her fade away into nothingness."

Wyatt gave a single, sharp nod. He would probably be holding onto his guilt for a long time. That was the way guilt worked. It wrapped its tentacles around you so tightly that it bit into your flesh, so the mark it left would be there forever.

"Is there anyone you can think of who might want to try to hurt her? Or extort money from her?" Jack asked.

"You think it's a kidnap for ransom?" Wyatt asked.

"Could that be a possibility?" Xavier asked.

"I don't know," Wyatt said thoughtfully. "Tessa doesn't really have a lot of friends. Even before Parker's death. Given what she's been through, she has major trust issues. And of the friends she does have, none of them would want to hurt her."

"She owns a lot of businesses … anyone from there who might try this?" Xavier asked.

"Tessa manages the businesses, but she doesn't really have much to do with the day-to-day running of them, so I don't know that she'd know any of them well enough to have any personal conflict with them. If this is purely about money, then I guess it's a possibility. Do you have someone going through all employees?"

"Yes, we do," Jack assured the man.

"Who's your crime scene person?" Wyatt asked. "There was blood in the car; there could be fingerprints in the house or the van. If we're lucky, we might get a hit in CODIS or AFIS. I'd bet anything this guy is in the system."

So would he.

Other than the car crash, the man had managed to get Tessa Bell—who was so paranoid she slept with a knife under her pillow—out of the house.

"Stephanie Cantini is working the case," he told Wyatt.

"I know her. She's good. If anyone can find this guy, then it's her."

"Did Tessa mention anything out of the ordinary happening over the last few days?" Jack asked.

"No, and if she had noticed *anything*, she'd have told me. Everything was the same as always. We ate dinner, we talked, we said goodbye, then we left, and she was going to head straight to bed because she was tired. She doesn't keep great health ever since that woman nearly killed her."

The *that woman* Wyatt was referring to was the same one who had killed Tessa's husband.

Maybe they should be looking into any workmen who had been at the house recently. From the smooth abduction, it was likely that the man had been inside the house before and knew the layout of it and the estate.

"Ryan, Sofia needs to talk to you for a moment." The door to the conference room swung open and Ryan's partner Paige and wife Sofia walked into the room.

"Just dropping off the keys, the mechanic is done already," Sofia said as she passed the keys off to her husband. Her gaze fell on the board and she froze. "Is that Tessa?"

"You know Tessa Bell?" Ryan asked, surprised.

"Yes. Since we were babies. My grandfather was good friends with Tess's grandparents. Sometimes when they visited each other, we'd play together."

"If you were good friends, why have I never met her?" Ryan asked.

"Because Tessa doesn't like to meet new people. Every time I suggested coming over to our place for dinner or bringing you over for dinner, she said no. Sophie has met PJ though. They're the same age, and PJ doesn't really have many friends. He's quiet and shy, and I thought Sophie would be good for him. Tessa was okay with Sophie coming over. I guess kids didn't freak her out as much as adults. What happened to her?" Her gaze circled the room searching each of their faces.

"She was kidnapped," Wyatt answered.

"Oh no." Sofia's hands flew to her mouth.

"When was the last time you saw her?" Xavier asked. Maybe Sofia would know something Wyatt didn't.

"We had lunch the day before yesterday. She was worried about PJ. She said that he was kind of freaked out when he found a plumber wandering around the house when he was supposed to be fixing something in the kitchen."

"She didn't tell me that." Wyatt looked upset.

"She probably didn't want to worry you. Do you think that's who kidnapped her?" Sofia asked.

It was as good a place as any to start.

* * * * *

12:09 P.M.

She liked it out here.

It was so quiet and peaceful.

Fifteen-year-old Sophie Xander paused and stared up at the blue sky. It was the kind of endless blue that you lost yourself in when you stared at it for too long. The trees were tall, stretching their branches right up to that blue sky as though they wanted to find out what was up there. The dappled light cast a beautiful pattern on the ground, and the butterflies that flitted about caught the sunlight, making them seem like they were sparkling. The only sound was the chirping of the birds and the buzzing of the occasional lazy honeybee or dragonfly.

The woods were like a little sliver of heaven.

Before she'd been abducted six months ago, she'd never really thought much about the outdoors. She'd enjoyed going camping with her parents and little brother Ned, but she'd never really paid much attention to the great outdoors.

Now, she loved it.

It was one of the few places where she felt truly safe.

She had never realized before just how much she'd taken that for granted.

Her dad was a cop. He dealt all day, every day with people whose lives had been thrown into chaos by crime. Her mom ran a center for women and children who had fled abusive homes. She knew that there were a lot of bad people in the world, and a lot of people who were suffering because of them, but it had still felt so remote.

Now, it was personal.

She had experienced firsthand what happened when someone wanted to hurt other people just because they could. Those people always had an excuse, a reason why they were doing it. But it was just that—an excuse. Really, they just did it because they wanted to.

As it always did when her mind wandered back to the basement she'd been held in, her gaze dropped to her right hand.

More specifically, to the small stump where her pinkie finger used to be.

The familiar wave of panic and terror began to build inside her.

It started in her stomach and worked its way out to her extremities.

She still wasn't very good at controlling these feelings.

And she was alone out here.

There was no one to come and hold her, to soothe her, to tell her that everything was okay, and that she was strong enough to get through this.

Sophie wasn't in a place where she believed that yet.

She needed to hear the words aloud.

She needed to hear them from other people.

She needed to know that her parents and her family and friends had faith in her.

When she got stuck in the dark place in her mind and all she could do was relive her ordeal and she couldn't find her way out, she needed the people who loved her.

She couldn't do this on her own.

Sophie was well on her way to a complete panic attack and she was stuck out here in the middle of the woods, in a place that, just moments ago, had made her feel safe and secure, but that now only served to remind her that she was all alone.

Her breath was coming way too fast and kept catching in her throat like there were lumps in there that grabbed at the air that wheezed in and out of her chest.

Little white dots started to dance in front of her eyes.

They seemed so real.

Like she could reach out and touch them.

Then her vision began to gray.

Great.

Now she was going to pass out.

She knew that she was having a panic attack, and all she had to do was some of the breathing exercises she had learned in therapy. She *knew* that; she just couldn't seem to *do* it.

Her panic was rising.

She didn't want to pass out.

She wanted to go home.

Why had she come here?

She should have stayed at home.

"Soph?"

She blinked and a fuzzy face came into view.

"Are you okay?"

She managed a single, sharp nod.

"Here, sit down." Strong hands closed around her upper arms, and she was eased down onto the rough ground and propped up against a tree. "Breathe slowly with me, okay? In and out ... in and out." The voice repeated that over and over again, and Sophie latched on to it and let her mind go blank, focusing only on the calm, controlled voice directing her breathing.

Eventually, it worked.

She was able to draw a breath that mostly filled her lungs, and she no longer felt like she was going to pass out.

"Thank you," she managed to whisper hoarsely, and she shot a smile at the guy kneeling in front of her.

"You're welcome." Parker Bell, Junior smiled back at her. "You okay now?"

"Yeah. Thanks."

"You said that already," he reminded her with a laugh as he moved around to sit beside her.

Sophie rolled her eyes at him. She and PJ had been friends since they were kids. Their moms had been friends since they were kids, and since PJ's mom was a virtual recluse since losing her husband, her mom had suggested that she might be a good friend for PJ, who didn't know many kids his own age.

They'd hit it off right away.

She liked the quiet, shy, sensitive boy who had an IQ off the charts and was lonely and yet, also comfortable in his solitary lifestyle.

PJ didn't attend school; he had a tutor, but he was already smarter than most adults, let alone most teenagers. And while his mother tried to make sure he spent time around kids his own age, she knew that PJ wasn't comfortable around his peers.

Except her.

Sophie also knew that PJ had a crush on her.

She just wished she had known that earlier.

Before she had fallen in love with Dominick Tremaine. The man who had ruined her life.

But she wasn't going down that road again. She didn't want another panic attack right on the heels of the first.

"So ..." She turned to face her friend, who was the spitting image of the father he was named after but had never met. "What did you want?" PJ had called her a couple of hours ago to ask her to meet him out here in their special place. They often hung out here and just sat in the shade of the trees and talked for hours about anything and everything.

"Oh, it doesn't matter … I don't want to worry you," he said, dropping his gaze to the ground.

"I'm fine, really," she said. She knew PJ, and he wouldn't have called her and asked her to come right here if it wasn't something important. "What's going on?"

"It's my mom." PJ still wouldn't look at her.

"What's wrong with her?" Sophie asked. She knew that his mom wasn't well. The same person who had killed Tessa's husband had also tried to kill her, and although Tessa had survived, she'd been left with several medical issues. "Is she sick? Is she in the hospital?" She hoped that Tessa was okay. She really liked PJ's mom.

"She's missing."

"What?" she asked, sure she must have misheard. "What do you mean she's missing?"

"Last night, someone broke into our house," PJ explained.

"Are you okay?" She scanned his body from head to toe in search of injuries.

"I'm fine. I didn't even know anything had happened until Wyatt woke me up. I didn't know, Sophie. I didn't know that anything was going on. My mom needed me, and I was asleep."

He sounded so distraught that Sophie reached out and took his hands in hers. "If you'd known that she was in trouble, you would have done anything to help her."

PJ nodded dismissively. "But she *was* in trouble and I didn't help her and now she's gone."

"But the cops are looking for her, right?"

"Your uncle and his partner. But I guess since my mom's husband was a cop who was killed in the line of duty that the whole police force will be looking for her."

He always referred to his father as his mother's husband.

Sophie guessed it was a way to distance himself from the pain of never having known his dad. Since they were all each other had, PJ and his mom were close. She didn't know how he was going to cope if anything happened to her. She prayed that her Uncle Jack and Xavier were able to find Tessa and bring her home. And from what she knew of Tessa and her past, if there was anyone who could keep herself alive until she was found, it was her.

"It'll be okay." She squeezed PJ's hands. "They'll find her. She'll be okay, and they'll bring her home. You can't give up hope. You have to believe in her. Trust me," she added. "She needs you to believe in her. She needs you to have faith that she'll come back home." Sophie knew without a shadow of a doubt that her parents' faith in her ability to fight, to survive, and their belief they would see her again, were the only reasons that she was still alive.

Sometimes, when you didn't have anything else, you had to have faith.

And sometimes faith was enough.

She hoped it was this time.

She hoped that PJ would get his mom back, just like her parents had gotten her back.

* * * * *

2:41 P.M.

He had thought they were done with this.

He thought he would never have to pace a room, barely able to breathe as helplessness and fear smothered him, wondering where his sister was and if she was even still alive.

Daniel Micah reached the living room wall, turned abruptly and started back toward the other end of the room.

He could do this all day.

He *had* been doing this all day.

Ever since Wyatt had told them about Tessa.

36

Moving was the only thing keeping him sane. If he stopped, he feared he would lose it. And if he lost it, he was pretty sure he was going to do something stupid.

It seemed like he was never there for his little sister when she needed him.

This was just another piece of the pattern.

He had split when he was eighteen and Tessa was twelve, and their mother had tried to kill Tessa. Because of that, he hadn't been there for her.

Daniel hated that.

He hated that he hadn't been the big brother she deserved.

Over the last fifteen years, they'd grown a lot closer. They were probably closer now than they had ever been. Tessa had inherited their paternal grandparents' estate, and after her husband's death, he had moved out here to be with her. Tessa had another house built on the property for him and his family.

"Would you please stop doing that?"

"Doing what?" he asked as he turned again and started back in the other direction.

"Pacing. You're making me dizzy," his wife, Matilda, said.

"I have to pace," he muttered.

"It's not going to bring her back."

He wasn't stupid.

He knew that.

But he had to do something. Even if it was just walk up and down the living room until his sister was found. "When it's *your* sister who's abducted from her bed in the middle of the night, then you can choose how you deal with it," he snapped at his wife. "Since it's *my* sister, I get to choose how I react. And I'm going with pacing."

"It couldn't be me worrying over my brother being abducted. My brother is dead," Mattie reminded him quietly.

Daniel finally stopped pacing.

He was being a jerk.

Sometimes he forgot that Matilda and Tessa's husband Parker were siblings. He knew how much Mattie had suffered when her twin brother died. The loss had brought her and his sister closer together.

He wondered if Parker had lived if the two of them would have liked each other by now. They had gotten off to a rocky start, and things had never really improved. Now, he wished that he'd made more of an effort, or *any* effort. Because he hadn't liked Parker and hadn't wanted his sister to marry him, Tessa had shut him out of her grieving process. He couldn't blame her, and he was glad that she had Mattie and the two of them were able to help each other, but he wanted to be there for her too.

Crossing the room, Daniel took a seat beside Matilda, taking hold of her hands. "I'm sorry."

"It's okay. I know you're out of your mind worrying about your sister." She gave him a reassuring smile.

He had really lucked out with her.

Daniel knew he didn't deserve this beautiful, sweet, kind, caring woman. And yet he had her.

She was the most amazing wife and mother, and he loved their life together. He couldn't stand it if anything happened to Matilda. The most important people in the world to him were his wife, his son and daughter, and his sister. With his sister missing, it terrified him that this might be someone with a grudge against their family and that his wife and kids could be in danger too.

"Just because I'm scared about what's happening to Tessa doesn't give me an excuse to take that out on you. I'm sorry. Really sorry." Daniel leaned down and touched his lips to Matilda's. "I love you so much," he said as he wrapped his arms around her and drew her against his chest.

"I love you too," Matilda said as her arms slid around his waist.

Daniel held his wife and tried to let the feel of her in his arms soothe him a little. Mattie was safe and so were their kids, and he knew that Wyatt would do whatever it took to find Tessa. Not only that, but he would make sure that the entire police department was working this case.

While he waited for the cops to bring his sister home, he was going to have to pull it together.

The family needed him.

Mattie and the kids were scared. His niece Winter and her husband and kids were scared, and so was his nephew.

PJ needed him to be in control right now. The kid had already lost his father. He must be out of his mind thinking that he might be about to lose his mother as well.

He nodded his head in PJ's direction and Mattie nodded. His wife stood and walked over to where Winter and her husband and Casey Wyatt were sitting, their heads together, deep in conversation. He stood and walked over to PJ. The teenager had been sitting in that chair, staring blankly into space for the last hour.

"Hey, PJ, how are you doing?" he asked as he perched on the arm of the chair his nephew was sitting in.

"I'm fine," PJ said immediately. "Mom will be fine. Wyatt will find her. I mean, every other time something bad happened to her, she was okay. This time will be the same."

Daniel wished he had PJ's faith.

His sister did have an uncanny ability to walk out of the worst of ordeals alive, even if the psychological damage done destroyed another piece of her. But that didn't mean she was going to survive this. Most of the times that Tessa had been in danger, it had been because someone she knew wanted to hurt her. As far as he knew, there wasn't anyone left alive who wished his sister any harm, which meant that this was a stranger. For some reason, that seemed to make it so much more terrifying. Maybe because it came with so many unknowns.

As much as he wanted PJ to have hope, he also wanted his nephew to be prepared in case the worst happened.

They *all* needed to be prepared for the worst.

"PJ," he started slowly, "as much as I want to believe that Wyatt is going to find your mom and bring her home, we have to consider …" He paused as he tried to think of the best way to phrase it. "Other possibilities," he finally settled on.

"You mean we have to be prepared for the possibility that mom won't come home," PJ said.

"That's what I mean," Daniel agreed, not liking hearing those words coming from his fifteen-year-old nephew's mouth, even if PJ was just paraphrasing what he himself had just said. "We're all praying that Tessa will be okay, and she probably will be, but yes, we all have to prepare ourselves for the worst."

"Mom will be okay," PJ said confidently. "Just have faith."

Daniel wondered if it was faith or denial that had PJ so confident his mother wasn't going to die. The kid had already lost his father before he even had a chance to meet him. The idea of losing the only parent he had was probably too much to even consider right now.

His phone chirped with an incoming message, and it wasn't until he was reaching into his pocket to pull it out that he realized it wasn't only his phone that had beeped.

Matilda, PJ, Winter, Winter's husband, and Casey were all reaching for their phones as well.

Bad news.

He knew it before he even got his phone out.

All he didn't know was just how bad the news was.

If Tessa was dead, he didn't think Wyatt would tell them in a text message.

So, they had either found Tessa alive, but injured, or they'd learned something about who had taken her.

Daniel was leaning toward thinking maybe Tessa had been found alive when he heard a collective gasp from the room's other occupants.

He'd been right.

It *was* bad news.

As much as he didn't want to, as much as he wanted to cling to denial for as long as possible, Daniel looked down at his phone.

The message was short.

Only one line.

She'll be dead in ten days.

He didn't have to guess who the *she* was.

It was Tessa.

And apparently, whoever had broken in here last night and abducted her planned to kill her in ten days.

"Did we all get the same message?" he asked, even though he already knew the answer.

"Yes," everyone else's scared voices confirmed.

How did this man know who they all were?

How did he know all their phone numbers?

Did he know that they were all here together?

And why tell them of his intentions?

Did he want them to find him?

Did he really not want to do this and was looking for them to stop him before he did something he regretted?

Did he want to extort money from them?

Daniel wished he could answer even one of those questions. Maybe then, he wouldn't feel like his world spinning out of control.

* * * * *

5:13 P.M.

It was such a gorgeous day.

The sunshine, the gentle breeze, the singing birds, the bright flowers—everything was so pretty.

She felt like bursting into song and dancing about the yard like she was still five years old.

Well, not really, Melanie Gardner thought as she stood in her front yard. She had never been this happy when she was a child. Her home life hadn't been the best. It certainly hadn't been the worst. There were a lot of kids in the world who'd had things a lot harder than she had, but still, she hadn't been happy.

Her parents were usually off at work. Her dad had travelled a lot, and her mother worked long hours. When they were both home at the same time, all they did was fight. With no siblings and no extended family, she hadn't had anyone to turn to when she was feeling alone and scared, so she'd started reading. She had learned to read when she was four, and that had opened up a whole new world to her. A world where she could be anything she wanted and go anywhere.

Little Melanie would spend most of her time with her nose buried in a book. Actually, it wasn't just *little* Melanie who would spend most of her time with her nose buried in a book. Up until just a year ago, reading and work had been pretty much all her life consisted of.

Now, she had so much more.

Now, she had someone in her life who made her feel loved for the very first time.

It was a little sad to say that it had taken her until she was forty-three to find it.

Besides her books, she'd had a great group of friends at school. They were all outcasts, shunned by their peers because of their intelligence. They'd grown very close, but that had also made them vulnerable to someone who wanted to hurt them. That time in her life had been dark, and she'd been the last one of their group to finally find her way into the light.

Now that she was there, she was never going back—not for anything.

She was happy.

Really and truly happy, and it was all thanks to Ross Hainer.

He was the complete opposite of her. While she was quiet and shy, he was outgoing and confident. He'd come up to her one morning when she was sitting by herself drinking coffee and eating breakfast in her favorite café. If he hadn't come up to her and started chatting away, she would never have gone up to him, and they would never have fallen in love. She'd actually noticed him long before that day. Most mornings they were in the café at the same time. He was good-looking, and she would often daydream about what it would be like to kiss him.

She had never been kissed before Ross.

And she never wanted to kiss anyone else.

She was one hundred percent completely and utterly head over heels in love.

Ross was two years older than her and had three kids: two sons who were nineteen and fifteen, and a seventeen-year-old daughter. Their parents had been divorced for a little over a decade, so they hadn't been angry or resentful when their dad had started dating her. They had been supportive of the relationship from the very first day and she got along really well with them.

It felt like so much longer than just eighteen months.

How could her life change that dramatically in such a short amount of time?

It was so amazing.

To think that one person could change your life like that.

That one person could make you feel loved after a lifetime of feeling unwanted. After what had happened to her when she was a teenager, she'd thought she was unworthy of being loved. Like she was broken inside and there was no one who had the skills to fix her.

But she'd been wrong.

So very wrong.

There was someone who could fix her.

And what was better—Ross hadn't fixed her; he had helped her see that she didn't need to be fixed. That there was nothing wrong with her, she wasn't broken.

Melanie couldn't wait to spend the rest of her life with this man. Helping him raise his kids and growing old together. They had even talked about the possibility of fostering or maybe even adopting. She was forty-three and he was forty-five and they had decided that having a baby of their own wasn't in their future, but there were so many older kids out there who needed a home and people to love them, that the idea of fostering had appealed to both of them.

She had so much to look forward to.

And top of that list was spending the night with her husband.

Melanie still got tingles every time she thought or said the word husband. She and Ross had been together for eighteen months, married for thirteen of those, and she still couldn't get enough of calling him her husband.

Ross had been away for the last few days, travelling for a work conference, and the kids would be here on the fifteenth to spend the rest of the summer with their dad. They had planned a family vacation. A *family* vacation. She'd never really been on one. Her parents were too busy to travel with her when she was a kid, and then she'd spent most of her adult life alone. She was so excited about this trip.

As excited as she was for the kids to arrive. She wanted to make the most of the last few days of alone time with her husband.

Taking a last look at the glorious afternoon, she headed inside. She was going to cook a special dinner, and then she'd bought some new lingerie that she couldn't wait to try out on Ross.

Collecting the grocery bags from the car, she headed inside. Ross would be back from the airport at seven, and it was already after five. She was going to have to hurry if she was going to get the table set and the meal cooked and then be in the lingerie before he walked through the door.

As she walked inside, she was thinking about where she would be when he got home. She could be in the bedroom … or maybe on the sofa in the living room … or she could be in the kitchen cooking, dressed only in the lingerie. That was sexy, right? She was so lost in thought that she didn't notice the figure in the corner.

It wasn't until she'd set the bags down on the counter, put the chicken wings in the oven, and flipped on the light—they had moved into a new place together after they got married, a fresh start for both of them, and it had a kind of dark kitchen even on the brightest, sunniest of days you needed the light on—that she saw him.

He was just standing there.

Staring at her.

Melanie blinked, sure that he was just a figment of her imagination and he'd be gone when she opened her eyes again.

But he wasn't.

He was still there.

Why wasn't he doing anything?

Why wasn't she doing anything?

She knew why he was here.

Well, not specifically, but there was only one reason someone would break into another person's house and lay in wait for them.

He was here to hurt her.

Kill her.

Probably rape or torture her first.

The man took a step forward.

She took one backward.

He took another step.

She took another back.

What was wrong with her?

Why wasn't she making a run for it?

When he took his next step, she bolted, grabbing a knife from the knife block on the countertop as she ran.

Melanie was halfway to the front door when something spiked her back and excruciating pain zapped through her body.

She groaned and slumped to the floor, the knife clattering

uselessly down beside her.

"Don't worry," the man said as he squatted beside her. "It won't hurt." He picked up her hands and tied her wrists together with a strip of fabric. Then he scooped her up and started walking through the house with her.

She couldn't believe this was happening.

She had survived a vicious psychopath who'd been intent on murdering her and her friends, only to finally find the happiness she had longed for her entire life, and now that she had it, she was going to die anyway.

He carried her through to her and Ross's bedroom and gently laid her out on the bed.

This was what Ross was going to come home to.

Instead of arriving back to find her draped out in her sexy lingerie, he was going to find her dead body waiting for him.

The man stood above her with a vial in his hand.

She tried to move, but she hadn't quite regained control of her body yet.

The needle pierced her skin.

If she was going to die, then she, at least, wanted to see the face of the man who was taking her life.

With a shaking hand she reached up and pulled off his mask.

Melanie gasped.

Then she couldn't do anything else.

Her hand dropped down to her side, and her eyes fluttered closed.

At least she was dying without regrets.

These last eighteen months had given her everything she had ever dreamed about.

Her last thought before she drifted away was gratefulness to Ross for making her so happy and sorrow that he would be the one to find her.

AUGUST 3ᴿᴰ

"Why did it take so long for this to be called in?" Detective Paige Hood asked her partner as she parked her car outside a pretty Cape Cod with a gorgeous garden and met Ryan on the curb.

"Husband freaked out when he found the body," Ryan replied.

"Freaked out how?" She didn't have any details on the case except that a middle-aged woman had been found dead in her home. When her boss had called twenty minutes ago, she'd been busy dealing with a sick kid. Her younger daughter, ten-year-old Arianna, had the flu, not fun at any time, but especially not when you were on summer vacation. She wished she could stay home with her; this year had been a rough one for her family, and she often found herself thinking about spending more time with them.

But the only way to do that would be to quit her job.

Paige wasn't sure that she wanted to do that.

She loved her job, but she loved her family more. She wished that there was a compromise that would let her spend more time at home without completely giving up work.

"He got off a plane at six last night; he probably arrived home around seven. He must have found the body almost immediately because whatever food Melanie Gardner was cooking was still in the oven. It eventually set off the smoke detector and that drew the neighbors' attention. It was the couple who lived next door," Ryan pointed to the house on the left of Gardner Hainer house, "who called it in."

"What did they find when they got there?" Paige asked. She knew they had found Ross Hainer and his deceased wife, but she wanted to know why the husband hadn't called in his wife's murder or tried to get her help.

"Apparently, the husband was still in the bedroom clutching his wife in his arms and sobbing."

"Shock," she murmured as the headed inside. That was understandable. Who wouldn't be in shock if they arrived home from a business trip expecting to find their wife waiting for them, probably with a romantic evening planned, only to find her lifeless corpse instead?

"It was lucky the dinner burned; otherwise; who knows how long Ross would have sat in there before anyone found him."

"How is he now? Is he still here or did the paramedics have to take him to the hospital?" she asked as they stepped inside.

"Paramedics checked him out, but he's still here. He's in the backyard."

That was good. They needed to talk to him and find out if he'd seen anything. He was the one to find the body, and given the timeline, they knew Melanie Gardner had left work a little before five with plans to stop at the grocery store on her way home, and that Ross probably arrived home around seven. He might have actually seen something that might help them.

"Knife on the floor," Ryan said as they surveyed the living room.

"She must have seen him and tried to defend herself." Paige wondered how long it had taken for her attacker to unarm her. "If he got her in here, he must have either knocked her out or restrained her in some way to get her to the bedroom."

"Her body is still in the bedroom, waiting for the medical examiner to arrive," Ryan said.

"Have you seen the body?"

"No, I was waiting for you before I came in here. We work better when we work the scene together."

That was true.

She and Ryan had been partners for two decades, and as well as working together, they were best friends. She considered Ryan and his family to be her family. Paige loved being Ryan's partner, and if she did decide to retire from the force, she would really miss seeing him every day.

"Let's go check out the bedroom," she said. Although she and Ryan were helping with the Tessa Bell case—as was pretty much every cop in the department—there were other cases that had to be dealt with, as well. But, since Tessa was the widow of a decorated cop who had been killed in the line of duty, everyone wanted to see her brought safely home.

The scene in the bedroom was not what she'd been expecting. The bed wasn't mussed up, and there were no signs of a struggle. Melanie Gardner's body was resting awkwardly against the headboard, which was probably where Ross had sat and cradled his wife's body.

There was no blood, and there were no wounds that Paige could see anywhere on the body. Melanie was still wearing the white and blue sundress she'd worn to work. One white pump was still on her foot; the other lay on the floor by the door, it had probably been knocked off as the killer carried her in here.

Melanie's hands drew her attention.

Her wrists were bound with a strip of white cloth.

That was the second case in as many days where the victim had been restrained with strips of cloth. It wasn't that that was particularly unusual. She'd seen it before, but it wasn't usually a killer or abductor's first choice of restraints.

"He used cloth to tie her wrists together," Ryan said, focusing in on the same thing she had.

"Think it could be related?"

"To Tessa's abduction?" Ryan asked. "I don't know."

"Do they know each other?" They hadn't gone through all of Tessa's acquaintances yet. They'd been focusing on people who worked in all of the companies she owned, working the case as a kidnapping for ransom. Especially after the message that Tessa's family had received, telling them that she would be dead in ten days. But if this was related, it opened up a whole new lot of possibilities about what had happened to Tessa.

"We'll ask the husband, and if he doesn't know, we'll ask Wyatt and Tessa's family. If they *do* know each other, then we could be looking at a serial killer."

The last serial killer case they had worked had ended in her fifteen-year-old daughter Hayley and Ryan's fifteen-year-old daughter Sophie being abducted as bait for the killers to get Ryan and her. The killers had been out for revenge against them, and although everyone had made it out alive, the psychological ramifications of the ordeal were still affecting all of them.

When she was already questioning remaining a cop, another serial killer case was the last thing she wanted to be dealing with.

"I don't see any obvious sign of death," she said, refocusing her mind on where she was and why. "There are no stab wounds or gunshot wounds. I don't see any ligature marks around her neck, no bruises around her mouth or anything."

"ME should be able to tell us that when she takes a look at the body," Ryan said. "If this is related to Tessa's case, then why abduct her and apparently decide to keep her alive for ten days, but kill Melanie?"

"I don't know. Maybe the cases aren't related. Maybe Ross Hainer killed his wife. And maybe one of Tessa's family members abducted her. Could be the brother, jealous that he didn't inherit the family fortunes, decides he'll try to get ahold of them in a way that doesn't involve actually hurting his sister," she suggested.

"Could be," Ryan agreed. "Maybe the husband can give us some answers."

"We're not going to get anything else from here until the medical examiner looks at the body, and CSU goes through the house. The husband is our best bet at getting anything useful right now."

Paige sucked in a breath as they stepped out into the backyard.

It was so hot.

It was only nine in the morning and already she felt hot enough to explode.

She wasn't really a summer person; she hated being too hot. Fall was her favorite season, she loved watching the leaves change color, fall, and cover the ground in a multi-colored carpet. But there was still over a month until summer ended, and probably another month at least after that before the weather started cooling down. For the time being she was stuck with hot.

"Mr. Hainer?" She announced their arrival as they came up behind the man who was standing under a large tree, staring blankly at its thick trunk.

The man turned around slowly, and it took a moment for his eyes to focus on them. "You're the cops?"

"We are. Detective Hood and Detective Xander." She introduced them.

"You're here because Melanie is dead. Melanie is dead. She's dead." Ross's eyes were staring right through them. It was going to take a while for the reality of what had happened to sink in.

"Did you see anything unusual when you got home last night?" Ryan asked.

Ross shook his head.

"You don't remember seeing anyone hanging around the house or any cars parked out front?" Paige pressed. They needed something to go on. Anything.

Ross shook his head again.

"Do you remember if the door was locked or unlocked?" Ryan asked.

"Unlocked. It was unlocked," Ross said.

"Was that unusual?" Paige asked. They wanted to try to get an idea of whether Melanie knew her killer. Since she'd made it to the kitchen, the killer could have surprised her inside, or he could have knocked at the door and she let him in. If she hadn't seen him as a threat, she might have let him in, especially if she knew him, then she'd grabbed the knife when she'd realized he was there to hurt her.

"Yes, Melanie was very safety conscious."

"Mr. Hainer, did your wife have a friend named Tessa Bell?" Ryan asked.

"Yes. Tessa was Melanie's maid of honor at our wedding."

So, they had been right.

Melanie's case *was* related to Tessa's.

Paige wished she knew what that meant and whether it increased or decreased Tessa's chances of surviving.

* * * * *

9:40 A.M.

"Find anything?"

Jack blinked and looked away from the screen. It wasn't even ten in the morning, and his eyes were already feeling the strain of staring at a computer for too long.

He and Xavier were still working their way through the list of employees from all of the companies and businesses Tessa Bell owned. They were highlighting anyone with a criminal history or who was currently suffering any sort of financial difficulties. So far, he had almost three dozen names marked to come back to and look into more thoroughly, and there were still several thousand more employees to look at.

"I have a list with names on it for us to go through in more detail, but so far, no one who jumps out at me," Jack replied. "You?"

"Same," his partner said, pushing back from the table and standing and stretching.

"This is going to take too long," he said, as he also stood and went to the coffee machine to pour himself another cup. He hadn't slept well last night. Even with the air conditioner on, it was too hot, and the threat that Tessa's family had received had been playing heavily on his mind.

Ten days.

According to the kidnapper, that was all the time they had to find her before he would kill her.

The threat in and of itself hadn't seemed all that unusual. They had already been thinking that this could be a kidnap-for-ransom case, so that the kidnapper would reach out to the family with threats was to be expected.

What had bothered him was that there had been no follow-up communication.

He had expected them to get more information. The amount of money the kidnapper wanted in return for letting Tessa go alive. Details on when the next communication would be. Threats not to involve the cops—although Jack supposed if the kidnapper did know Tessa and who she was then that would be pointless. As a widow of a decorated cop, they were bound to get involved as soon as she went missing. Threats that if they didn't comply with instructions, Tessa would be hurt, and possibly even a body part included.

Those were the things he'd been expecting.

But there had been nothing like that.

They had heard nothing else, and that had him on edge.

That and the fact that this case hit way too close to home for his family. The events of six months ago, standing in this very building, opening a brown cardboard box that had been addressed to his brother Ryan and Paige, finding two small pinkie fingers inside—one belonging to Ryan's daughter Sophie, the other to Paige's daughter Hayley—all of that was too fresh in their minds.

He didn't want Tessa's family—or Tessa herself—to have to go through that, but how could he stop it from happening when he didn't have enough information to go on?

"Maybe we'll get a hit on the blood," Xavier suggested. The sample from the front of the van was being run through CODIS and they were all hoping it would get a hit, and they'd get their guy.

"Our murder case is related," Ryan announced as he and Paige entered the room.

"What case?" Jack asked. As far as he knew, Ryan and Paige were working this case, but new cases that came in still had to be assigned and worked even if the department's focus was locating Tessa Bell.

"Where's Wyatt?" Paige asked.

"Right here," the older man said as he stepped into the room, shoving his phone back into his pocket. "I was just checking in with my family. What's up? Do you have something?"

They all waited expectantly for an explanation.

"Paige and I went to a house this morning where a husband returned home to find his wife dead," Ryan explained, taking a seat at the table. The rest of them joined him there.

"And?" Wyatt prompted.

"How is that related to Tessa's abduction?" Xavier asked.

"Well, at first, we weren't sure it was," Paige continued. "The victim had been restrained with cloth rather than rope or string or plastic ties. Given that it's not the most common choice of binding, unless it's clothing the victim was wearing, which this wasn't, we wondered if the cases could be linked."

"Is that it?" Wyatt demanded. His green eyes were sharp. He might have retired from the force fifteen years ago, but he hadn't lost his cop edge.

"No," Ryan replied. "We asked the husband if his wife knew anyone by the name of Tessa Bell, and he said yes. He said his wife had a friend by that name who'd been the maid of honor at their wedding."

Wyatt paled. That obviously meant something to him.

"Her name was—"

"Melanie Gardner," Wyatt interrupted Ryan.

"That's right," Paige nodded. "You know her?"

"Oh yeah." Wyatt drew in a deep breath and then puffed it back out.

"How?" Jack asked when the other man didn't elaborate.

"It was the case where Parker and I first met Tessa."

Jack knew a little about the case but not all the details. And if they were going to find Melanie Gardner's killer and Tessa's abductor, then they needed details. "What happened with the case?"

"It started as an abduction. A twenty-five-year-old woman went missing, and whoever took her, left a note in her apartment with clues to nine other women he planned on killing. He claimed that if we found the other women, he would kill his victim, but if we didn't and he killed them all, then he would let her go alive. We knew it wasn't true; we just didn't know what he really wanted. During the investigation, we met Tessa. She drove us crazy insisting she didn't know who was after her. Parker was so mad at her." Wyatt gave a sad smile. "But he couldn't stop thinking about her. He was in love with her from the first time he saw her."

"But you solved that case," Xavier said.

"We did. It wasn't until Tessa ran off to sacrifice herself to save her friends that they finally cracked and told us what was going on. We ran off to try to save Tessa, but she had already saved herself. The killer had intended to whisk her away, keep her alive; he was obsessed with her. Like I told you earlier, Tessa is always prepared for the worst. She was able to get free from the ropes he'd used to tie her up, they fought over his gun, it went off, and he was killed."

"So, if he's dead, then that man couldn't be the one who abducted Tessa and killed Melanie," Paige said.

"Could her friends have lied?" Ryan asked. "Could it really have been someone else who was after them?"

"They didn't lie. Everything they said was backed up. That was the man who was killing them off one by one. But …"

"But what?" Jack asked.

"But they could have left something out. They weren't very forthcoming with information, and what they told us, they only did so because they were backed into a corner. There could be more to the story than they let on. Tessa has this strategy where she lets you think something and doesn't correct you, so you think you're on the right path, but really, you couldn't be more off base."

"We need to talk to them," Xavier said immediately.

"Lauren, Carrie, and Michelle are all that's left now. And one other woman, but I have no idea how to contact her, and unless one of the women is prepared to call her and let her know what's going on, we'll never find her."

"Do you really think there's a chance that it's related to that case?" Jack asked. Parker and Tessa had met almost twenty years ago, and it had been fifteen years since his death. Why would a killer wait this long before coming back for the women he wanted to kill?

"If you had asked me this ten minutes ago, I would have given a definitive no, but now …" Wyatt trailed off.

"Paige, Ryan, I might have cause of death for you in the Melanie Gardner case."

"Already?" Paige asked the medical examiner.

"It's not official," Jenny Buckley said as she joined them at the table. "But, as I was examining the body, it looked like she died of a heart attack, and I started wondering what would cause a forty-three-year-old woman who is in good physical health and doesn't have any medical condition to have a heart attack. Since we know that she was attacked, I started thinking, and then it hit me, potassium chloride. In large doses, it causes severe heart arrhythmia and mimics a heart attack. I checked the body, and I found a small puncture wound on her right bicep. Since potassium is released into the bloodstream whenever there is muscle tissue damage, I probably can't prove that's what he gave her, but I'm pretty confident." Jenny beamed at them.

That made sense.

And it fit in with their idea that he was using the cloth to restrain his victims to minimize their suffering. A heart attack, while not the best way to die, certainly wasn't the worst. He could have tortured them, stabbed them or shot them, or anything else, and yet, he seemed to have chosen something that would be quick and relatively painless. He hadn't spent long with Melanie Gardner; he'd been in and out in less than two hours. It was almost like he had a job to do, and he just wanted to get it done as quickly and as efficiently as he could.

"Did you get anything else?" Ryan asked.

"I found evidence that she'd been tasered—two small puncture marks on her back. Probably how he subdued her," Jenny replied.

"Tessa too," Jack said, casting a cautious glance in Wyatt's direction. He still wasn't sure the man could hold it together until they found Tessa.

Wyatt winced, but then nodded. "Makes sense. You found a knife on the floor beside her bed, right?"

"We did," Xavier replied.

"Tessa sleeps with one under her pillow. She probably tried to get to it to defend herself but dropped it when he tased her."

That made sense.

And between what Jenny had told them about Melanie's murder, and what Wyatt had said about the history between Tessa and Melanie, they actually had a direction to move in.

Maybe they *would* find Tessa before her ten days were up.

* * * * *

11:58 A.M.

"Where exactly are we going?" Hayley Hood asked her best friend as she followed Sophie through the woods.

"We're going to go meet someone," Sophie replied.

"And we couldn't have done that at your place?"

"He doesn't want to."

"Oh," she smiled knowingly, "it's a he."

"He's just a friend," Sophie said quickly.

"Sure," Hayley snickered. She had known Sophie since they were five years old and she'd been adopted by Paige and Elias Hood.

She had been rescued, along with four other girls, from a maniac who'd kept them locked in a house and intended to keep them there forever. Back then, she'd been a terrified and very emotional child who didn't know how to live in the real word. Sophie had been her lifeline. As much as she loved her parents and knew she wouldn't be where she was now without them, a lot of the credit definitely went to Sophie.

They had been through a lot in the last ten years.

Particularly, what had happened six months ago.

Hayley didn't think she would have survived being chained up in that basement without Sophie.

Every time she looked at where her finger used to be, she couldn't help but think about it. She still saw her therapist, and she and her parents made sure they talked about it sometimes. They wanted her to know that she could always talk to them, and Hayley knew it helped her mom to feel less guilty knowing that they were both dealing with what had happened as best as they could.

She and Sophie talked about it sometimes too. It was something they shared that no one else could really understand. Some nights when one of them couldn't sleep, they would call the other up and talk for hours.

Although what had happened had affected both of them, it

had touched Sophie in a completely different way.

Sophie had lost faith in herself.

She didn't trust her own judgment anymore.

Especially when it came to guys.

But maybe some of that confidence was returning.

"He likes you?" Hayley asked as she stretched to step over a large tree root.

"Yeah, he does." Sophie stopped and stared out over a small trickling stream.

Hayley stopped beside her.

Sunlight seeped through the canopy of trees and sparkled on the water.

It was so beautiful.

She could see why Sophie and her friend liked it out here. It was peaceful, like you could switch off your brain and the mess of thoughts that swirled constantly through your head and just be. Just exist without being afraid or overly cautious. She was going to spend more time out here.

"Do you like him too, Soph?" she asked gently. Hayley knew that Sophie had sworn off guys, but she didn't want to see her friend punish herself for something that wasn't her fault. They were teenagers. They had their whole lives ahead of them, and she would hate to see Sophie miss out on meeting someone great just because she was afraid.

"I don't know."

Despite her friend's answer, Hayley got the feeling that she *did* know exactly what her feelings were for this so-called friend. "I think you do know. You like him."

"It's too soon," Sophie said, sounding more like she was trying to convince herself of that than anyone else.

"How long have you known this friend?"

"My whole life. His mom and mine were friends since they were babies."

"How long has he liked you?"

"Since we were like, nine."

"So a guy that you have known your whole life, who your family knows and I'm guessing likes, who you have a special place to meet and talk, and has had a crush on your for the last six years, and that's too soon?" Hayley asked.

"Okay, I guess you're right about that. I have known PJ for a long time, and yes, I'm comfortable around him. He's been a good friend to me. But he's going through a lot, and the last—and only—guy I ever dated turned out to be a killer."

"That's not going to happen again." She wrapped an arm around her best friend's shoulders. She couldn't imagine having to go through what Sophie was. It was hard enough dealing with their ordeal without the added bonus of knowing that you had fallen right into a trap and were in love with the man who wanted to hurt you.

"You don't know that."

"Well, he's *your* friend. Do you think he's a deranged killer?"

"No, of course not. PJ's dad was a cop who was killed before he was born, and his mom is a really sweet woman who has been through a lot in her life. He's a great guy; any girl would be lucky to go out with him."

"So ..." She knew that Sophie was scared to put herself out there again and fall in love. But this PJ sounded like a great guy. He was the perfect person to help her move on.

"So, what?" Sophie deliberately played obtuse.

"So, maybe you should see if there could be anything between you two. It can't hurt."

"Maybe," Sophie mumbled, then started walking again. "Enough about my love life or lack of, are you going to do anything about the pianist?"

"No," Hayley murmured. Now, she was the embarrassed one, wishing they could be talking about anything else.

"Why not?"

She may as well tell Sophie the truth. They were best friends;

they shared everything. "I was never really that interested in him."

"Oh? Why did you say you were?"

"No reason."

"You like someone else, don't you?" Sophie asked delightedly.

"Maybe," she said reluctantly.

"Who is it?"

Hayley couldn't help but smile at the glee in her friend's voice. It was nice to just talk about normal things like boys, just like two normal teenage girls would. Sometimes she forgot that they were still fifteen; she'd always been one of those kids that was like an adult in a child's body, and after the ordeal they'd gone through, she felt so much older than fifteen.

"Hales? Who's the guy?"

"Nothing can ever happen between us," she hedged.

"How do you know? Maybe they could."

"He's too old."

"It's Brian, isn't it?" Sophie spun around, a huge smile on her face.

"How did you know that?" she asked. How did Sophie always know her so well?

"It really is, isn't it? You like my cousin Brian."

Hayley shrugged. "I have a teeny, tiny crush on him. But he's twenty-one and in college studying premed, and I'm fifteen and about to be a high school junior. We have nothing in common, and he thinks I'm just some kid."

"It's a bit of an age gap now," Sophie acknowledged, "but in a couple of years, it won't seem so big. Have you told him how you feel?"

"No. And you can't either. Promise me." She didn't want to have to go through the embarrassing conversation of being turned down. Sophie might have lost her confidence with guys, but Hayley wasn't sure she'd ever had any, or that she ever would.

"Hayley," Sophie groaned.

"Promise me," she repeated.

"Yeah. I won't say anything. Look at us, we're a mess, aren't we?"

"We are, but we have each other. And we have amazing families."

They really did.

When she and Sophie had been abducted, it had been as a trap for the killers to get her mom and Sophie's dad. Those hours that she'd spent knowing that her mother had traded herself for her and not knowing if she was going to make it out alive had been amongst the worst of her life. She knew how lucky she was to have such an amazing mom. Her dad was just as amazing.

She was one lucky kid, and she reminded herself of that every single day.

"So, you said your friend PJ is going through a lot. What's going on?"

"PJ's mom was abducted. She's the only parent he has, and he's so freaked out."

"Oh, poor PJ." She wished she didn't know exactly what he was going through.

"He's probably going to be nervous around you," Sophie warned. "He's a genius like his mom and studies from home with a tutor, so he doesn't really have many friends."

"Does he know I'm coming?" She didn't want to get in the way of Sophie and PJ, especially while he was going through something so rough.

"Yes, I told him I wanted him to meet you because you're my best friend, and we both know what he's going through. It's just up there." Sophie pointed to a small clearing with a large log in the middle. "And there he is."

A teenage boy with messy black hair stepped out from the tree line. He looked in their direction and waved when he saw them.

Immediately, Sophie quickened her step. Her friend might claim that she wasn't ready to date again, but she obviously had feelings for PJ.

If PJ liked Sophie and Sophie liked PJ, then they should go for it.

Maybe there was something she could do to bring them together.

They all deserved some happiness.

* * * * *

3:36 P.M.

Thankfully, they'd been able to track down Tessa's remaining friends who had all readily agreed to come down to the station and answer some questions.

Wyatt wanted to go running into the room where they were waiting and shake them until whatever they were still hiding came tumbling out. The only thing stopping him from doing it was that he knew Jack Xander and Xavier Montague were watching him like a hawk.

One wrong move, and they would block him from this case.

While he still had some sway here at the department, he wasn't a cop anymore, and the only way he was remaining on this case was to play nice with the detectives.

So he was.

He would do whatever it took to keep on their good sides because the only thing that mattered right now was bringing Tessa home.

"You think they're holding something back?" Jack Xander asked him.

Wyatt liked the detective. He seemed competent—he was smart, intuitive, and hardworking. He'd done a little research on the detectives that were working this case. If he hadn't thought they were good enough, he would have done whatever he had to, to get them removed. When looking into Jack Xander, he had learned that the man was married to a woman who had once been a victim of crime and was now a psychiatrist who helped run a center for abused women and children. The guy had two kids, a twelve-year-old son, and a ten-year-old daughter who had witnessed a crime a few months ago.

He trusted this man, which made "playing nice" to stay on the case easy enough.

"I don't know," he said in answer to the cop's question. "They are all really good at keeping secrets. They've been doing it most of their lives. But Tessa was the leader. She was the glue that held them together. If they *are* hiding something, then I think it will be easier to get information out of them this time than it was last time."

"Do you think they'll be more or less likely to open up to us or to you?" Xavier Montague asked.

Wyatt liked this detective too. Xavier was also married to a woman who'd been a victim of a crime and who helped to run the same center that Jack Xander's wife worked at. He had five-year-old twins who had been named after their mother's deceased siblings.

Xavier and Jack worked well together. From what he'd heard, they had been partners for the last fifteen years, and they had developed that same closeness and ability to read each other and play off each other that he and Parker used to have.

Losing Parker had been a double blow. He hadn't just lost his partner; he'd lost the man who'd been his best friend since he was fifteen. After being abandoned by his mother when he was three months old, Parker and his twin sister Matilda had bounced around the foster care system before being adopted by the family who had lived next door to his.

He still remembered meeting sullen, angry ten-year-old Parker. He remembered hearing a bit about what the kid had gone through and deciding then and there to help Parker adjust to being part of a loving home.

They had been friends ever since.

When Parker died, he'd made a promise to take care of Tessa and the baby. Parker was family, and so were Tessa and PJ, and you did whatever you had to for family. There wasn't anything he wouldn't do to honor the promise he'd made.

"They'll be more likely to open up to me," Wyatt said. "They don't like strangers and they know that I care about Tessa, so it'll be harder to lie to me."

"Then let's get in there," Jack said, opening the door to the interview room.

"What's going on?" Michelle Joseph demanded the second they stepped into the room.

"You haven't been paying attention to the news?" he asked as he slid into a seat.

"Of course we have been," Lauren Angel rolled her eyes.

"We know that Tessa was abducted, and Melanie was murdered," Carrie Marble replied. "We just don't know why. What is going on?"

"We don't know," he replied honestly.

"Just like old times," Lauren muttered.

"Is it?" he asked. "*Is* it just like old times?" Last time Parker had been the one impatient to get answers from Tessa's friends so they could find her before it was too late, and he'd been the one to try to keep things smooth so they could get what they needed. This time things were reversed. He was the one desperate to get whatever information they needed to find Tessa, and it would have to be Jack and Xavier who played nice and smoothed things over.

"What do you mean?" Carrie asked, eyes all wide and innocent.

"You know what I mean. Are you keeping secrets again? Do you know what's going on? Do you know who took Tessa?"

"I can get why you would think that, given that we weren't very forthcoming with information last time, but this time is different," Michelle said. "We don't know what's going on."

He wished he could believe that.

He wanted to.

But he couldn't be sure.

When he looked into their eyes, he saw that look of practiced blankness which came from many years of hiding things.

"I don't believe you," he said. "That's exactly what you said last time."

"Last time, Tessa's life wasn't at stake," Lauren shot back. "Well, it was, but not the same way it is this time. Last time, she knew what she was doing—she had a plan—but this is different."

"For all I know, this time Tessa has a plan too." Wyatt didn't believe that. He had heard the tone of Tessa's voice when she called him. She had been afraid; she wasn't faking or lying or up to something. But he had to push her friends. He had to be sure they weren't lying to him.

"Look, we know what happened to all of you when you were kids." Jack stepped in to try to smooth things over.

From what Wyatt had heard, the man was good with victims. Really good. Apparently, he could get information out of them that no one else could. He hoped that was true.

"I'm so sorry about what happened," Jack continued, "and I understand that it formed a bond between all of you. But if you know anything at all about what might have happened to Tessa and Melanie, then you need to tell us. Was there anyone else involved in what happened to you?"

"There really wasn't," Carrie said. "Honestly. There wasn't anyone else that hurt us back then. We aren't keeping any other secrets. And even if there *was* something, I think this time we would just tell you." She looked at the others who both nodded their agreement.

"We all learned from that," Michelle said. "We're just sorry that our friends had to die for us to see that he was still controlling our lives and hurting us all those years later. But we did learn, and we've all moved on with our lives. Tessa had Parker, Melanie met Ross, Lauren is married with three kids,

Carrie is married with a son, and I'm married with two daughters. We're still all friends, real friends now, like we used to be in school, not just people tied together by a lie and a gigantic secret."

"Do you think we're in danger?" Lauren asked.

"I don't know," Wyatt answered honestly. "It depends on who took Tessa and killed Melanie and why. But after what happened with Dylan Riley, there were only five of you left—and of those five, one is now missing, and one is dead. We can't rule out that this involves the rest of you as well."

"We're going to have you go through everyone who was connected with you during your time at school and see if you can think of anyone who might want to hurt you," Xavier said.

"I can't think of anyone," Carrie said.

"Me neither," Lauren said.

"Or me," Michelle added.

"We'll pull up lists of all the teachers and students at the school while you were there," Jack told them. "We'll go through all of them and run them for criminal records or financial problems."

"Financial problems?" Lauren asked.

"We were wondering if this could be a kidnapping for ransom when Tessa was first taken. Now that Melanie was murdered, we're not sure if that's what this is, but we're still keeping that angle open," Wyatt explained.

Part of him wished that Tessa's friends had been keeping secrets. That there was someone connected to what had happened twenty-five years ago who might have done this. At least then he would have known for sure who they were after.

But now he didn't think that was likely.

As far as he knew, Tessa wasn't keeping any more secrets of her own, and there was no one else from her past who might want to hurt her.

So, who had kidnapped her?

TEN

* * * * *

4:18 P.M.

He was watching.

Reconnaissance.

It was an important part of his plan.

He knew how important it was that he be careful about this. If he wasn't, the cops were going to find him and that couldn't happen.

It was too soon.

There was more he needed to do, and having the cops on his tail was only going to slow him down.

He couldn't quite explain this driving desire inside him. He needed to do this; it was as simple as that. He didn't know why he did, and he didn't care. He knew it was the right thing to do, possibly even the only thing to do.

Sometimes life just put you in a situation that you hated and knew needed to be rectified.

That burning passion had always been inside him.

He wished he'd done this sooner. It was a relief to finally be doing something about it. Maybe now, he'd be able to find the peace that had eluded him for so long.

If this didn't work, if he didn't end up getting the peace that he so desperately sought, he didn't know what he was going to do. He needed this so badly.

Which was why it was so important that he not mess up. Just one little slipup could ruin everything. So, he was taking this seriously. He was making sure he thought through everything and came up with plans and backup plans.

So far, his attention to detail was paying off. Tessa was safely tucked away in her new room. His partner's body was disposed of and, as far as he knew, was as yet undiscovered. Melanie Gardner's murder had gone off without a hitch, and now he was preparing for the next one.

Because he needed everything to run smoothly, he'd done most of his reconnaissance before he started. If he was going to get through this, he was going to have to do it quickly, keep moving. Any pause just gave the cops a chance to find him.

So, it was a murder a day until he reached his goal.

That would keep the cops too busy just chasing around after him and wouldn't give them a chance to get ahead. Because if they got ahead of him, they would catch him, and everything would be ruined.

Since he had been so diligent in learning everything he could about his intended victims, it was easy to move at a fast pace. There wasn't anything new he needed to learn. He just needed a couple of hours to make sure that there were no last-minute issues that were going to crop up.

Which was why he was here.

He was sitting in his car outside the house of his next victim.

This one wasn't going to be quite as easy as the last one. This woman didn't live with only one other person, who'd been away and on an airplane. This woman lived with her physically-disabled mother, her mentally-disabled brother, her husband, and ten-year-old daughter.

It would almost be easier if he could just kill them all.

But that wasn't the plan.

And he had to stick to the plan, even if it did make things harder.

His plan was to wait until everyone was inside except the husband, who usually worked late most nights and wasn't home until around eight. Then all he had to do was lure the woman out into the backyard, kill her, and disappear.

It wasn't important to him that they suffered; in fact, he preferred that they didn't. He just wanted them dead.

That was it.

Plain and simple.

Hacking into the house's home security system, he watched on his phone as images of the family popped up on the screen.

The brother sat in his wheelchair in the living room watching the TV, at least that's what it looked like he was doing. It seemed to be what he spent most of his time doing. From what he'd seen as he'd been studying the family, it seemed to be one of the few things that kept him calm.

He wondered why they didn't just put him in a home. He couldn't care for himself, and even with the help of a nurse who came to the house for a couple of hours every day, it must be a lot of work to care for him. Personally, he wouldn't bother.

The mother was in the kitchen, also in a wheelchair. She was puttering about preparing dinner. Although she was paralyzed from the waist down, she seemed to be able to get about fairly easily. He wondered why, if she could move about easily, she didn't get out and get her own place.

Maybe the daughter liked taking care of her mother.

He didn't have to wonder about why an adult child would take care of a parent. That he understood. He had been there and done that. His circumstances were very different than those of this family, but still, he knew that a love of a child for their parent knew no bounds.

The kid was upstairs in her bedroom, lying on her back on her bed, a phone in her hands. He knew kids, and he knew that once they entered the land of the cell phone, they lost touch with reality. The girl wouldn't notice anything was wrong until it was too late.

And the woman he was looking for was, as luck would have it, outside in the backyard. The fully fenced-in backyard.

Everything was ready.

The family were busy all doing their own thing, and the woman was in her yard tending to her vegetable garden. He could go for it now.

Right now.

That familiar rush started in his stomach.

The ruse he was going to use wasn't a clever or overly imaginative one.

Stick with simple.

The more complicated you made something, the greater the chances that something could go wrong. And since he couldn't afford for anything to go wrong, he was going to go with simple whenever he could.

Climbing from his car, he started to search around, pretending he was looking for something. A very specific something. A something that no one would think it was odd that he was looking for.

"Hello?" he called out as he walked down the side of the house.

"Hello?" the woman called back, standing and brushing dirt off her hands as she shot him a wary glance.

He shot her a warm, but worried smile, and he saw her relax a little as he got closer, and she got a good look at him. "I'm really sorry to bother you and interrupt your gardening." He looked down at the vegetable garden like he hadn't just been watching her via the security cameras surrounding her house.

"That's okay. Can I help you?"

"I was walking my dog, but the leash broke." He held it up so she could see the broken lead.

"Oh, your puppy got away?"

"Actually, she's an old dog, going on sixteen, but she still loves her daily walks. A car's tires squealed as it turned a corner, she got spooked and jolted against the leash. It broke, and she ran. I thought I saw her come this way. Did you see her?"

"No, I don't think so, but I guess she could have snuck by me as I was weeding. I love gardening. It's kind of my happy place, and I tend to get pretty distracted, just letting my mind wander."

"She's old and it's hot today. If she came in here, she would have headed for a shady place to rest." He pointed to some trees down by the back fence. "Maybe she might have gone there. I don't mean to interrupt your afternoon, but might I just check really quick?"

"Of course." She stood and walked with him toward the back of her yard.

He stayed a step behind, ready to pounce as soon as he was sure they were out of sight of anyone who might be watching. He slid the prepared syringe filled with potassium chloride from his pocket.

"There … is that her?" he asked, pointing to a shadow behind the last tree.

"It could be." The woman moved closer, no longer paying him any attention as she searched for his fictional dog. People were such suckers for a dog. Tell them one was in trouble, and they lost all their inhibitions and sense of potential danger.

When she bent down to look behind the tree, he made his move.

In one fluid motion, he swung the syringe up and then plunged it into her back.

When he had chosen the drug, he wasn't really sure just how quickly it would act. But he had been very pleasantly surprised last night at Melanie Gardner's house. It took effect almost immediately.

He watched with interest as the woman's face contorted in pain, and she clutched at her chest. He wondered what it was like to die. He wondered what death itself was like.

He would no doubt find out soon enough.

It was over quickly.

She was dead.

He'd done it.

Another successful murder.

It was time to start preparing for the next.

* * * * *

7:22 P.M.

"You have plans for tonight?" Sofia Xander asked her fifteen-year-old daughter.

"Not really," Sophie said, looking up from the book she was reading.

That was the same answer Sophie had given every night of her summer vacation so far. All her daughter had done since school finished was hang around the house or at the house of her best friend Hayley.

As much as Sofia loved having her daughter around, especially after almost losing her six months ago, she didn't want what had happened to affect Sophie to the point where she shut herself away from the rest of the world. Sofia knew what it was like to lose your sense of self when your true identity was blown wide open, and then on the heels of that, have to fight for your life. She knew what it was like to feel like giving up and letting the dark close in around you. But she'd fought to get her life back and she so badly wanted to help her daughter find her own way back from the dark.

She hated that she couldn't just pick her daughter up, kiss her, and make everything bad in the world go away.

But Sophie wasn't five years old anymore.

She was fifteen. She was growing up, and as much as she would be there for her daughter and give her all the support she could, this was something that Sophie had to figure out on her own.

Sofia went and sat beside her daughter. "Sweetheart, it's your summer vacation, and you're a teenager. Don't you want to go and hang out with some friends? Maybe go to the lake or a party or you could have some friends over here for a sleepover."

"I'm sure. I spent half the day with Hayley, and tonight I just want to hang out here, at home, with you and Dad."

She could never get enough of hearing that.

Last summer, she and Ryan had sat Sophie down and told her that she was adopted, and that her biological parents were a woman who wanted to extort money by selling her child and a man who paid women to have children for him. That same man was the man she had grown up thinking was her father but had turned out to be her grandfather. That was why she understood what Sophie was going through, because she had gone through it too.

When they'd told Sophie the truth about who her parents were, she had been so angry with them.

She had started to spin out of control, her grades had dropped, and she started staying out till all hours and refusing to come home. She'd started dating an eighteen-year-old, and she started saying how much she hated them. They had tried to give her space and time, but that had only added to the problem.

Now, everything was back to normal. Better, in fact, than it had been before. She and Sophie had grown so much closer the last six months.

But as much as she loved hearing her daughter say that she wanted to hang out at home with them, she wanted Sophie to be okay, and part of a teenager being okay was them wanting to be with their friends.

"As much as I love hearing you say that you want to spend time with your dad and me, it's really fine if you want to spend more time with your friends."

"I know, Mom." Sophie smiled at her. "But I'm not ready yet. Maybe, once school starts again. When I was in that basement, all I wanted was to come home and tell you and Daddy how much I love you. Right now, I just need to be with my family."

"All right, honey," she agreed. Maybe Sophie was right. Maybe she did just need a little more time; maybe they all needed a little more time.

"Who's ready for dinner?" Ryan called out as the front door

slammed closed.

"What did you bring?" Sofia asked. With her crazy schedule at the women and children's center she had started with the money she had inherited when the rest of her family was annihilated, and Ryan's crazy schedule, they ate takeout more than they probably should.

"Pizza and ice cream for dessert," Ryan replied, appearing in the doorway with three large pizza boxes and a tub of Sophie's favorite ice cream.

"Yum," Sophie beamed as she jumped up to grab the ice cream and stick it in the freezer, then got out plates and glasses and set the table.

"Ned," Ryan called out. Clambering on the stairs said that their twelve-year-old son was on his way.

Sofia had missed this.

Just hanging out with her family.

When she was a kid, she'd been so lonely. Her family was wealthy, but her older brothers—who turned out to be her father and two uncles—had been much older than her. Her sister—who was Sophie's biological mother—was much younger. The woman whom Sofia believed to be her stepmother was truly her biological mother and wasn't interested in her at all. And Sophie's father—who was really her grandfather—worked all the time.

She had always wished for a family like the one she and Ryan had made. It was one of the many things she loved about him. When she had felt so alone, Ryan had brought her into his family. His parents and brothers had accepted her as one of them. Then he had given her the most amazing daughter and son. She didn't care that Sophie wasn't biologically theirs she couldn't love her any more if she were.

This was what life was all about.

Sitting around having pizza and ice cream with your husband and your children. Talking and laughing and just enjoying being together.

Sofia cherished every single one of those moments because she knew better than most just how fragile life could be. She could blink and all of this could be gone.

Just like Tessa.

She used to love visiting Tessa when they were little girls. Tess always had some crazy scheme cooked up, and because they were both lonely little rich kids, they could commiserate and have fun running wild around her family's estate or Tessa's. She remembered when Tessa had changed. She'd gone missing one weekend when she was eleven. No one had noticed she was gone until she was found wandering at the side of the road covered in blood. After that, Tessa had never been the same. They had remained friends but grown apart, reconnecting after Tessa's husband was killed

She prayed that Tessa was okay. Her friend had been through so much, and she didn't deserve this.

"You okay?" Ryan asked as he slipped an arm around her waist and drew her against his chest, planting a kiss on her cheek.

"I'm fine," she assured him.

"Thinking about your friend?"

"A little. I just wish you knew where she was and if she was okay. I can't imagine PJ having to lose his mom on top of already having lost his dad."

"We're doing everything we can to find her."

"I know you are." She smiled up at her husband.

Fifteen years later and she still loved him as much today as she did on the day they'd gotten married. She was such a lucky woman. She had found the love of her life. That, in and of itself, was no small feat. That she had then married him and had a family with him and remained happily married for over a decade was even more amazing.

"Let's just enjoy tonight," she murmured as she rested her head on his chest. "Let's just enjoy spending time with our kids and hanging out like a normal family." With everything they'd been through, sometimes they didn't feel like a regular family. Regular families didn't deal with twisted family relationships and abductions.

"Let's," Ryan said, then touched his lips to her temple. "So ... who's up for a movie night like we used to have when you guys were in the single digits?" he asked their kids.

"With popcorn?" Ned asked. "And cookies. Oh, and pretzels if we have any of the ones that Aunt Laura makes. And maybe we could make s'mores later too."

Their almost teenage son was obviously due for another growth spurt. He'd been eating nearly constantly the last few weeks. He was growing so quickly. Next year he'd be a teenager, and he was already taller than her and Sophie. Soon, he'd be as tall as Ryan, and then he and Sophie would be graduating and going away to college.

She had to make the most of evenings like this while she still had them; before she knew it, it would just be her and Ryan alone in the house again.

"We can have all of those," she told Ned, as they opened the pizza boxes and started eating.

"Maybe we could get out the sleeping bags and all camp out in the living room tonight," Sophie suggested. "Just like when we were kids."

Sofia smiled. Her kids might be growing up way too fast, but they weren't all the way grown up just yet. She still had plenty of time to enjoy them, and no matter how old they got, they would always be her little babies, and she would always be there for them.

AUGUST 4TH

Tessa felt ill.

Part of it was probably from the concussion she'd sustained, but that was two days ago now. This was more than that.

She was sick.

If she had to guess, then she was *really* sick.

The wound on her leg was infected.

It was red and enflamed and filled with puss. Her leg was swollen and tender to the touch, and she was burning up.

The infection in her leg was slowly invading her body.

She had lost her appetite and hadn't eaten any of the dinner he'd brought her last night. And she was tired. The kind of tired that seeped inside you so you could barely function.

Without access to a doctor and antibiotics, she didn't see how she was going to get any better.

If she was lucky, the infection wouldn't progress to septicemia. And, if she was unlucky, then it would progress past septicemia to sepsis.

He had cleaned her wounds the same day he brought her here, and several times since, but it wasn't enough. Clean water wasn't enough to help her right now. She needed real medical care.

Since he'd taken the time to try to close the wounds on her head with strips of tape, and he had cleaned and bandaged all of her other wounds, she didn't think that he wanted to hurt her, even though he claimed he was going to kill her in ten days.

Ten days.

Apparently, that was the sum of the rest of her life.

Unless Skylar found her first.

Tessa wasn't sure how much faith she should put into that. He knew she was missing, and he would, no doubt, find the knife on the floor in her bedroom where she had dropped it when her kidnapper had tased her. For all she knew, the van might still be there too. It had crashed, and since there were two people involved in her abduction, they might have fled in a different vehicle. If the van was still there, Skylar would have blood evidence of the man who'd been in her bedroom. Hopefully, he would get DNA leading them to her abductor.

Or, at least, one of them.

But she had no idea if there were any connections between the two men involved that the cops would be able to find.

If they couldn't find the connection, they couldn't find this second man. And tracking down the first man was no good. He was dead.

She groaned.

Thinking about this wasn't doing her any good.

She had to figure out a way out of this room.

Every time he left, he relocked the door, and since the window was boarded up, she didn't like her chances.

She wasn't prepared for this.

She'd had the file in her watch to cut through the material binding her back in the van, but that was it. She didn't have any other tricks up her metaphorical sleeve.

Between her leg, her arm, her head, and the knifing pain in her chest every time she took a breath, she didn't even like her chances of talking her way out of this. She was usually very persuasive, and she was good at reading people. It was a skill she'd been born with and then honed with the help of an evil man who was so obsessed with her only death had broken that hold. But, right now, her head was too muddled to get a good read on his motives for abducting her, so she couldn't figure out how to use that against him.

The bathroom.

She needed the bathroom.

There was an en suite, so she had access to one to use the toilet or take a shower. She hadn't made it into the shower. It just took more energy than she possessed. But she had been up and down to the toilet a few times. It was just that it took so much out of her.

If a simple task like that drained her to the point of needing a couple of hours of sleep to recover, how was she going to be able to take advantage of any opportunities that presented themselves to escape?

He'd said he might let her out of her room later.

If she had free range of the house, she was sure she could find a way out.

Unless all the doors were locked.

And all the windows boarded up.

Then she wasn't sure what she was going to be able to achieve.

But she couldn't give up.

Not yet, at least.

The bathroom.

Right.

That's where she was supposed to be going.

With a painful moan, she pushed herself up into a sitting position. Even that hurt so much that it almost made her think it was too much of a bother. There were painkillers in the bathroom cabinet, but she was wary of taking any. She was already having trouble concentrating, and if she took any, she might not be able to keep focused enough to even give her a chance at coming up with a way to get back home.

Using her good arm to push herself off the bed, she kept most of her weight on her uninjured leg. It was getting harder and harder to use her bad one. With each passing hour, it got stiffer and more swollen. It wouldn't be long before she couldn't walk on it at all.

Maybe she could find something to use as a crutch.

With an awkward hop, she managed to make it to the bathroom. She took care of business as quickly as she could, then paused at the vanity, using it to help her keep her balance.

Tessa stared at her reflection.

It didn't look good.

Aside from the gash on her forehead and the one on her cheek, there were black smudges under her eyes, and her face was way too pale.

Her eyes met her reflection's and she stared into them.

They were a mix of blue and green, depending on her mood.

Parker always used to say that they were like staring into the ocean. He used to get lost just staring into them. When they first met, he always thought that just like the ocean, he knew there were things lurking beneath them, but he couldn't see what they were.

As time went on, and he started to earn her trust, she let him in on some of the things that lurked inside her head.

She just wished that she had let him in on everything.

Now, she couldn't even remember why it had seemed so important to keep her secrets.

Secrets had destroyed her marriage.

She had loved Parker. He was the best thing that had ever happened to her, but she had been betrayed by too many people, and it was so hard for her to let anyone in. She'd been so afraid, she couldn't take another betrayal.

Because of that, she'd wasted the short time she and Parker had shared.

She had continued to shut him out, no matter how many times he promised her that he was there for her. If it hadn't been for her, Parker would still be alive. She was the one who'd attracted that lunatic woman. She was the one who'd let distance grow between them, giving that woman the opportunity to take advantage of both of them. Because she'd let herself get abducted,

Parker had to come running to her rescue. Then, instead of coming to the hospital with her as she had begged him to, he'd gone off after that woman, knowing that she was dangerous and wanting to eliminate her as a threat, and gotten himself killed in the process.

Parker wasn't the only one she'd gotten killed.

Her friend Maisy had been abducted along with her and hadn't survived until Parker and Skylar found them.

She had died from an infection.

And now, things had come full circle.

She was probably going to die of an infection before she was found.

Then she and Parker would be reunited in death.

She missed him so much.

So much that it physically hurt.

He was her heart, and she wished that she had told him more often just how much he meant to her. She wished that she had told him everything that had been going on inside her. She wished that she hadn't spent the three years they'd known each other being terrified that he would leave her just like everyone else had.

She had learned her lesson about shutting people out and trying to do everything on her own, but unfortunately, it had been too little, too late.

Tessa just wished she'd had a chance to tell Parker just how much his love had changed her.

* * * * *

12:21 P.M.

"I think we can drop the ransom theory," Xavier said.

"I agree," Jack said. "No one has received any communication from the kidnapper demanding money."

"I don't think this has anything to do with Tessa's friends and what happened to them when they were kids. If it did, then he wouldn't have gone after Elizabeth Landry. He would have gone after Carrie, Michelle, or Lauren." Xavier shrugged out of his jacket. It was too hot to be wearing one; he wasn't even sure why he'd put it on this morning.

He'd left in a hurry. He and Annabelle had taken the kids out to the lake last night, and they'd stayed until after dark. By the time they got home, wrangled the twins into bed, and they enjoyed a little adult time, it had been after midnight by the time he'd fallen asleep. He was forty-seven now and late nights were starting to get to him. For the first time, he was starting to feel his age. It wasn't just the late nights making him feel old. Katie and JP were going to be starting kindergarten in the fall.

His kids were growing up.

Xavier couldn't believe it.

His babies were going to be off to school.

It was like he had blinked, and they'd gone from being tiny little things who fit in his hand to children who were about to take their first step into having independent lives.

"Yeah I agree," Jack nodded. "This has to do with Tessa. She was abducted, then her friend Melanie Gardner was killed, then her friend Elizabeth Landry was killed. She's the target. We can use that to find him."

"He's getting more brazen," Xavier said thoughtfully. "He kidnapped Tessa in the middle of the night, using the fact that she was asleep to his advantage. He timed Melanie's murder so she would be home alone, but she was awake and conscious when he came after her. But with Elizabeth, he killed her in broad daylight in her own backyard while her mother, brother, and daughter were in the house."

"He didn't want anyone to know she was dead right away though," Jack said. "Hiding her body in the tree gave him plenty of time, so even if anyone had seen him around, they wouldn't have connected him to the crime."

His partner was right. At first, Elizabeth had just been reported missing. It wasn't until a neighbor's dog got into the yard and wouldn't stop barking at the tree that anyone realized the body was even up there. They had spoken with the neighbors, and no one had seen anyone coming or going from Elizabeth's house.

"Wyatt, what do you know about Elizabeth and her relationship with Tessa?" Jack asked.

Wyatt looked up from his phone. "We met her in a case Parker and I worked about a year after we met Tessa. She was almost a victim of the serial killer The Iceman."

"I remember that case," Xavier said. The notorious killer had stalked the city every winter for several years. The killer would abduct a victim, keep them alive for a month before killing them and taking another victim on the same night. It was Wyatt and Parker who had eventually found the killer when Tessa had figured out the identity.

"Me too," Jack said. "You guys were able to save one of the victims, right?"

"We did. She's married now with four kids. Elizabeth was the victim he was going for, and when the abduction was interrupted and he couldn't take her, he went after her instead. Lizzie was eighteen then. She was in college and worked part time at a café to support her family. They were in a car accident when she was ten. Her father walked away with scrapes and bruises. Lizzie had internal injuries but made a full recovery, but her mother was left paralyzed from the waist down, and her younger brother Devon was left brain damaged. Her father couldn't cope and split, so Lizzie kind of took over with looking after her family."

"She sounds like she was an amazing woman. That was a big responsibility to take on at ten," Xavier said.

"How did she and Tessa become friends?" Jack asked.

"They met at the station when they both came in to make an ID. The killer had gone after Tessa as well. They started talking, and because Tess had been through something traumatic, she kind of looked out for Lizzie, tried to help her wherever she could, and they just kind of became friends," Wyatt explained.

"Could The Iceman be the killer?" Xavier asked.

"Cordelia was killed," Wyatt reminded them.

"Could Daniel have lied about it?" he asked. He didn't think it was a likely scenario, but they had to look into everything.

"Why would he?"

"Because Cordelia was his sister," Xavier said.

"His sister who had just killed several innocent people and who was planning on killing him too. His sister who had just shot and almost killed Tessa. Her heart stopped beating. She was dead; we were lucky to get her back alive."

"Daniel shot and killed the woman who was found in the hospital. Maybe he lied so he wouldn't get in trouble. Maybe he was The Iceman," Xavier suggested.

"Tessa backed him up," Wyatt said. "She said her sister snuck into her hospital room and was going to abduct her when Daniel showed up and Cordelia shot her."

"Well, Tessa isn't here to confirm that right now," Xavier reminded him.

"We ran DNA tests. Cordelia was The Iceman, and she was the woman found dead on the hospital room floor."

"Okay," he conceded, convinced. "Where is Daniel?" Tessa's older brother was supposed to be meeting them here so they could talk about possible suspects.

"He should be here any minute," Wyatt said. "That's who I was on the phone with before. He got held up because PJ is really having a hard time. He thought his mother would be back home by now." Self-recrimination was written all over Wyatt's face as though he were personally responsible for them not having found Tessa yet.

"Hey guys, I have news," Jenny Buckley announced as she entered the room.

"You got a hit from the DNA in the van?" Xavier asked.

"Actually, I got more than that."

"What could be more than that?" Jack asked.

"I found him," Jenny replied.

"You found the man who abducted Tessa?" Wyatt's emerald green eyes lit up.

"Yes."

"So, you know where Tessa is?" Xavier asked.

"Nope."

"So, what do you know?" he asked, confused.

"The man who abducted Tessa was killed," Jenny told them.

"Like in an accident or something?" Jack asked.

"His body was found dumped in the woods. He was shot."

"There were two of them." Wyatt looked shocked.

"How do you know this is the kidnapper?" Xavier asked.

"When the body was brought in, I noticed the injuries. He had recently been in an accident, and the injuries matched those that I would have expected the man who was driving the van involved in Tessa's abduction to have had. I ran his DNA against the sample from the van and they matched. His name was Joey Geller."

"So, someone killed him and then dumped his body," he said slowly. This opened up so many more possibilities. He just didn't know if that made Tessa's situation better or worse.

"They scrubbed him down from top to bottom," Jenny added.

"When was he killed?" Jack asked.

"Looks like he died just after Tessa was abducted."

"The partner didn't like that he almost messed up the abduction, thought he was a liability and took him out," Wyatt said.

Xavier agreed.

"What's going on?" Daniel Micah asked as he came into the room and looked at all their faces.

"We just learned there were two men involved in Tess's abduction, and one of them killed the other," Wyatt told Tessa's brother.

"What does that mean for Tess?" Daniel anxiously looked from one of them to the other.

"We don't know," Xavier answered honestly. There was no point in lying to Daniel. He could be the only person who could help them find his sister. "Can you think of anyone who would do this to your sister?"

"You already asked me that, and I already told you no." Daniel sounded frustrated as he flopped down into a chair at the table.

"There has to be someone," Jack pushed.

"Someone is out to get your sister. They abducted her, they threatened to kill her in ten days, they've killed two of her friends. He has to know her," Xavier added.

"*Two* of her friends?" Daniel asked.

"Lizzie Landry is dead." Wyatt broke the news.

"So, you think he's going after people that she cared about, to what? Punish her? Hurt her? Make her suffer before he kills her?" Daniel asked.

"At the moment, it looks like that. Are you sure you can't think of anyone who would want to hurt your sister?" Xavier asked again. Daniel had to know something; he just didn't realize it was important. But if this guy hated Tessa like they thought he did, he didn't just appear out of thin air. He was a part of Tessa's life in some shape or form.

"I wish I had something to tell you, but I don't." Daniel looked helplessly back at him.

"Then we're going to go through every single acquaintance and friend and relative until we find who they are." It would take them a long time, but at the moment, it looked like it was the only option they had.

* * * * *

8:39 P.M.

It had been another good day.

For a long time, there hadn't been any of those in his life.

Lucas Mianta turned the corner and picked up speed. When he went for his daily run he worked on a series of sprints and jogs, and it was time to sprint the last half mile home. This was his favorite time of day to run, the sun was just starting to go down, the sky starting to change color, the whole world was a mix of reds and golds and deep purply blues.

The air was hot, and when he picked up his pace it was like running through an oven. An oven that was turned up as high as it would go.

He didn't mind though.

He loved running.

It had saved his life.

That and bodybuilding.

If he didn't have them, he would still be stuck back in that same place that had almost gotten him killed. Or perhaps thrown into prison to spend the rest of his life behind bars.

His life had been a mess, basically, from day one.

Pretty typical stuff. His dad was an abusive alcoholic, his mom was a druggie who didn't care about her kids, only about getting her next high. He had an older sister who had followed down the same path as their parents, and an older brother who had managed to get out. Way out. He had graduated early and gone off to college, and none of them had heard from him since.

Lucas had been following in his father's footsteps. He started drinking when he was nine, and by the time he was sixteen, he was already an alcoholic who started getting into more and more fights.

Then he got expelled.

Turning up to school drunk, as he did most days, he had gotten into a fight with one of his teachers, shoving the woman so hard she fell down a flight of stairs and broke her back.

Which landed him in prison.

As it should have.

He knew that he'd been spinning out of control, and if it hadn't been for that instance and what happened next, he didn't know where his rock bottom would have been, but he knew that sooner or later—probably sooner—he would have hit it.

But the universe must love him.

Or at least like him.

After pushing the teacher, he had run. He'd managed to evade the cops for almost a month before they finally tracked him down. When he'd been found and dragged off to prison, he had met someone. Not a romantic someone, but someone who had helped him get his life in order. Someone who had made him realize that he could waste his life, throw it away like his parents had done, or he could straighten up and make something of himself.

It was the first time anyone had ever said that to him.

No one had ever made him feel like he was worth anything.

That someone had cared enough to tell him that he was being stupid and that he could change if he wanted to, stirred something inside him.

A desire to be a better person.

So, he had become one.

It hadn't been easy.

He'd had to draw on every ounce of strength he had, but he'd made it. He had served his time, which had helped him to get sober. Once he had gotten out of prison, he had gone straight to rehab. He hadn't been confident that he would be able to stay clean once he no longer had the constraints of prison.

While in prison, he'd finished high school, so once he was confident that he could remain sober, he'd gone to college. Once he graduated, he'd gone to work at the same rehab center that had helped him stay clean

That was almost two decades ago.

Anytime he got the urge to drink, he ran or he lifted weights. His gym membership had been his lifeline these last eighteen years, and he had the body to prove it. Every time he looked at himself in the mirror, he was reminded of his strength. His inner strength as well as his physical strength. And he still needed the reminders. Life was still a struggle, a daily battle against the desire to drink.

But he continued to overcome it.

Because someone had believed in him and helped him learn to believe in himself.

Now he was thirty-six, and for the first time since he'd gotten out of prison, he actually felt like he was ready for a relationship. He wanted to meet the woman of his dreams, fall in love, have a family of his own.

A family of his own.

That terrified him as much as it excited him.

He didn't want to mess up. He didn't want to do to any kids he might have what his father had done to him. He was afraid that the stresses of marriage and raising kids would push him to drink. He thought he was strong enough to stand up to his urges, but what if he wasn't?

What if being a bad father was in his genes?

What if being a bad person was in his genes?

What if no matter how hard he tried, alcohol would end up claiming him?

Before these thoughts and doubts could get a foothold, he pushed through the tightness in his chest and ran faster.

He would find a way to be a good husband and a good father. He would find a way to keep those fears at bay, and he would find a way to keep fighting the fight. He owed it to the woman whose life he had destroyed; he owed it to the people who believed in him, and he owed it to himself.

With a last burst of energy, he ran down the block and into his own front yard.

Downing the last of the water in his bottle, he sucked in some breaths and let his racing heart calm. The rush of the run was still buzzing through his system. He'd grab a quick dinner, and then he'd hit his weight room. Lifting weights always calmed him down at the end of the day. Then a hot shower and off to bed. He wanted to be well rested because tomorrow was the day.

The day he was going to garner enough courage to finally ask out the gorgeous woman who owned his favorite café.

He ate lunch there every day, just so he could watch her.

She had long, dark blonde hair with red highlights that were always catching the sunlight and shining like a sunset. Her eyes were the warmest shade of brown and he would love to lose himself in them. Her smile was the kind that lit up a room, and she was always flitting about the café like a beautiful butterfly.

She was someone he could fall in love with.

Lucas was almost to the front door when he spotted the man with the dog leash walking up behind him.

* * * * *

10:57 P.M.

She could sit here like this forever.

Although she hated to see her kids sick, Paige loved just sitting and holding them. Arianna was asleep on the couch in the living room where she had drifted off earlier. Not wanting to risk moving her and waking her, she and Elias had decided to let her sleep down here tonight, and Paige just hadn't been able to leave her.

Her daughter's head was in her lap, and Paige was stroking her long black hair. She treasured every single moment like this because her girls were growing up fast.

Next month, Ari would be starting middle school, and Hayley was going to be a junior this year. Ari was already starting to show more of an interest in boys and less in toys and would soon be turning eleven. And Hayley would be getting her license this year, and they were already planning her sweet sixteen party.

She wasn't ready for them to grow up yet.

After being attacked and almost killed by a stalker fifteen years ago, she had received life-saving surgery that had resulted in her uterus being removed. She had been pregnant, although she hadn't known at the time, and learning that, not only had she lost her baby but also the ability to have children of her own had been a terrible blow.

For a long time, she'd thought that she would never get to be a mother. She and Elias had had several adoptions fall through, and after the last, she had decided that she couldn't take it anymore. She and Elias were obviously not meant to be parents.

Then they had worked a case that changed everything.

Four girls had been kidnapped and kept prisoner by an insane man who wanted to recreate the family he'd lost. He had begun abusing the girls after they turned thirteen, and the oldest had become pregnant.

When the girls made a daring bid at escaping, they were finally saved. The older three returned to their families, but the second youngest no longer had a family to return to. They had died while she was a prisoner, and the youngest couldn't be cared for by her mother who felt after the ordeal they'd been through, she couldn't love her daughter the way the child deserved to be loved.

The two children, then aged five and just a few months old, needed a home and parents to love them.

She and Elias needed children to love.

So, Hayley and Arianna became theirs.

The last ten years had been the best of her life. While it wasn't always easy, and it involved a lot of juggling since both she and Elias worked jobs with unpredictable hours, she loved having a family. And somehow, with the help of family and friends, they managed to fit everything they needed to into the day.

Paige loved the hectic lifestyle they lived—her job, her husband's job, school, the kids' activities, family time, and volunteering at the center for abused women and children that she helped run with her friends. It was a lot to balance, but every second was so precious. As much as she loved it, she just couldn't shake the feeling that she was ready for a change. She just didn't know what that change was yet.

Returning to work after the case that had almost cost her and Ryan their daughters' and their lives had been tough. Not because almost being killed had made her wary or afraid to do her job, but because she felt like she was abandoning her daughter when she needed her the most.

Hayley was doing well, and seemed to be coping okay with everything that she'd been through, but knowing that her precious child had been hurt because of her, because someone wanted to punish her for something they believed she'd done wrong, was something Paige still hadn't come to terms with. She wasn't sure she ever would.

Some nights the guilt was still so crushing that she couldn't sleep.

Her beautiful daughter would forever bear the scars—both physical and psychological—of her ordeal, and to Paige, that just felt so unfair.

She not only suffered the usual doubts that came with parenting, like whether or not she was doing a good enough job, but she had also spent the last ten years living with the fear that she would lose her daughters.

Not to some evil person intent on harming others, but to Arianna's biological mother. While the woman had at first given up her infant daughter—and Hayley whose elderly grandmother and only living relative had offered her custody since she couldn't care for the child herself—because she wasn't psychologically in a place where she could raise two children, Paige had always been afraid that once Eliza had her life back on track, that she would want the girls back.

Despite constant reassurances from Eliza that she didn't, that she knew she had made the right decision. She was happy with her husband and their kids and content just to remain a part of Hayley and Ari's lives. It wasn't until what they had all gone through six months ago that Paige had finally been able to lay those fears to rest.

The look on her daughters' faces when she woke up in that hospital room were enough for her to know that to them, she would always be Mom despite what biology might say.

It was such a relief to be able to let go of that fear.

To finally be confident that her daughters were never going to wake up one day and throw in her face that she wasn't really their mother. And that no one was going to knock on her door one day and demand she give up the children she would gladly die to protect.

They were hers and she was theirs, and that was all there was to it.

In her sleep, Ari groaned and wriggled a little.

"Shh, sweetheart," she whispered as she leaned over to press a kiss to Arianna's cheek.

It wasn't just Hayley and her who were still dealing with the fallout of what happened six months ago, but Arianna too. She and her friend Rosie had witnessed Hayley and Sophie's abduction, and it had left Arianna fearful of being alone anyplace other than at home.

Paige was grateful that at least her younger daughter felt safe here. With all the doubts that came with parenting, it was nice to know that she and her husband had created a home that was warm and nurturing and loving, and especially secure.

The light in the kitchen flicked on, and she wondered who was up. Elias or Hayley? Since Elias had just finished a twenty-four-hour shift that she knew had been particularly hard because he and his crew had been unable to save a couple trapped in their burning home, he was probably still passed out.

"Hayley?" she called out quietly, trying not to disturb Arianna.

A moment later, the partially closed living room door swung open and Hayley stepped into the room, glass of water in hand.

"Everything okay?" Paige asked. She hoped her daughter hadn't been having nightmares. Thankfully, Hayley didn't suffer from them often, which was a blessing, since Paige knew how crippling they could be, having suffered from them after her stalker's attempts on her life.

"Yeah, I just couldn't sleep. I kept thinking about a friend of Sophie's that I met today. He's going through a rough time with his mom, and it made me think of how scared I was when you traded yourself for me." Hayley grabbed some pillows and dropped them on the floor at Paige's feet and curled up on them, leaning against the side of the couch.

"I hate that you were so scared, but you know how much I love you, and I would do anything to make sure you or your sister or your dad were safe," Paige said, resting a hand on top of Hayley's head.

"I know, and it makes me love you even more."

Paige could never get enough of hearing her girls tell her they loved her. "So, this friend of Sophie's, is it a guy she likes?"

"Yes," Hayley giggled. "They like each other, but Sophie is still a little nervous to try dating again."

"And what about you?" she asked. Sometimes with their busy schedules they didn't get as much time to talk as she would like, but she always tried to make sure she knew what was going on in her daughter's life. "Any boys you like?"

Hayley's cheeks turned bright pink.

Which was pretty much her answer.

"So, who is he?" she asked, nudging Hayley's shoulder.

"Mo-om," Hayley groaned, sounding like the teenager she was and not the old woman she sometimes seemed to be.

"Someone you really like if you don't want to say," she teased.

"If I tell you, you can't tell anyone. Promise?"

"Promise."

"It's Brian Xander," Hayley said in a rush.

Huh.

Paige couldn't say she was surprised to hear that.

Brian was a little like Hayley in that they had both been through a lot, and it had aged them in a way that only happened when you were forced to carry a heavy burden at a young age.

From the way Hayley was looking up at her, she suspected that her daughter was waiting to hear that she was too young to like a guy so much older than her. But Paige wasn't going to say that. Although Hayley was too young right now to be dating a guy who was six years older than her, in the future, she could actually see them as a couple.

"If you still like him when you're a little older, then I think you should go for it," she told Hayley.

"Really? You don't think it's crazy that I like him when I'm fifteen and he's twenty-one?"

"It seems like a big age gap now, but when you're both in your twenties, it won't seem so big. And I actually think you two would make a great couple."

"Who would make a great couple?"

They both turned to see Elias standing in the doorway.

"No one," Hayley said quickly.

"That's right, no one," Elias said firmly. He wasn't ready to see his little girl dating, and he'd already scared off a couple of boys from Hayley's school who had shown an interest in her.

"Dad," Hayley sighed.

"What?" Elias asked, all innocently. "A father can't look out for his daughter?"

"Of course, he can." Hayley smiled. "But sooner or later, I am going to meet someone and fall in love."

"Let's make it later rather than sooner." Elias groaned as he came and joined them, perching on the arm of the couch beside her.

"What are you doing up?" she asked her husband.

"I heard voices. What are you two doing?"

"Hayley came down to get some water and we were just talking," she replied.

"Without me?" he asked with mock disappointment.

"You can join us," Hayley said with a quiet giggle.

"About time I was asked." Elias poked his tongue out. "So, who is this guy that you like? I assume that was the couple you and your mom were talking about."

"It's no one," Hayley said.

"No one, huh? It didn't sound like no one."

"Really, Dad, it's not anyone that I'm going to date," Hayley assured her father, but Paige heard the unsaid words as well as the spoken ones.

Yet.

It wasn't anyone Hayley was going to date *yet*.

"Mom?" Arianna's sleepy voice asked as she lifted her head.

"Go back to sleep, baby," she whispered.

"Why is everyone here?" Ari asked.

"We're just talking," she told her daughter.

"Without me?" Arianna asked the same question her dad had. Although their kids were adopted, Paige couldn't deny that Elias and Ari were two peas in a pod.

"You needed your rest. How are you feeling?"

"I'm feeling better." Arianna pushed herself up into a sitting position.

"That's great." She wrapped an arm around Ari's shoulders as her daughter snuggled against her side.

"Is it too hot for cocoa?" Hayley asked.

"No," Arianna said excitedly; cocoa was her favorite drink.

"I'll go make some and maybe we can hang out together for a bit," Hayley suggested.

"I'll help," Elias said as he followed Hayley to the door.

Paige watched her husband and oldest daughter go, chattering away together, as her younger daughter rested her head on her shoulder.

She was lucky.

Despite everything that she'd been through that could have made her angry or bitter or too terrified to live. She didn't feel any of those things.

She felt so incredibly lucky to be alive and to have been blessed with such an amazing family.

AUGUST 5TH

10:34 A.M.

"We just wasted three days," Wyatt growled in frustration. There was nothing he hated more than spending days working a case only to find that you were going in the completely wrong direction. "This isn't about Tessa, it's about Parker."

How had they not seen it earlier?

It seemed so obvious.

Tessa was Parker's wife, Melanie Gardner was a potential victim in a case Parker had worked, and Lizzie Landry was a victim in a case Parker had worked. They all tied back to Parker.

But who would hate a dead man so much that they would go to such lengths to hurt people just because they'd had something to do with him?

"We had no way to know that this was about Parker and not Tessa," Jack Xander reminded him.

"Before this, everyone involved was linked to Tessa just as much as they were linked to Parker," Xavier Montague added.

That was true, but right now it didn't make him feel any better.

He should have seen it.

He should have figured it out.

He had promised to look after Tessa, and now she was missing. If the killer had been telling the truth, she only had a week left to live.

He had promised to help raise Parker's son, and now, he was going to have to tell PJ that he had messed up and his mother would pay the price.

"Stop beating yourself up," Xavier said. "There was no way we could have known that we were looking at this all wrong until this." He gestured at the house they were standing in front of.

The house belonged to a man named Lucas Mianta.

At least, it had, before he was murdered.

Any victims who appeared to be in good health but had suffered what appeared to be a heart attack were being referred to them—so they'd been alerted to this case right away. Then they were running checks to see if there were any links to Tessa, and if there were, then the case was theirs. Technically, the case was Jack and Xavier's, but he wasn't going anywhere until Tessa was back home where she belonged.

"We still don't actually know for sure that Parker is at the center of this," Jack said. "For all we know, it could be you. Tessa is your friend, and you and Parker were partners, so you worked Melanie, Elizabeth, and Lucas's cases as well."

"No," Wyatt said immediately. He knew this wasn't about him. Sure, he and Tessa were friends, but she was Parker's wife. And yes, he had worked the same cases as Parker, but if this killer was really targeting him, he wouldn't have gone after Lucas Mianta.

"How can you be sure?" Xavier asked.

"Because Parker was the one who really connected with Lucas. When we met him, he was a sixteen-year-old kid from a bad family with a drinking problem. Lucas had pushed a teacher down a flight of stairs, which had broken her back. She told us that Lucas had had a tough life and asked us to go easy on him. Parker really went all out to help him. He sat the kid down, shared about his own rough childhood, and that the only person who could change Lucas's life was Lucas himself. Even after the kid got out of prison, Parker kept in touch with him, encouraged him to stay clean, and to find what he wanted to do with his life and then go for it."

"You're sure that Lucas had no connection to Tessa?" Xavier asked.

"As far as I know, they've never even met. Lucas came to the funeral, but Tessa was so out of it that day that they never spoke to each other."

"And you and Lucas never had anything to do with each other?" Jack asked.

"Other than spending almost a month looking for him and then arresting him, nothing. I'm telling you, this is about Parker." He just wished he knew why.

"Parker has been dead for fifteen years," Jack said.

Wyatt knew it wasn't just to state the obvious, but because they were all having a hard time figuring out why someone would go after people connected to someone who'd been dead for so long.

"If this guy is just going to go after people from old cases that you and Parker worked, then how are we going to figure out who he's going to go after next?" Xavier asked.

He'd been wondering the same thing.

It made no sense.

None at all.

"Can you think of anyone who might want to hurt people that were connected to Parker?" Jack asked. "Anyone who hated him or who might be angry with him? Anyone who had a grudge against him? Anyone who caused a scene at the funeral? Or who was happy that Parker was dead? Has Tessa mentioned anyone contacting her and expressing any sort of hatred toward her husband? Anyone who has tried to ask Tessa out who she turned down because she's still in love with Parker that was angry or made a scene about it, or who kept asking, even though she had already said no?"

Responding to each of the fired-off questions, he answered them in order. "Off the top of my head, no, I can't think of anyone who would want to hurt people connected to Parker. There is no one angry enough at Parker to do this. There was no one who hated him. The funeral went smoothly, and I was mostly focused on Tessa and getting her through it. There wasn't anyone I knew of who was happy to see him dead, but again, in the months after Parker's death, we were all focused on Tessa. Tess keeps to herself and if anyone has ever asked her out, she never said anything to me about it."

"You're going to have to go through all your old cases and see if you can identify anyone who could be a likely target for this killer, so we can try to get ahead of him," Xavier suggested.

"So far, he seems to be going after people Parker either had some sort of relationship with outside of just the case, or who had something to do with Tessa as well," Jack said.

"But who would have access to all of Parker's cases?" Xavier asked.

"Could we be looking at another cop?" Jack asked.

Wyatt hadn't thought of that, but it made sense. A cop or someone in law enforcement would have access to old case files, and who else would? The only other thing he could think of was a hacker.

Was it possible that someone had managed to hack the department's system to get into one deceased cop's files?

"If it *is* a cop or someone else in law enforcement, it could explain why he's done such a good job at cleaning up the crime scenes and making sure no one sees him come or go," Xavier said.

That was true.

They were starting to build a profile, but that wasn't getting them the answers they needed. A profile might help them narrow down their suspects—if they got any—but it wasn't going to give them a name. And they needed a name. Tessa's time was quickly running out.

Seven days.

That was all the time they had.

It wasn't enough.

At best, they had a few vague theories. What they needed was something concrete. Like the blood in the van that had given them DNA which they'd been able to use to find the kidnapper.

That's what they needed now. They needed this guy to slip up, make a mistake, give them something they could use, but so far, he'd been too smart.

"This guy must be huge," Xavier was saying. "If he could take down a guy this big without a struggle."

Lucas Mianta was a runner and a bodybuilder; the guy worked out several hours a day. Every day. Wyatt still worked out regularly, and he thought he was still in pretty good shape for a fifty-three-year-old, but even he would have had trouble taking down someone of Lucas's size without using a weapon of some sort.

Maybe the killer did.

"He might use a weapon to keep his victims under control," he suggested. "Make sure they don't fight back until he can inject them with the potassium chloride. Assuming that's how he kills them."

"I don't think so," Jack called out. "I think he uses this." He held up a broken dog lead.

"So, that's his ruse," Wyatt said. "He approaches them claiming he's looking for his dog that got free when the leash broke. They believe him because he had the lead in his hand, so they don't view him as a threat. Then he stabs them with the syringe when they aren't looking and hides the body so it won't be found right away, allowing him to put enough time and distance between himself and his victim so no one will connect them." The killer had shoved Lucas Mianta's body behind the shrubs that surrounded the house; it had been discovered by the postman.

But what did that tell them about the man they were looking for?

Did it mean he was physically weak and needed a ruse to get close enough to his victims to kill them? Or did he just like playing games?

They were making progress, learning more about the killer with each crime scene, but it wasn't enough.

They needed more.

And they needed it now.

* * * * *

1:24 P.M.

He was getting worried.

Tessa was sick.

He had tried to take care of her as best as he could, but he was starting to think that it wasn't enough. He had cleaned out all her wounds with water and bandaged them up. He had even put antibiotic cream on them.

Why wasn't it working?

What was he doing wrong?

What did he need to do to make sure that she didn't die?

Well, at least before he was ready to kill her.

Although, to be completely accurate, he didn't really think of it as killing her. He was helping her.

Setting her free.

Ending her suffering.

Tessa had been unhappy for so long; she was sad and grieving. She deserved to be at peace.

And that was what he was going to give her.

He had spent so long working it out, thinking about it and dreaming about it, and playing out in his head exactly how it would go. Only he had never envisioned it being like this.

Never had he expected that she would be sick and getting sicker by the hour. Most of the time, she was just sleeping, and even when she was awake, she had no appetite and no energy and just lay in the bed.

That wasn't what he wanted.

He'd thought that they would be able to enjoy these days together—that they'd be special days, and the two of them would laugh and talk and have fun together.

Instead, these days were being wasted, and they didn't have many of them left.

One week.

In one week today, Tessa would pass from this life to the next, where she would be able to enjoy eternal rest.

It was hard to believe.

It was a weird feeling when your dreams came true. More often than not in life, they didn't. Bad things happened to good people. They had parents who ruined their lives or some evil person hurt them or they lost the people they loved, and they were left with scars that would never completely go away.

Which was why he was doing this.

He wanted to make his life mean something.

He wanted to leave something behind when he died.

He didn't want his life to be a waste.

So, he was going to send as many people off to eternal peace as he could before his end came.

And it felt good.

It really did.

He had never felt like this before. He'd always been so sad, so lost, and now he had a purpose.

He stood and walked the couple of steps so he was beside Tessa's bed. He wanted to tell her everything that was rolling around inside his head and his heart. He so badly wanted her to understand. He didn't want her to be afraid. He knew deep down inside that she wanted to die because she knew that in death, she would be reunited with the man she loved.

He just wished he had been the one to bring her here. That stupid man had ruined everything. Not only had he almost gotten himself caught, but he'd hurt Tessa. He wished that he hadn't given the man such a merciful death. Instead of just killing him to get rid of him, he should have made the man suffer the same way Tessa was suffering now.

"Hey," he said softly, reaching out a hand but stopping just short of touching her. He was almost afraid of touching her. Like, if he did, it would ruin the magic that hovered between them.

"Hmm," Tessa groaned and seemed to struggle to open her eyes. Her cheeks were bright pink, but the rest of her skin was paper pale.

Just how badly hurt was she?

He ached to take away her pain.

He would do anything to make her feel better.

He would do anything for her.

Anything.

Maybe he shouldn't wait the last few days and end her suffering earlier than he had originally planned. He didn't like to deviate from his plans—he was, by nature, a creature of habit—but if Tessa was suffering and he could end it, then maybe he should.

"Please," Tessa said when she fixed her glassy eyes on him. "I need a doctor. I know you think you're doing this for me, but I need to go to a hospital."

He knew she was right in that she needed a hospital, but he couldn't take her to one. If he did, it would be over, and he would never get another chance to do this.

It was now or never, and he couldn't let it be never.

So, for now, he was just going to have to keep her here and continue to give her painkillers so she didn't feel too bad until he could decide what he was going to do.

"I can't, I'm sorry," he said sincerely.

"You can. This is a mistake. You know that it is. You know that you shouldn't be doing this, that it's wrong. I know that you do. It's not too late … you can still do the right thing. You can take me home and we can find a way to fix this. We can get you the help that you need. Please," she implored, her large blue-green eyes were shimmering with unshed tears.

She made it sound so simple.

Just go home and get help.

Like psychological help was all it took to get rid of the dark pit of despair that lived inside you.

But that was a joke.

He knew from personal experience that talking with a shrink didn't do anything.

How could it?

It was just talking, and to get better, to finally find a way to exorcize that pit of despair, you needed so much more.

He needed this.

Needed it.

There wasn't any way he could go back and live the rest of his life like he had been before.

No, it had to be this way.

Besides, he wasn't even sure that it was possible to go back. He thought he was in way too deep to walk away now. He was in this to the end. Sometimes, once you started down a certain road, there was just no turning back, and that was what was happening now.

"I can't, I'm sorry," he told Tessa. "I brought you something."

He reached into his pocket and pulled out a small sealed plastic bag.

He stared at what was inside, transfixed.

Another to add to his collection.

Another suffering soul he had saved and set free.

"Here, this is for you." He handed her the bag.

Tentatively, she took it until she saw what was inside, and then she dropped it like it was on fire.

"Is that what I think it is?" she asked in a shaky voice.

Sweet Tessa.

He wasn't offended that she didn't want to look too closely at the gift he'd brought her. She wasn't like him; she dealt with her own personal pit of despair in a different way.

"It is," he acknowledged.

"Who?" she asked, although her expression said she wasn't sure she really wanted an answer.

"Lucas Mianta," he replied. He'd been honest with her up until this point, and he didn't intend to change that now.

"Oh." Her face fell and tears began to slowly trickle down her cheeks. "Parker tried so hard to help him."

Parker had.

But it wasn't enough.

All that man brought into the lives of others was pain and misery.

Well, he was going to undo that.

He was taking those whose lives had been damaged by Detective Parker Bell, and he was finally setting them free and giving them the peace they'd been seeking for so long.

He was going to right those wrongs.

Melanie Gardner, Elizabeth Landry, Lucas Mianta ... they were all happy now, and finally at rest.

There were a few more to go. He couldn't save them all, but he could save as many as he could before his time ran out.

Some were better than none.

That was what he had to keep reminding himself of whenever he felt guilty that there were so many he was leaving behind in this dark, cold, cruel world.

"You should rest now," he said as he picked up the small plastic bag containing a lock of Lucas Mianta's hair from the mattress where Tessa had dropped it.

Tessa needed more sleep, and he needed to get back to work. He had another soul to release tonight.

Tucking Tessa in, he made sure she had a glass of water on her nightstand, and a bottle of painkillers should she need them, then he left the room, locking the door behind him. He would put Lucas's lock of hair with the others, and then he would start preparing for tonight.

No rest for the wicked, people said.

There was no rest for the righteous either.

He should know.

His righteous quest required constant thought and attention.

Still, it was worth it, because when it was over, he too, would find the peace that he so desperately sought.

* * * * *

3:06 P.M.

"What's wrong?" Jack looked up from the file he was reading as Wyatt stepped back into the room.

"He's out of prison," Wyatt replied slowly as though he couldn't quite believe what he was saying.

"Who is?" Xavier asked.

Ever since they'd returned from the Lucas Mianta crime scene, they'd been going through all of Parker Bell's old case files, trying to find anyone who might have a grudge.

That someone had a grudge against a cop who had been dead for fifteen years and would go after people related to him seemed so strange.

What purpose did it serve?

Parker was dead. Hurting his widow or anyone else wasn't going to affect him. He wasn't going to find out about it. He wasn't going to know that this person hated him, and he wasn't going to get the message they seemed to be trying so hard to get across.

But, as strange as it was, that seemed to be what they were dealing with.

The facts were that someone had abducted Parker's wife and threatened to kill her in ten—now seven—days, and he now appeared to be working their way through his old cases killing people off one by one.

In a relatively quick and painless manner.

Which to Jack seemed to be at odds with the presumed goal.

This guy was angry at Parker Bell yet killing people in a humane manner to get back at him.

The whole thing was weird.

This was definitely up there amongst the most unusual cases he had worked in his twenty-five years as a cop.

"Who's out of prison?" he asked, echoing his partner's question when Wyatt didn't offer an answer. The man appeared to be hanging on by a thread. Jack was pretty sure that Wyatt hadn't slept since Tessa's abduction, despite the fact that he and Xavier insisted he go home at the end of each day. Jack was worried about Wyatt, but he wasn't sure he could tell the man that he was no longer able to work this case. Skylar Wyatt had been a good cop, and both Jack and Xavier still believed he was their biggest asset in solving this case.

"Lachlan Mountain." Wyatt looked like he was in a daze as he dropped into a chair.

"Who is Lachlan Mountain?" Xavier asked.

Wyatt sighed and ran his hands through his hair. What did he know about this Lachlan Mountain man that had him this freaked out?

"Who is Lachlan Mountain?" Jack asked, once again echoing his partner's question. As much as he understood what Wyatt was going through, he knew what it was like to have someone you loved snatched away from you and not know how to get them back. He'd been through that with his wife Laura, and this was a case where time was definitely not on their side. The killer had told them they only had ten days before he killed Tessa, and three of those days were already gone. They had to keep working.

"Parker and Matilda grew up in foster care." Wyatt started speaking but the blank look in his eyes remained. "It wasn't a good time in their lives. In the last home they lived in before they were adopted, they were both abused. Parker physically and Mattie sexually. Matilda decided that she was going to run away.

She was scared and took her foster father's gun. When she saw a car pull up the driveway she panicked, thinking it was one of her foster father's friends come to hurt her, so she fired the gun. She killed the man, only he turned out to be a social worker who was coming to get all the children who lived there and take them someplace safe."

Parker would have been forty-eight had he still been alive. If this happened when he was a child, then they were looking at something that had happened around four decades ago. That probably ruled out the social worker's widow and the abusive foster parents and foster father's friends. The killer they were looking for couldn't be someone in their seventies or eighties. They had to be able to hoist a body up into a tree because that was where Elizabeth Landry had been found.

"So how does Lachlan Mountain fit into that?" Xavier asked.

"The social worker had a son who was a couple of years older than Parker and Mattie. They were ten when it happened, and although they were adopted by a great family, Matilda was never able to overcome her guilt over what had happened."

"It was self-defense," Jack said immediately. His daughter was ten and the idea of her having to arm herself with a gun and then use it to protect herself chilled him. He hated that any child had to do that.

"It was, but she still killed a man. A good man who had done nothing wrong, and I know that still eats at her to this day," Wyatt said. "Matilda left as soon as she and Parker graduated. She came back a couple of months after Parker and Tessa were married. Tess and Parker were going through a rough time, and Parker started acting out of character. Tessa was pregnant and the thought of being a father terrified him because all he knew about his own father was that the man had walked out on his pregnant girlfriend. So, when Parker abruptly disappeared, we all thought that he'd split."

It was clear that Wyatt still felt guilty about that, as though he had betrayed his friend by thinking the worst of him.

"Parker didn't leave of his own free will, did he?" Jack asked.

"No, but Tessa was the only one who believed that. We all thought she was losing it, but it turned out she was right. Someone had kidnapped Parker and that same person had been drugging Tessa's drinks so we would all think she was crazy."

"That someone was Lachlan Mountain," Jack said, a statement not a question.

"He hated Parker and Matilda for what happened to his father, and he wanted to destroy them. What he didn't plan on, was falling for Tessa. The man became obsessed with her, and since he pretended to believe her when she said someone had kidnapped her husband, he was able to wriggle his way into her life because she was angry with the rest of us for not listening to her. Eventually Tessa was able to get proof he was spying on her, and she followed him. He ended up knocking her out and taking her to Parker. They almost managed to escape, but not before Lachlan found them. Thankfully, Tessa left a clue for me to find so that I would know that she was in trouble, and I found them before Lachlan was able to kill Parker and run with Tessa, but Tessa lost the baby. Lachlan didn't let go of his obsession with her. He would write her letters from prison. I didn't find out about it at first, but apparently, he would send them almost daily telling her how much he loved her."

"And now this man is free," Xavier said.

Free and quite possibly the very man they were looking for.

Lachlan Mountain was obsessed with Tessa, so it would make sense that he would kidnap her. And while he couldn't think of a logical reason for why Lachlan would start killing people from Parker's old cases, that didn't mean that Lachlan didn't have a reason that made sense to him. Jack had long since accepted that lots of the things criminals did made no sense to anyone other than themselves.

"Has Lachlan still been sending letters to Tessa?" Jack asked.

"I don't know. Tessa doesn't like to talk about things like that, and I would assume that, if he is, she just throws them away. You could ask PJ. He might know since he's the only one who lives in the house with Tess. Lachlan had put cameras all over Parker and Tessa's house, so he could spy on her and torture Parker with images of him and Tessa together. I believe that he worked in computer programming for a security company before he was arrested."

"So, he could probably quite easily hack into our systems and search for old case files," Jack said.

"How long has Lachlan been out of prison?" Xavier asked.

"Nearly a month."

Which was plenty of time to set this plan into motion.

"We should find out if Lachlan and Joey Geller spent time together in prison," Jack said.

"And we should go and speak with Lachlan's cellmate," Xavier added. "See if he can tell us anything. If Lachlan was as obsessed with Tessa as you say, then he no doubt talked about her often. Maybe he mentioned a plan to try to get her back."

"Now that we know who we might be looking for, you can go through your cases and see if you can figure out who Lachlan might target. If we can figure that out, we can post cops on them and try to catch him in the act," Jack said.

This was exactly the break they'd been waiting for. Now they just had to hope it panned out and they were able to stop Lachlan Mountain before anyone else died and bring Tessa safely home to her family.

* * * * *

4:19 P.M.

Sophie was nervous.

She never used to be nervous when she saw PJ. He had been a

part of her life for as long as she could remember. There had never been a time when they hadn't known each other. She'd always loved when her mom had taken her over to Tessa's house to play with PJ. Tessa had always baked some delicious treat, and she and PJ would play hide and seek in the enormous house, or chase each other around the gardens, or sometimes Tessa would take them to ride her horses.

Those had been great times, and she was scared they'd never have more times like that if they started dating. If dating PJ would ruin their relationship, she wasn't sure it was worth giving it a try.

But how did she tell PJ that?

What if he was so angry with her that their friendship was over anyway?

Or what if she and PJ could have something really special and she missed out on finding the love of her life just because she was afraid?

She *was* afraid.

She had loved Dominick, and it had turned out that she'd never really known him.

While Sophie knew that things with PJ weren't the same as things had been with Dom, she was still scared. She knew PJ, his family, she knew about his past, and she knew what he liked and disliked. She knew practically everything about him.

Most importantly, she knew that PJ would never hurt her like Dom had.

But it was such a big risk to take.

She had changed so much from the girl she used to be.

Ever since what happened six months ago, she wasn't comfortable in big groups of people anymore. She felt like they were looking at her and whispering about what had happened to her. She hated that feeling. Some days it was hard enough just to know that her family was talking about her and her progress behind her back, and she knew *they* were doing it out of love and concern and not just to gossip.

And there was one other thing that might be stopping her from going for it with PJ.

She may or may not still have unresolved feelings for Dom.

Okay, not may not.

May.

She *did* have unresolved feelings for Dom.

Sophie knew what he'd done, and she knew she could never forgive him for it. He had hurt so many innocent people. But in the end, he had killed his brother because Victor was going to come after her.

He wrote her letters.

She hid them in her bedroom, so her parents didn't know. She wasn't really sure why. Maybe it was because she knew that if they found out, they would put a stop to it, and she wasn't sure she was ready to sever all ties to Dom just yet.

But she couldn't live in the past.

Dominick was going to be spending the rest of his life in prison.

Even if he wasn't, she would never get back together with him.

It was just that knowing all of that didn't change the fact that she still felt something for him.

Those feelings would fade, and even though Hayley was right that she was nervous about the idea of dating someone else, she couldn't deny that she could do a lot worse than PJ Bell.

Maybe she should take a chance.

It couldn't hurt, right?

And if it didn't work out, she and PJ could still be friends. Surely he would want that.

"Hey, Soph."

Her head snapped up at the sound of PJ's voice. He smiled at her and sat down beside her on the log.

"Your friend Hayley didn't come with you today?" he asked.

"No ... she ... uh ... she knew that I wanted to talk to you," she said. Her hands were sweating, and she tried to unobtrusively wipe them on her shorts. She'd never been nervous with Dom, but a lot had changed in the year since they started dating.

"Oh?" PJ raised a hopeful brow.

He really was good-looking.

He was tall, with a mess of thick black hair, and the most amazing golden-brown eyes that she'd ever seen. Although he was quiet and shy, he was so loving and caring and really sweet. And despite his love of reading and studying, he worked out every day and had a great body.

PJ was everything a girl looked for in a guy.

She would be lucky to have him.

She should be excited that he was interested in her.

And she was. She was just so unsure of things these days. She didn't trust her feelings anymore, and the fact that she had feelings for Dom and PJ at the same time certainly wasn't helping.

"What did you want to talk about?" PJ asked. His fingers drummed on his knee, and she wondered if he wanted to hold her hand.

"Is there any news on your mom?" she asked. She needed a couple more minutes to gather her courage, and she really did want to know if the cops were any closer to finding PJ's mom.

"Wyatt said that they thought they might know who took her," he said. "But they don't really know anything for sure."

"I'm sorry. I love your mom. I've been praying every night that she's okay and that she'll come back to you. I'm really sorry," she said again because she didn't know what to say to comfort PJ. Was this how other people felt when they were around her? They wanted to make her feel better, but they knew there was no way words could help. But what did help was just knowing they were there, and that she could definitely do for PJ.

"I know you are." PJ tentatively reached out and lightly rested his hand on hers. When she didn't pull away, he curled his fingers around hers and then they were holding hands. It was so innocent and yet she couldn't deny she got a tingling feeling in her stomach.

"I'm here for you, PJ," she told him. And she meant it. Whatever he needed, she would do for him. "No matter what happens, I'm here for you. You know that, right?"

"I know. You're a good friend, Sophie, a really good friend."

He was looking at her and she could feel the tension building between them.

Heat.

There was heat there. She could feel it inside her. PJ wanted to kiss her, and she couldn't say that she didn't want him to. She wanted him to kiss her, but she wasn't ready to take it any further than that. She and Dom had talked about having sex, but now she knew what a mistake that would have been, and she was so glad that they hadn't taken that step.

When she did take that step, she wanted it to be with someone she knew she loved.

Whether or not that was PJ, she didn't know yet.

"Sophie," PJ said, his voice gone all husky. He lifted a hand, and she could see it shaking. It reassured her a little to know that he was nervous too. Very gently, he touched his fingers to her cheek, cupping it in his palm.

She stared into his eyes, transfixed.

Maybe their friendship really could develop into more.

She was attracted to PJ; she liked him; she had fun when they were together—today notwithstanding. She was comfortable around him. Maybe that was the basis of building a real relationship.

Something that could last.

Something like what her parents had and her grandparents and her aunts and uncles.

She wanted that someday.

She just wasn't sure that that day was today.

She didn't think she was ready.

And yet she couldn't tear her eyes away from PJ's, and when

his dead dipped and he touched his lips to hers, she was the one who deepened the kiss.

Sparks.

There were definite sparks.

But when his tongued pressed between her lips, she lifted her hands to his chest and gently pushed him away.

"What's wrong?" he asked, hurt and confusion written all over his face.

"I'm sorry," she said.

"For what? Why?" His golden eyes searched hers, seeking answers.

"This," she waved her hand between the two of them. "I can't do this."

"Why not?" PJ's face fell.

"Because I'm not ready. I'm so sorry. It's just that what happened a few months ago is too fresh. I'm not ready for another relationship this soon." She hoped he understood; she didn't want to lose him.

"Oh." A smile slowly crept over his face.

"Why are you smiling?"

"Because there *is* something between us. I felt it when I kissed you. You felt it, too, didn't you?" His smile grew when she nodded. "I can wait. I've liked you since we were nine. I can wait a few more months or a year or however long it takes for you to be ready."

"It's not fair of me to ask you to wait," she said.

"You didn't ask. I want to. I would wait for you forever," PJ told her as he slipped his arm around her shoulders.

Sophie relaxed. Nothing had changed between them. Or maybe it had, but for the better. She might not be ready for a relationship right now, but PJ was right, there was something between them, and maybe one day they would be able to explore it.

Content, she rested her head on PJ's shoulder.

She was lucky to have him in her life.

* * * * *

6:30 P.M.

Cassandra Stanton giggled as she and her new husband walked hand in hand down the street.

It wasn't that anything funny had happened, although her husband did have the ability to make her laugh like no one else ever had. She was twenty-six now, but when she was eleven, she'd been abducted and almost sold into the sex slave industry. Ever since, she hadn't been much of a laugher.

It's not that she never laughed, but before Leon, she didn't laugh very often.

Now, she laughed all the time.

It was so freeing.

It was by far the best form of therapy she'd ever had, and she'd had a lot of therapy over the last almost-sixteen years.

"What's so funny?" Leon asked.

"Nothing, I just love being with you." She smiled up at him. Leon was tall, really tall. She was five feet, ten inches, and he towered over her. She kind of liked that; it made her feel safe. She knew that as long as she was with Leon, no one would ever hurt her again.

"Well, I love being with you, too." Leon stopped in the middle of the busy sidewalk, pulled her into his arms, and kissed her long and hard.

People streamed past them, but Leon didn't care, and because he didn't, Cassandra didn't.

She never would have guessed even a year ago that she would be fine with public displays of affection.

But she was.

She really was.

It was so amazing. She'd thought that she would never be able to feel like this. She'd thought that what had happened to her and her little sister, Olivia, had scarred her forever, that it had broken the part of her that could fall in love and trust another human being. If it wasn't for Leon, she'd have never gotten to this point.

She was one lucky woman.

"What do you want for dinner?" Leon asked as he broke the kiss, then casually took her hand and resumed walking down the street.

"I don't care. Anything is fine … we can have whatever you want," she said, swinging their hands like they were two high school kids in love.

Only when she was a high school kid, she had been closed off and withdrawn. But she knew that Leon would have been as carefree and full of life as he was now.

She was so grateful to the mutual friend who'd introduced them a little over a year ago.

And what a year it had been.

After a whirlwind romance of only two months, Leon had taken her away on a short vacation at the beach and proposed to her at sunset while they stood in the shallows. Cassandra hadn't even hesitated to say yes. She'd been in love by the end of their first date.

Planning her wedding with her mom and her little sister had brought her closer to both of them, and it had almost been like old times—before the abduction. And she knew that since Olivia looked up to her, that seeing her happy and in love might give her the confidence to go after love as well.

It had.

Olivia was now engaged to Leon's cousin.

It was all so perfect.

"Want to start with dessert?" Leon asked, waggling his eyebrows at her.

Cassandra giggled. Giggling about sex was something she'd

never thought would happen. Even after she met Leon.

But, once again, Leon's calm and relaxed demeanor had rubbed off on her, and even their first time had gone smoothly and been something that she had enjoyed.

"We sure can," she smiled bashfully.

"Then we could order in something, pizza maybe. We could eat it in the backyard, kind of like our own little picnic."

Leon made everything fun, even eating in the yard. "Maybe we could make out a little under the stars," she said. Leon even made her comfortable enough to be forward and tell him what she wanted instead of waiting for him to read her mind like he'd had to do the first few months they were together.

"We better." He nudged her with his shoulder, then laughed a nice, deep, throaty laugh.

Their yard was small, but she loved spending time in it. There was something about the freedom of being outdoors that she found soothing. Her therapist thought it was because subconsciously she believed that being outside gave her more opportunities to flee should danger arise. Maybe there was some truth to it, but the vow she'd made to herself when she got married was that she wasn't going to overthink things anymore. She was going to live in the moment.

"I'll just pop upstairs and change into something a little more comfortable," Cassandra said as they turned into the small path that went through their front yard to the porch. "We should really plant some flowers or something," she said as Leon fished around in his pocket for the keys.

"Sure, anything you want," he said.

"Fruit trees. I think I'd like to grow some fruit," she said. Her dad had grown some when she and Olivia were kids, and she had loved picking apples or plums or apricots straight from the tree and eating them. And at the end of the summer, they would cook up the last of the fruit in pies. "Definitely fruit trees."

"Sure thing, babe," Leon said as he turned the key in the lock and pushed the door open. "We can go tomorrow after—"

Leon broke off abruptly and with a groan slumped to the floor.

Instantly, Cassandra was on high alert.

Her husband was a young healthy guy; he wouldn't just collapse for no reason.

Something was wrong.

She grabbed her phone and was just dialing 911 while trying to look into the house and see what was going on when the barrel of a gun suddenly came into view.

"Put the phone down and step inside," a low voice rumbled.

Cassandra weighed her options.

She could probably dart sideways around the side of the house and out of the line of fire. She could probably make it to the street where she could scream for help.

But if she did that, she'd be leaving her husband—the man she loved, the man she had pledged to love and support in good times and in bad—completely at the intruder's mercy.

She couldn't do it.

She couldn't leave him.

She knew Leon would be furious with her for not trying to save herself, but she just couldn't run and leave him here alone.

Feeling defeated, she dropped her phone and stepped inside her house. The house she and Leon had owned for only three months that in one instant had ceased to feel like her home and now felt like a prison.

"Go over there by the wall," the man ordered, slamming the door closed the second she was inside.

While her every instinct was to try to fight back, the man had turned his gun on Leon, who was stirring and trying to struggle to his knees. She couldn't risk her husband getting hurt, so she did as the man told her to.

"I didn't come here for him. If you listen and do as I tell you, I won't hurt your husband," the man said.

So, this was personal.

He hadn't chosen their house at random.

He was here for her.

She looked at his face and tried to see if she'd seen it before. Was this one of the men from the sex ring? She didn't recognize him, and that was a long time ago, but what other reason could he have for breaking in here to get to her?

The man pulled a Taser out of his pocket.

He was going to fire it at her and then probably drag her off to the bedroom, rape her, and then kill her.

But he didn't turn the Taser in her direction. He pointed it at Leon and fired it at him.

Her husband jerked and groaned in agony.

Cassandra wanted to run to him, hold him, but she couldn't. If she did, the man would likely shoot Leon.

"Walk to the bedroom," the man ordered, finally pointing the gun at her.

She should run.

Now was her chance.

But if she did, he would kill her husband and then come for her anyway. Maybe if she did what he wanted, he really would leave her husband alive. She'd be dead, but at least Leon would be okay.

With a sigh, she turned and walked up the stairs, the man on her heels.

An idea occurred to her.

They were on the stairs.

He thought that she was obeying him, so he was off guard.

If she spun around quickly and threw her entire weight at him then she could probably knock him off balance, sending them both tumbling down the stairs. Hopefully, the gun would fly out of his hand, and as long as she wasn't hurt too badly in the fall, she might be able to get to the weapon first.

It was risky, but it was worth a chance.

Cassandra took one more step. They were almost to the top. It was now or never.

Just as she was turning around, a needle pierced her bare shoulder.

* * * * *

8:42 P.M.

It was such a gorgeous evening.

Laura could sit out here for hours just enjoying the gentle breeze, the sunset, and watching her husband play in the pool with their kids.

It had taken her a long time to get here, but she was finally in a place where she could enjoy being outside again. As long as there weren't too many people about.

She had suffered from agoraphobia ever since she'd been abducted and taken to a remote wooded area where she was chased and raped and tortured for four days before being stumbled upon by a group of hikers.

She and Jack had known each other since they were born. Their families had lived next door to each other, so they'd grown up together and dated all through high school. Their relationship had ended abruptly, and by the time they'd stumbled upon each other again, she was a recluse who hadn't been outside her apartment in ten years.

His love and strength had helped her find the strength she hadn't thought she had, and although it had taken her another fifteen years, she'd finally managed to mostly overcome her agoraphobia.

When they'd first moved into this house, she hadn't been able to sit in the backyard. Even that had been enough to send her into a panic. Her pulse would pound, her heart would race, she would sweat, and her entire body would shake uncontrollably.

Now, as she sat at the edge of the pool with her feet dangling over the edge in the cool water, watching her husband and son and daughter toss a ball around, her heart fluttered a little, but that was it. It was a completely manageable feeling that she hoped would continue to fade over time until she felt nothing when she went outdoors.

She was a lucky woman.

A husband who had stood by her as she struggled to reclaim her life. A tenacious son who was no doubt going to follow in his father's footsteps and dedicate his life to helping people. And a daughter who was just the sweetest, kindest little person she'd ever met.

Laura wondered if Zach would probably follow his father and grandfather into the police force and if Rosie would follow in her footsteps and become a psychiatrist.

"Hey, Mom," ten-year-old Rosie called out.

"Yeah?"

"Why don't you come in with us?"

She wasn't really a swimmer. Sitting dangling her feet in the water was one thing, particularly at the end of a long, hot day, but getting right in the water was a whole other thing. "I don't think so, honey."

"Please," Rosie begged.

"Please," Zach, who was twelve echoed his little sister's plea.

How could she say no to that? "I'll have to go put on a swimsuit," she told them. Well maybe not a swimsuit, scars from her assault covered most of her body, and she didn't like people to see them, so she'd probably throw on an old pair of shorts and a light sweatshirt. "I'll be back in a few minutes. And only another fifteen minutes or so, then you both go inside and have your showers and get into your jammies."

"Can we stay up late and watch movies?" Zach asked. He was making the most of the summer and no school and had been going to bed close to midnight most days. The start of the new school year was only a couple of weeks away and they were going to have to start getting back into their regular routine.

"Ooh, ooh, can we play board games?" Rosie asked. She was going through a major board game phase.

Zach rolled his eyes as though that were the uncoolest thing he had ever heard in his life.

"We'll see," she told the kids as she turned sideways and pulled her feet out of the pool and then stood.

She didn't see him until she was turning around.

He came running at her, and other than shriek, she didn't have time to do anything else.

Too late, she realized she'd been played.

The kids had kept her distracted so she wouldn't notice that their dad had snuck out of the pool.

Jack picked her up and tossed her into the water.

She landed with a gigantic splash, and even from under the water she could hear the kids delighted squeals and giggles as their little plan worked.

Something splashed beside her, and then a few seconds later, Jack's arms came around her, and they both burst up to the surface together.

"My clothes are drenched." She pretended to frown at Jack and the kids.

"You can wash them." Zach smirked.

"*I'm* drenched." She pouted.

"You can take a shower." Rosie giggled, splashing through the water toward her.

"Oh yeah, we'll take one together," Jack whispered in her ear so that only she could hear him.

"Jack!" She swatted at him. Every night this summer after the kids had gone to bed, he'd wanted to fool around a little. They were forty-six-year-olds with two kids, and he'd been acting like they were two teenagers in love.

Well, the in-love part was right.

She had loved Jack since they were in middle school, and over time that love had only deepened and grown.

Laura knew how lucky she was to have found her other half, and she also knew that there was nothing that could come between them.

They had been through a lot, dealt with a lot, and yet, in the end, all of those things had only served to strengthen their relationship.

"Water fight," Zach said as he grabbed one of the water pistols and began to fire at them.

"Girls against boys," Rosie shrieked, grabbing two water pistols and passing her one.

For the next few minutes, they all splashed about the pool, squirting each other and laughing.

She lived for moments like these.

All those years she'd spent alone, locked up in her apartment living out her self-imposed exile, she had convinced herself that she could spend the rest of her life alone. That it was no big deal.

But she had been lying to herself.

She hadn't really wanted to spend her life alone; she had just been afraid and hurting.

This was what she wanted.

Fun nights just hanging out and being silly with her family.

She almost hated for it to end, but it was mostly dark now. It was time for them to be heading inside. Once they were all showered and in their PJs, they could play a board game, whatever one Rosie wanted, then they'd watch a movie, Zach's choice. Then once the kids were tucked in, she and Jack could enjoy a little grown-up time.

"Okay, guys," she called out. "It's time to go in."

"Aww," Zach whined.

"Can't we stay just a little longer?" Rosie stuck out her bottom lip.

"No, it's time to go inside," she said firmly.

"But—"

"No buts." Jack cut off Zach. "You heard your mother. Go. Out of the pool."

The kids grumbled under their breaths but knew better than to argue back. She and Jack were always on the same page when it came to Zach and Rosie; it was the only way they could be successful parents. Especially as the kids entered their teenage years, they needed to know that playing one parent off the other was out of the question.

"Here," Jack said, holding out his hand as he started up the steps at the side of the pool.

"You know I'll never be able to get the chlorine out of my shorts," she told him, accepting his hand.

"You can't fool me. You loved playing in the pool with the kids." Jack grabbed a towel and wrapped it around her, rubbing her arms to warm her as she shivered.

"Maybe." She grinned up at him.

"No maybes." He leaned over and kissed the tip of her nose. "So, a shower?" Jack asked, and she could see in the fading light that he had raised one brow in that way he did because he thought it made him look sexy.

Okay, so it *did* make him look sexy.

"The kids will be ready for a game and movie in less than thirty minutes," she warned.

"That's okay; we can be quick." Jack winked, then scooped her up into his arms.

"Jack ..." She laughed as she curled an arm around his shoulders. "We don't have time."

"I beg to differ," he said, taking off across the backyard with her. He managed to open the door one handed, then close it behind them. Then he was up the stairs, down the hall, and into their en suite in record time. "See?" He smirked as he set her on her feet. "We have a whole twenty-five minutes before Rosie will be out of the shower. You know how long it takes her these days."

He was right.

Rosie was ten but quickly heading toward being a teenager. She would be starting middle school in a couple of weeks. And Zach was already interested in girls. He'd had some girl who'd been in his class last year over to the house several times already since school had let out.

Her babies weren't babies anymore.

"Want to make another one?" Jack asked.

"I think we're a little too old. Grandchildren is next for us," she said, although the idea of having another baby did hold a little appeal. She missed having an infant around.

"I'm willing to try if you are." Jack took hold of the hem of her long-sleeved T-shirt and pulled it up and over her head, then unsnapped her jean shorts and tugged them down her legs.

"I guess it can't hurt to try." She smiled and untied the cord of his board shorts.

AUGUST 6TH

8:51 A.M.

Want to make another one?

Jack couldn't believe he'd said that to Laura last night.

They were forty-six, they both worked jobs with erratic hours that took up a lot of time and mental energy, and they already had two kids.

And yet, it was true.

He hadn't meant for it to slip out. He hadn't even been thinking about having more kids, but then he'd seen Laura playing in the pool and having more fun than he'd seen her have in a long time. It had just come out, but the second the words were out there, he realized they were true.

He would love to have another kid.

He knew that with their age there was a chance they wouldn't be able to get pregnant, and even if they did, there were no guarantees Laura could carry to term. If the baby did survive, then there were higher risks that it would be born with problems.

But none of that mattered.

If they couldn't have another biological baby, he would love to look into fostering or even adopting. His brother Ryan had an adopted daughter, and Paige's daughters were both adopted, and he liked the idea of being able to give a home to a child who needed one.

"You're quiet this morning," Xavier said.

"Last night I said to Laura that I wanted another kid," he told his partner.

"You do? It's been ten years since you had Rosie. I just

133

assumed you guys were happy with two."

"We were. Or I thought we were. But then last night it just kind of came out, but I realized it's true. I would like to have another kid. I want to talk to Laura about looking into adoption."

"Annabelle and I have been trying for another child ever since the twins celebrated their first birthday," Xavier admitted.

His partner's twins were five going on six and would be starting kindergarten in the fall. Jack knew that Annabelle had struggled to get pregnant last time and just assumed that Xavier and Annabelle had decided two kids were enough. "I'm sorry it hasn't happened already."

"I haven't said it to Annabelle—although I'm sure she's already thought about it—but I don't think it's ever going to happen for us."

Disappointment was written all over Xavier's face, and Jack wished there was something he could do.

"Annabelle is thirty-eight now, so her chances of getting pregnant are diminishing. If it never happens, it's not like we're going to be unhappy. I love JP and Katie, and I love being their dad, but I'd like another kid. Maybe if it doesn't happen for us soon, we'll look into adoption too."

The idea of adoption was growing on him.

Not that he wouldn't be thrilled if Laura did turn up pregnant. She was in her mid-forties, and the chances of her naturally conceiving were dropping. She could still get pregnant, but he thought either way he would like to look into adoption. There were so many kids who'd lost parents for one reason or another and needed someone to love them and take care of them.

Like PJ Bell would if they couldn't find his mother in the next six days.

The killer had struck again last night.

Twenty-six-year-old Cassandra Stanton had been discovered by her younger sister Olivia, who had turned up to discuss her wedding plans. Cassandra had been lying dead in the master bedroom. Her husband, Leon, had been tied up and left in the bathtub, alive.

Cassandra Stanton had been a victim of the same gang of child traffickers who'd gone after Tessa and her friend Eleanor Matthews when the girls were eleven. Parker and Wyatt had worked the case about six months before Parker was murdered.

Another victim from Parker's cases.

Another victim with a connection to Tessa.

Right now, Jack wasn't sure what to think. Wyatt might have said that Lucas Mianta had more of a connection with Parker than with him, but Wyatt and Parker had arrested him together. And although Wyatt thought that Tessa had never met Lucas, that didn't mean that she hadn't.

Jack wasn't sure who the intended target was, but he *did* like Lachlan Mountain as a suspect.

Which was why they were here.

As if on cue, the door to the interview room at the prison where Lachlan Mountain had served his time swung open, and a shackled Rick Caretta was led in.

"Whatever you think I did, I didn't," the man said without preamble.

Rick Caretta was seventy-nine years old. He'd been in prison for the last forty-three years after he was convicted of murdering his wife, four kids, the family who lived behind his house, and one of his next-door neighbors.

That the first thing out of his mouth was a claim of innocence, probably meant there was something he was afraid they'd found out about. There had been a couple of other neighborhood teenage girls who'd been raped and strangled in the months leading up to the murders, and it had always been the theory that his wife found out what he'd done so he killed her, then their kids, and the neighbors so there would be no witnesses. If it hadn't been for the fact that the sixteen-year-old boy who lived next door had come home and seen bloody footsteps on his porch, then Rick probably would have killed a lot more people.

"We're not here about you, Mr. Caretta," Jack told the man.

"Oh." He looked disappointed as though he almost wanted them to have come to speak with him about his other crimes. Maybe as he neared the end of his life, he wanted to confess so he could die with a clear conscience.

"We're here about Lachlan Mountain," Xavier said.

"Oh," Rick said again, this time accompanied with an eye roll. It seemed he wasn't fond of his ex-cellmate.

"What can you tell us about Lachlan?" Jack asked.

"He was boring."

"Boring? In what way?" Xavier asked.

"He only had one topic of conversation. One. In sixteen years. Trust me, that gets old pretty quick."

Jack was almost positive he already knew the answer, but still he asked, "And what was this topic of conversation?"

"Tessa Bell. That was it. That was all I heard about. How much he loved her, how one day they were going to be together, how much he hated Tessa's husband Parker. How he was going to kill Parker and then have Tessa all to himself, and well, you get the picture, it was all variations on that one theme."

Lachlan hadn't known that Tessa's husband was dead. Maybe that was where this idea to kill off people that Parker had helped came from because he couldn't kill Parker himself.

It didn't make a lot of sense, but that didn't mean it wasn't true.

"Did Lachlan mention anything specific?" Jack asked. They needed something so they could get ahead of Lachlan before he killed anyone else.

"No. Mostly he just rambled about Tessa: how beautiful she was, how smart she was, how sweet she was, how much he loved her, how much she loved him, how they were going to be so happy together."

"Did he mention Matilda Bell?" Jack asked. Maybe they could

talk to Parker's sister about the possibility of her playing bait so they could try to catch Lachlan. If Lachlan still hated Parker as much as they thought he did, then it made sense he still hated Matilda too. She was the one who'd killed his father, after all. It was likely he was going to go after her at some point.

"The woman who shot his father." Rick nodded. "Yeah, he hated her and Parker. He talked about how much he hated them almost as much as he talked about how much he loved Tessa. He wrote her a letter every single day. He would read them to me."

"Can you remember anything specific from them?" Xavier asked.

Rick paused, then nodded. "He talked about coming for her as soon as he had a place for them to live. He said that he wanted to give her the peace he knew she'd been searching for, for a long time. He said that he wanted her to be happy and that he wanted to take away her pain. He thought that Parker was the source of that pain, and without him, she could finally be free."

"Anything else you can remember?" Jack asked.

"What did Lachlan do?" Rick asked.

"We think he might have kidnapped Tessa and killed some people," Xavier replied.

"I'm not surprised," Rick said smugly. "The guy was obsessed, and that kind of obsession always leads to no good. Oh, there was one more thing. August twelfth was the date that his parents were married; it was the day that he wanted to marry Tessa."

August twelfth.

That was ten days after the second.

That was the day that the kidnapper had claimed to be going to kill Tessa.

Coincidence?

Jack didn't think so.

Instead of just killing Tessa on the twelfth, Jack wondered if Lachlan was instead planning a murder suicide.

That way, instead of being joined together in holy matrimony they would be joined together in death.

* * * * *

9:17 A.M.

She hadn't missed Parker this much since he died.

Matilda was pacing aimlessly around Tessa's house.

She felt lost.

And very alone.

As much as she adored her husband and their two kids, Parker was her twin brother. They'd grown up together, and because their first ten years of life had been so awful, they'd grown so close.

In a way, she missed those days.

Not the hell they'd lived through in some of the foster homes they'd been sent to, but being close to her brother.

After she'd accidentally shot and killed that social worker, her entire world had changed. She had become withdrawn and so guilt ridden she could barely function.

Parker hadn't understood.

He had said he did, but he hadn't.

And when they'd been adopted by the Bells, he had thrived. He'd turned into a normal, happy, well-adjusted child.

But she hadn't.

No one could save her.

So she and Parker had grown further and further apart.

Then she had fled.

Now she wished so badly that she could get those years back. At the time, it had seemed like there was plenty of time. She had thought that they would have the entire rest of their lives to reconnect, so she'd stayed away. Swamped in guilt and struggling to make it through each day.

When she had finally returned, her timing couldn't have been worse. Parker and Tessa had been going through a rough patch, and her reunion with her twin brother had not been what she had been dreaming about.

Things had gotten a little better, and they'd had a couple of good years together before he died.

But he had died, and now she was an only child with no parents.

All she had in the world was Daniel and his family.

Now Tessa was gone, and Daniel was out of his mind with worry, and her kids might lose another relative.

Mattie wished that Mary and Michael had met Parker; they would have loved him so much. Michael reminded her a bit of her brother and what he had been like as a preteen.

She liked that.

It was like a piece of her brother was still alive.

Parker had loved Tessa so much, and she was so glad that she'd gotten to know Tess. The woman felt more like her sister than her sister-in-law. They'd grown so close over the last fifteen years, and she felt lucky that she'd been able to help raise Tessa and Parker's son.

PJ.

He was an interesting kid.

He was quiet and shy and not really much like his father. He wasn't much like his mother either. Tessa might have become quiet and a little withdrawn since Parker died, but she was still confident and self-assured. But PJ was so unsure of himself that she worried about him sometimes.

Especially if his mother wasn't found alive.

She wished there was something she could do to help.

But there wasn't.

So, she was reduced to wandering around the main house where they'd moved, so they could stay with PJ and he could remain in his own home. Mary and Michael were thrilled. They loved running around the mansion and often asked to spend the night here with Tess and PJ. But she found this house creepy. Probably because she knew what had gone on here. It was hard to enjoy sleeping in a house where she knew that Tessa had almost been killed by her own mother when she was just a kid.

This house held so many bad memories for Daniel and Tessa, and now for PJ too.

Mattie sighed.

She had to do something. If she just kept wandering around the house, she was going to drive herself crazy. Wyatt and the cops were doing everything they could to find Tessa. She just had to believe that they *would* find her.

Maybe she would go and do some baking. Tessa had always enjoyed baking and cooking, and they'd spent many hours together in the kitchen talking and laughing. It was when Tessa had been the most relaxed and at ease.

She'd make lasagna for dinner; that had been Parker's favorite, and it was PJ's too. One of the few things, other than his looks, that he had in common with his dad.

Matilda tried to talk to PJ about Parker, so he would know what kind of man his father was. Tessa had been only two months pregnant with PJ when Parker had died. It was a miracle that she and her unborn baby were alive. It had been touch and go for a few days after she was rescued, and losing Tessa and the baby on the back of losing Parker would have been too much to bear.

As much as she tried to talk to PJ about his dad, he never seemed too interested in listening. He always said it was too painful, and she got that. It was painful for her to think about and talk about her brother.

She worried about PJ keeping himself locked away here on the estate. He had attended a regular school until he was ten, but then he'd begged and pleaded to be allowed to study from home with a tutor, and Tessa had conceded, so PJ didn't have many friends his own age. He loved his cousins and spent a lot of time with them, but he should have friends, like a normal kid. With his high IQ she knew that he felt awkward around other teenagers, but she didn't want to see him become a recluse like his mother.

Mattie was so lost in thought that she didn't notice the man standing behind the kitchen door until it was too late.

As she stepped into the kitchen, he snapped out an arm and wrapped it around her neck, yanking her up against his body.

The arm squeezed and she clawed at it, desperate to draw a breath.

Her kids.

Where were the kids?

It took her a moment to remember that Casey Wyatt had taken them out for the day.

They weren't here.

They were safe.

She sagged in relief.

Then her mind started to spin.

Was this the man who had Tessa?

Had he come back to kill the rest of them?

Did he just want her, or was he going to kill Daniel, and Mary and Michael, and PJ as well?

She started to panic, flinging her body from side to side, and clawing with her nails, trying to dislodge his arm.

"Stop," a voice ordered, shaking her viciously.

That voice.

She recognized it.

She knew who this was.

It was Lachlan Mountain.

He hated her.

With good reason.

She had killed his father. His father who was a good man who had dedicated his life to helping kids like her who, with no one to care for them, had been dumped in the foster care system.

If she could change just one thing from her past, it would be that.

But Lachlan was in prison, wasn't he?

After kidnapping Parker, then getting his hands on Tessa, too, he had intended to kill Parker and flee with Tess and her unborn baby.

Wyatt had shown up in time, and although Parker had nearly died and Tessa had miscarried, they'd all survived, and Lachlan had been sent to prison.

So why was he here?

The man was obsessed with Tessa.

He sent her letters all the time. Usually Tessa threw them out, but Matilda saw them from time to time.

"Matilda Bell," Lachlan drawled. "Just who I was looking for."

So he was here for her.

Hopefully, that meant that her husband and children were safe.

"We're going to have a little fun together. Well *I'm* going to have a little fun. I doubt what I have planned is going to be much fun for you," he snickered as he shoved her into the middle of the room.

A knife.

If she could make it to the counter, she could arm herself with one.

"Uh, uh, uh." He smiled and shook his head. "You try anything stupid, and everything I do to you, I'll do to your kids."

That threat was enough to keep her standing still.

"Strip," he ordered.

He couldn't be serious.

But one look at his face said he was.

With shaking hands, she pulled her green sundress over her head and tossed it on the floor. She wasn't wearing a bra, so she was left mostly naked.

"Underwear too," Lachlan said.

Terrified of what he would do to her children if she didn't comply, she slipped out of her panties and dropped them on the floor beside her dress.

Naked now, she shuddered as Lachlan gave her a once-over.

"By the time I'm done with you, you're going to wish you were dead."

The malevolent look in his eyes filled her with icy dread, and yet, at the same time, Matilda couldn't shake the feeling that she somehow deserved this.

She had killed his father, after all.

* * * * *

9:32 A.M.

"Hello?" Daniel said as he answered his phone to an unknown number.

"Daniel?"

"Yes. Is this Detective Xander?" Something in the man's voice set his stomach churning.

It was bad news.

He knew it was even before the detective said anything.

Had they found Tessa?

Had the killer decided not to keep her for the full ten days?

"It is. Where are you?" Detective Xander asked.

Where was he?

That was not what Daniel had been expecting the cop to ask. He had expected it to be news on Tessa. Why did it matter where he was? What possible bearing could that have on anything?

"I'm on my way back from the store. Why?" Despite Detective Xander not having given him any bad news about his sister, that sick feeling of dread in his stomach just grew.

"You need to get back to your place as quickly as you can. Get Matilda and drive to the station. We'll meet you there as soon as we can. Is anyone else there? PJ? Your kids?"

"PJ, Mary, and Michael are all out with Casey. Matilda is home alone. What's going on?" If Detective Xander didn't tell him what this phone call was about in the next few seconds, he was going to explode.

"Don't panic," the cop started.

Of course, when someone said that to you, the first thing you did was panic. His sister had already been kidnapped, and now it sounded like his wife was in danger as well.

"I'm panicking," he snapped. "Hurry up and spit it out."

"After speaking with Wyatt, we thought that the kidnapper and killer could be Lachlan Mountain—"

"Lachlan Mountain?" he interrupted. That man hated Matilda. *Hated* her. He couldn't—or didn't want to—comprehend that what had happened with his father was nothing more than an unfortunate accident, and that Matilda had just been a traumatized child, not a hardened criminal.

"I said don't panic," Detective Xander repeated in an irritatingly calm voice. "He's been out of prison for a month, and he hasn't made any move to go after Matilda."

"But you think he has Tessa. He's obsessed with her, and he said that he was going to kill her in ten days. That's just six days away, which means he's probably going to go after Matilda before then. Which you already figured out, that's why you're calling."

"We *do* think he's going to go after Matilda, but there is no reason to think that he will today. We spoke with Lachlan's cellmate, and he said that Lachlan's parents' wedding anniversary was the twelfth, and he spoke about him and Tessa getting married on the same date—"

"You think he's going to kill Tessa and himself on that day. That will be the ten days." Daniel could feel himself starting to panic. There was no way Lachlan wasn't going to kill Tessa in six days' time. And if Lachlan was planning on killing himself, then there was no way he wasn't going to make sure Matilda was dead too. He pressed his foot down on the accelerator. "Are you sending cops to the house?"

"We are. Xavier and I are on our way there too. We just left the prison. We're probably an hour out, but there should be officers there within the next fifteen minutes. When you get home, be careful. I really don't think that he's going to go after her today, but that doesn't mean he won't. Just get Matilda and leave. We're going to set up surveillance there and have an officer remain there at all times. When we get to the station, we want to talk to you and Matilda."

"No."

"No, what?" Detective Xander sounded confused.

"No, you can't use my wife as bait to catch this guy." He knew what cops were like. They were always wanting to use innocent people to help them do their job. Well, Mattie wasn't going to be helping them. No way, no how. "He already has my sister. I'm not letting him get his hands on my wife as well. I'm turning into the driveway. I'll call you back once I have Matilda and we're leaving."

Daniel hung up and tossed his phone onto the passenger seat.

This was a nightmare.

Life had been so quiet and peaceful the last fifteen years.

Yes, Tessa had been grieving, and yes, as part of her grief, she had pretty much locked herself away here on the estate, but they had all been happy. He had his sister back in his life, and he had been glad that he'd been able to be there for her this time when he hadn't in the past. Their lives had been simple. They went horse riding or swam in the pool, hiked around the woods that surrounded the property, had dinner together, played board games, and talked.

Now, everything was just like it had been in the past.

Completely out of control, and he desperately wanted to be back in control.

Parking the car in front of the mansion, he climbed out and walked around to the rear of the house. He knew his wife, and when she was feeling lost, she liked to spend time in the kitchen, because that was what Tessa always did. If he had to guess, then Matilda would be making lasagna because that had been Parker's favorite meal, and it was PJ's. She was probably making it for them for dinner to try to cheer them all up.

For some reason, he looked in the kitchen window as he passed it.

And froze.

He'd been right. Matilda was in there, but she wasn't alone.

Lachlan Mountain was in there too.

So much for the cops not thinking he would come for Matilda today.

Matilda was in the middle of the large kitchen, naked, with a knife in her hands.

If she had a knife, why wasn't she using it on Lachlan?

He shifted slightly so he could get a better look at Lachlan, and saw that the man had a gun.

It was trained on Matilda's head.

As he watched, Lachlan's mouth moved, and Matilda took the knife she clutched and pressed the tip into her forearm, slicing it through her flesh.

Daniel tensed as blood began to flow from the wound.

Why had Matilda done that?

What had Lachlan said to her that would make her cut herself?

He knew Matilda, and she would do whatever she could to fight for her life. If Lachlan was going to shoot her anyway, then she wouldn't play his games. He bet that Lachlan had threatened their kids. If he'd told her that he would hurt their children if she didn't do what he said, then Matilda would do anything he asked without protest.

Lachlan threw some sort of liquid at Matilda, splashing it all over the gash in her arm and she screamed in pain.

Daniel felt his blood begin to boil.

This man had caused Tessa to lose her first child, and in doing so, started a chain of events that ended in Parker's death. Now he had Tessa in his clutches again, but that wasn't enough for him. He wanted Matilda too.

Well, he wasn't going to get her.

Circling back around to the front of the house, Daniel headed inside. Tessa owned a gun, but it was upstairs locked away in the gun safe and he didn't know the combination. He could probably guess it, but Matilda didn't have that kind of time. The cops were on the way, but there were no guarantees they would arrive in time either.

There was a heavy wooden statue that his grandparents had bought on one of their travels that sat on an occasional table by the front door.

That should do the job.

Picking it up, he ran as quickly as he dared through the house. He didn't want Lachlan to know he was there.

As he approached the kitchen, he heard Matilda scream again.

Daniel saw red.

His blood boiled, and all he wanted to do was hit Lachlan over and over again until the man lay in a bloodied mess at his feet. The only thing stopping him from doing it was that they needed Lachlan to tell them where Tessa was.

The kitchen door was open, and Daniel knew that if he hesitated, Lachlan could hear him or turn and see him.

Without pausing, he pushed through the door, just as Matilda let out another pained scream, and swung the statue up then brought it down again, connecting with the back of Lachlan's head.

The man dropped instantly.

A bottle of bleach and the gun clattered to the floor.

Lachlan had been throwing bleach on Matilda's open wounds.

He couldn't help slamming the statue into Lachlan's head one more time.

The man deserved a lot more.

Sirens sounded, so he didn't bother tying Lachlan up. He just kicked the gun to the other side of the room and ran to Matilda, picking up her dress and wrapping it around her then gathering her up in his arms.

"Are you okay?" he asked her, scanning her body. There was the cut on her arm, another on her thigh, and a third on her stomach. All three were oozing blood, but none looked life threatening. Just horrendously painful, thanks to the bleach Lachlan had doused them with.

"He said he'd hurt Mary and Michael if I didn't do what he said," Matilda explained through clenched teeth. She rested her head on his shoulder, tears streaming down her face.

"I love you, Mattie." He kissed her wet cheek.

"I love you, too." She turned her face sideways and kissed the side of his jaw. "I'm okay, Daniel."

She would be.

But she would have scars, and she'd forever be apprehensive in her home.

Half a dozen officers burst into the room and snapped handcuffs on Lachlan Mountain, dragging him away.

At least now this was over.

Matilda was alive, and hopefully, Tessa was as well.

But he had come so close to losing both of them.

Daniel clutched his wife tighter and sank down to the floor, cradling her on his lap. He tucked her head under his chin and buried his face in her hair, dragging in her scent.

She was okay.

She was okay.

Maybe if he kept telling himself that, it would eventually sink in.

* * * * *

10:44 A.M.

The Micah Estate was abuzz with activity.

Cop cars, forensic vans, and a couple of ambulances.

If Daniel Micah hadn't arrived when he had, then the coroners van would also be here.

Thankfully, it had worked out. Matilda was injured, but alive, and so were all the other people on Lachlan's kill list. Now they just had to get the man to give up where he was holding Tessa, so they could bring her home to her family too.

Xavier pulled the car to a stop in between a squad car and an ambulance, and he and Jack climbed out and headed inside where Lachlan was waiting for them.

The man was in his late forties, his sandy hair was more white than blond, freckles covered his face, and the blue eyes that tracked their progress from the front door were shadowed with pain, but otherwise sharp. In comparison to the pictures they'd seen of him from when he had been arrested sixteen years ago, Lachlan had bulked up over his decade and a half in prison.

"He okay to be interviewed?" Xavier asked the medic who was hovering close to Lachlan Mountain. He didn't want anything the man told them thrown out when they went to court because some defense lawyer claimed that Lachlan's head injury invalidated everything he said.

From the look of the blood that still coated the back of his head and his white T-shirt, Daniel had done a bit of damage with the two blows he'd delivered. Given what the man had done to Daniel's sister and wife, Xavier admired the man's restraint. And he guessed that if they didn't need Lachlan to tell them where Tessa was, then Daniel would have killed him.

"No concussion. He knows his name, the date, where he is, what happened to him, what he was here to do. He's fine to be interviewed," the medic replied.

Lachlan didn't look concerned as they came and took seats on the sofa in front of the one he was seated on. It was like he was so consumed with his plan and trying to achieve his goals that he just didn't care that he was going to be punished for it.

"I shouldn't have played with her." Lachlan's voice was clear when he spoke. "If I had just killed her right away, then I'd have been out of here before the husband showed up. I got greedy."

Complete and utter lack of remorse.

The man was a true sociopath.

That Lachlan would be spending the rest of his life in prison was some small consolation.

"That you're going to prison is a given," Xavier said.

Lachlan nodded.

"Matilda can testify to what you did to her," he continued. "You're never getting out. Telling us where she is isn't going to affect your sentencing, but it's the right thing to do."

"Tell you where who is? Matilda? You know where she is. She's here somewhere. And life in prison is a bit of a harsh sentence just for holding a gun on her and making her cut herself."

Xavier sighed.

He had been hoping that Lachlan's obsession with Tessa went deep enough to do the right thing. If for no other reason than now that Lachlan was in custody, Tessa wouldn't be left alone to die a slow death from dehydration.

"There's the assault on Matilda, the murders of Joey Geller, Melanie Gardner, Elizabeth Landry, Lucas Mianta, Cassandra Stanton, the assault of Cassandra's husband, and the abduction of Tessa."

The man paled.

So dramatically and instantaneously that the paramedics immediately moved to check his vitals.

Maybe the shock of being confronted with what he'd done to the woman he claimed to love had finally sunk in.

If he wouldn't tell them where he had stashed Tessa, then she would die.

Surely Lachlan cared about that.

It was one thing to have planned a murder suicide, but to leave Tessa to die a slow death was something else.

"Where is she, Lachlan?" Jack asked.

"She needs you to tell us," Xavier added.

"If you love her like you say you do, then you need to do the right thing," Jack said.

"Otherwise, she's going to die," Xavier continued. They didn't want to give Lachlan time to think they wanted to hammer him about Tessa until he had no choice but to blurt out where she was.

"She was injured in the accident; she probably needs a doctor."

"Tell us where she is, so we can go and get her."

"Her son needs her."

"Where is Tessa, Lachlan?" Xavier asked.

"Tessa?" Lachlan squawked. "What happened to her?"

"You took her," Xavier said. Why was the guy playing stupid about Tessa when he had been so open and blatant about his intentions with Matilda?

"I didn't take Tessa," Lachlan spluttered, no longer calm and in control. Now he looked like he was in a panic. If he wasn't handcuffed, Xavier wouldn't have been surprised if the man had lunged at them.

"I suppose that's technically true," Jack said. "You paid Joey Geller to kidnap her, and then you killed him when he delivered her to you."

"I didn't pay anyone to kidnap Tessa. And I don't even know anyone called Joey Geller. I came here to get Tessa today. I was going to kill Matilda then take Tessa. She loves me, you know, and the two of us would have been happy together." He glowered at them. "And now you're saying she's gone. That someone took her. Who? Who has my Tessa?" The last was said in a booming shout.

Was Lachlan telling the truth?

When they'd thought he was the man they were looking for, they'd been surprised that Lachlan had come after Matilda so soon. They had expected him to kill Matilda on the eighteenth, and then kill himself and Tessa on the twelfth.

If Lachlan wasn't the man they were looking for, then who was?

Xavier shot Jack a look and saw that his partner was doubting Lachlan's guilt just like he was.

"You didn't abduct Tessa?" Jack asked.

"No. And I didn't kill anyone. I already told you I was going to kill Matilda, but her husband interrupted. Now tell me who has Tessa!"

Lachlan was looking worse by the second. By the sheer panic and terror rolling off him in waves, Xavier didn't think that he was the man they'd been looking for. If he had Tessa, he might refuse to tell them where she was, but he didn't think he would lie about it. He would be more likely to try to convince them that Tessa wanted to be with him and that the two of them were in love.

"If it's not you, then we don't know who has her," Xavier told Lachlan.

"Well, it's not me," Lachlan snapped.

Then they were back to square one.

Lachlan Mountain had been the only solid lead they had.

Now it was gone.

One look at Jack said his partner was convinced as well.

He was innocent.

Lachlan had tried to kill Matilda Micah, and he would have kidnapped Tessa had she been here, but he wasn't their killer.

Xavier didn't relish having to tell Tessa's family that they were back to square one.

"You can take him to the hospital," he said to the paramedics. "Make sure you stay with him and take him down and book him as soon as a doctor clears him," he said to the pair of officers who had been assigned to stay with Lachlan until he was booked.

"No. Stop. Wait," Lachlan screamed as he was pulled to his feet and dragged away. "Who has Tessa? Who took her? Tell me who they are. I'll kill them. I'll *kill* them."

Xavier ignored him. They didn't have time for Lachlan now. They only had six days left if they were going to find Tessa and bring her home.

"I guess we're back to the possibility we're looking at a cop or someone involved in an old case of Parker and Wyatt's," Jack said as they both stood and headed to the living room across the other side of the foyer where Daniel and Matilda were waiting for news on Tessa.

"Do you know where she is?" Daniel demanded the second they stepped into the room. Matilda was wrapped in a blanket, curled up in Daniel's lap, but she lifted her head from his chest to hear their answer.

"He said he doesn't have Tessa," Xavier broke the news.

"And you believed him?" Daniel growled.

"He was very honest about what he did to Matilda, and he admitted that he *was* here to abduct Tessa, but he was shocked and scared when we told him that Tessa had been kidnapped," Jack explained.

"So, that's it, then," Daniel said, sounding hopeless. "Before Lachlan, you didn't have any suspects. Tessa's time is running out. You're never going to find her, are you?"

Xavier wanted to offer assurances to this suffering family. He wanted to tell them that they would find their loved one and bring her home and that their lives could return to normal.

But he couldn't.

Because he would be lying.

He didn't know if they were going to find Tessa Bell, but it was looking less likely with each passing day.

* * * * *

2:50 P.M.

So far, his luck was holding.

The cops were clueless.

Really, he thought they were stupid. How could they not have figured it out? He was glad that they hadn't, but it didn't really engender much trust in the people that were supposed to make you feel safe when they couldn't solve what should be a simple case if they would only open their eyes and look.

But people didn't do that.

Hardly any of them anyway.

They saw only what they wanted to see, no matter how much what they didn't want to see was staring them in the face.

He thought that was interesting.

It certainly wasn't how he saw the world.

He accepted things for what they were, even when he didn't like it, and he tried to make changes for the better in the lives of those he cared about.

Be the change you want to see in the world.

He'd heard that once, and it had stuck with him. It was true. How could you expect something to be different when you weren't prepared to put in the work to make it different?

You couldn't.

It was as simple as that.

There were big changes that he wanted to see in this world, so instead of just sitting back and moaning about the fact that there were problems he wished weren't there, he was doing something about it.

He was being his own change in the world.

He was doing something about all the pain and suffering that existed.

He was helping people who had already suffered so much to find peace.

He was on his way to help another person right now.

Kelita McNamara.

She was next on his list.

Kelita was a fifty-six-year-old woman. She had lost her first husband when they were young and had raised her two sons, Sam, now thirty-three, and Jordan, now thirty-five, on her own. After a falling-out when both boys decided to move away from home to attend college instead of staying close by, leaving Kelita feeling abandoned by the only people she had left in her life, she was now close with both sons. She had remarried fairly recently and appeared to be happy, spending a lot of her time caring for her three young granddaughters.

Fifteen years ago, she'd been tricked by a woman out for revenge, and had been kidnapped, chained up in an old abandoned warehouse, and left for dead.

Miraculously, she'd been saved at the last minute and was the only survivor of the ordeal.

It had been that ordeal that was the catalyst for her reconciling with her sons, and it seemed like, although she'd been through something horrific, she'd come out of it all with a better life than she'd had before.

At least on the outside.

But he knew better.

He knew that you never recovered from something like that. Those scars would forever be there; you were forever haunted by what had happened to you. It was always there, lurking just underneath the surface, ready to pounce whenever it felt like it with no care for the fact that you might be trying to move on and find happiness.

Well, he was going to rid that darkness from Kelita McNamara's soul forever.

He was going to send her off into eternal bliss.

But he was going to have to move quickly. He only had a short window of opportunity if he was going to end her life today.

Most days she babysat either her son Sam's two little girls, or her son Jordan's daughter, to save her sons and their wives the cost of placing their small children in daycare.

The days and times varied, which had made things extremely difficult choosing a time when she was alone so he could get to her. He didn't want to come for her when the children were with her. They were only two, four, and five, and he didn't want to traumatize them for life by scaring them, so he had to wait for a time when Kelita was alone.

But most of the time, when the children weren't there, her husband was. And unlike Cassandra Stanton's husband, Kelita's husband was an ex-cop. He wouldn't be as easy to incapacitate as Leon had been.

He absolutely could not risk getting caught when he was this close to finishing what he'd started.

If he got caught now, then what would happen to Tessa?

Instead of having her suffering relieved and being ushered into eternal peace, she would be left alive to continue suffering for maybe another thirty or forty years.

That was unacceptable.

He could not allow that to happen.

No matter what.

Every decision he made, every move he made, it all had to be done with care and precision.

It was a great motto for life in general, but particularly when you had to operate outside the law for the greater good.

He turned the car into Kelita's block and drove about halfway down before pulling to a stop in front of the house four down and on the opposite side of the street than the house Kelita shared with her husband. He didn't like to park right outside the homes of his victims because if any of the neighbors or anyone walking past happened to notice it, they'd tell the cops when they canvassed the street.

Play it safe.

It was always the better option.

He had left the dog lead behind at Lucas Mianta's house. He hadn't needed it for Cassandra's murder. He had known the only way he would get to her was to lay in wait indoors, incapacitate the husband the second they came inside, then use threats to get Cassandra to comply. It almost hadn't worked. She had been going to try to knock him down the stairs. It was just lucky that he had anticipated that and managed to inject the potassium chloride before everything spun out of control.

For today, he had cooked up another scam.

He had a picture of a cat that he'd pulled off the internet, and he was going to claim that someone had run over his cat a couple of days ago and that he was just asking around to see if anyone had seen anything. It should work; he could see no reason why it shouldn't.

His hand was on the door handle when he suddenly stopped.

Something felt wrong.

He couldn't say what, but something was telling him not to get out of the car.

Were the cops out there?

Had they figured out who he was going to go after next and set a trap?

Were they out there laying in wait for him?

Were they ready to pounce on him the second he got out of the car?

Instead of getting out of the car, he picked up his phone and pretended that he was deep in conversation while he surveyed the street.

There were a few more cars parked than he would have suspected, including a florist delivery van. It was the perfect place to hide out and wait for him if the cops really had figured out who was next on his list and were here waiting for him.

Kelita McNamara was in her front yard.

Again, that was unusual. The house had a simple yard, just lawn and a single large tree, and they hired a gardener to mow the grass. Kelita didn't usually spend time in the yard unless she was out there playing with her grandkids, but it was at least an hour before they were due to arrive.

That cinched it.

This was a trap.

A setup.

Kelita was supposed to hang around outside as the bait, waiting for him to hook himself.

But that wasn't going to happen.

He wasn't stupid, and he was a little insulted that the cops seemed to think that he was.

He would have to call this one a loss. He didn't like it, but it wasn't worth risking getting caught by trying to kill Kelita. If they knew that he was after her, then they were going to keep cops on her around the clock. As much as he hated to admit defeat, it was what it was.

In the end, it wasn't the worst thing in the world.

He wanted to help some of these other poor victims find peace, but it wasn't what he really longed for.

What he really wanted was to join himself and Tessa together forever.

And that he could still have.

She was back at the house waiting for him to return. She wasn't doing any better, and he was starting to get extremely concerned about her.

They were close.

So close.

She only had to hold on for a couple more days.

A couple more days and then *the* day would be here.

The day where they would be joined together for all eternity.

* * * * *

8:48 P.M.

"Can we watch one more movie?" Katie pleaded the second

the one they were watching ended.

"No," Annabelle firmly told her daughter. "It's almost bedtime."

"But it's summer," Julian Paul, nicknamed JP, followed up his twin sister's plea.

It wasn't a surprise that the kids wanted to stay up late; she and Xavier had been pretty relaxed about bedtimes the last month or so. The kids didn't have preschool in the morning, so it didn't matter if they stayed up late and slept in. But they would be starting school next month and they had to start getting back into a routine, so she was going to make sure they cut down on the number of stay-up-late nights.

"No staying up late tonight," she said again.

"But—" Both twins immediately began to protest but broke off when she gave them *the look*. The look that said, "Continue with this at your own peril."

Annabelle adored her twins more than anything else on earth, other than her husband. JP and Katie were as identical as it was possible for twins of the opposite sex to look; they both had the same straight brown hair and brown eyes. She had been so pleased when they were born and she saw that neither had her near white eyes or their dad's heterochromia. Both she and Xavier had been self-conscious about their unusual eyes their entire lives, and she was glad her kids would never go through that.

But as similar as Katie and JP looked, their personalities couldn't be more different. JP was loud and boisterous. He liked to play outdoors, in the mud, climbing trees, wrestling and playing sports with his friends. He was the one who liked to push the boundaries. Katie was quieter, more reserved. She liked to play inside, coloring or drawing, playing board games, playing with her dolls. She was the one who Annabelle thought was probably never going to cause them any trouble.

She loved those kids, and yet, she couldn't get over wanting another baby.

It shouldn't bother her so much.

She had two gorgeous children who had owned her heart from the second she knew they were growing inside of her. It shouldn't matter that she couldn't seem to get pregnant again.

Both she and Xavier had gone to see a fertility specialist, had numerous tests done, and all of them had come back normal.

There was no reason why she couldn't get pregnant.

And yet, she wasn't.

They'd been trying for four, coming up five years now, and nothing.

Annabelle knew she was going to have to let it go.

As though reading her mind, Xavier reached out and wrapped an arm around her shoulder, pressing a light kiss to her cheek.

Maybe it was for the best. She was thirty-eight, and Xavier was forty-seven. They weren't getting any younger. Plus, he worked long and irregular hours, as did she. She ran the children's programs at the Matilda Warren Women and Children's Center. It was a place for women and children who were victims of violence that she'd started and helped to run with her friends Sofia, Laura, and Paige.

Yes.

It was for the best.

"Okay, you two, upstairs now," Xavier told the kids. "PJs on, teeth brushed, into bed, and Mom and I will be up to read you a story in ten minutes. Ten minutes," he repeated as the kids took off up the stairs.

Once they were alone, he drew her closer. "I'm okay," she assured him. She really would be, even if they never had another kid.

"I want to talk to you about something once we put the kids down," he said to her.

Because of who she was and her ingrained sense of expecting the worst, something she was trying to overcome but hadn't quite mastered yet, she immediately thought it was going to be bad news.

Xavier laughed. "It's nothing bad. Just something Jack and I were talking about today."

"Oh." She relaxed. If Xavier and Jack had been talking about it, it couldn't be all that bad. "We better get up there before JP finds some sort of mischief to get himself into."

Hand in hand, they walked up the stairs. By the time they reached the second floor, they could hear the kids flushing the toilet and giggling as they climbed into bed. They still shared a room although they were in the process of making the change of JP moving into his own room. All his stuff, except his bed, had already been moved, but the twins were struggling sleeping on their own, never having been on their own before. And even though it was only a Jack and Jill bathroom that separated their rooms, to them, it was half a world away.

They had made a deal with the kids that one week before school started was the day. From then on, they would be sleeping in their own beds in their own rooms. Annabelle expected a lot of sleepless nights that week as the kids adjusted to sleeping alone.

"What books do you want tonight?" she asked as she and Xavier stood at the bedroom door.

"*Fox in Socks* and *Cat in the Hat*," JP replied from his sister's bed where the two of them were under the covers and propped up against the pillows.

The kids were going through a major Dr. Seuss phase, and they read those same books pretty much every night.

For the next twenty minutes or so, the four of them cuddled together on Katie's bed, reading and giggling. Annabelle lived for moments like this. As a child, her parents had been distant with her after she was abducted as a four-year-old. It hadn't been until about ten years ago that she learned the reasons why. Finally having answers had helped her to come to terms with it and understand why the distance had been there. Because of that, she made sure that her kids never once doubted that she loved them.

There may be times—especially as they grew and reached their teenage years—where they wouldn't always like her decisions, and she knew that at times they would be angry with her, but they would never doubt as she had that their parents loved them more than life itself.

"The end," Xavier said as he closed the second book. "Okay, munchkins, it's time to go to sleep."

There were the obligatory groans, but both kids looked exhausted, and neither really protested when Xavier picked JP up and carried him to his own bed, tucking him in. Annabelle helped Katie scoot down, then laid the pillow down against the mattress and pulled the covers up.

"Sweet dreams, I love you," she told her daughter as she kissed Katie's little head.

"Love you too, Mommy." Katie smiled up at her.

She and Xavier switched, and she kissed her son's head. "I love you."

"Love you too, Mom," he said, then yawned.

"Sleep tight, sleep right, no bad dreams at all tonight." They recited their little nighttime saying, then she and Xavier walked to the door, switched off the light, making the hundreds of glow-in-the-dark stars that covered the ceiling start to shine.

Once the door was closed behind them, she turned to her husband. "I love them so much, sometimes it hurts. I want to be okay if we never have another, but I don't know if I can be."

"I know." Xavier pulled her into his arms. She knew that whenever he looked at their kids, he thought of the daughter he had lost. His first child with his first wife had been stillborn, and had she lived would have been eighteen by now, and Annabelle knew, an amazing person. How could she not have been with Xavier for a father?

"So, what were you and Jack talking about today?" she asked as they walked down the hall to their bedroom.

"Adoption."

"Jack and Laura want more kids?"

"I think Jack does. And he knows with their age, they might not have any more biological kids, which got him thinking about adoption, which got me thinking about adoption. What do you think about it?"

"I love it." She beamed up at him. She still wanted another child of their own, but she would love to give a home to a child who needed it. So many kids came through the center who were in desperate need of love and stability, and she loved the idea of being able to give that to a child in need.

"So, you want to look into it?" Xavier asked.

"Absolutely."

"Okay, I'll start doing a little research. But ..." He picked her up and laid her down on the bed, then climbed on top of her. "That doesn't mean we have to stop trying."

"Good," she said, "because I don't ever want to stop trying."

Xavier's lips met hers, and his hands found their way under her sundress and to the hem of her underwear, pushing it down her legs so he could gently push his way inside her.

As they moved in well-practiced harmony, Annabelle knew that adopted child or biological child or both, whoever joined their family next was already loved.

AUGUST 7TH

She was burning up.

Tessa kept kicking the covers off because her skin felt like it was on fire, but as soon as she shoved them aside, a couple of minutes later, she was freezing cold.

Her whole body ached now.

A combination of the injuries she had received in the crash and the infection that was quickly spreading through her body.

The infection was in her blood now.

Septicemia.

And quickly progressing to septic shock.

She doubted she would last another five days when he planned to kill her.

Her breathing was too fast, as was her heartbeat. The nausea was still there, and she was finding that, although she drank all the water he left for her, she wasn't needing to go to the bathroom as often. It was also getting harder and harder to concentrate.

All she wanted to do was sleep.

Given that she didn't think she was ever walking out of here alive, she didn't fight it.

Tessa was just drifting off when the sound of a slamming door jarred her awake.

Was he back?

She wearily lifted her head off the pillows, but her room was empty.

He must have gone out.

A moment later, she heard a car engine and then tires squealed.

He was gone, and obviously in a hurry to get somewhere if she could hear the tires through the boarded-up window.

Had he locked her door?

Earlier he had talked about not wanting her to feel trapped and that she wasn't a prisoner here, and he had mentioned leaving her door unlocked so she could have use of the house.

She didn't think that he would have left the front or back door unlocked, but if she was lucky, she might be able to get her hands on a phone. If she could, then she still stood a chance at getting out of here alive.

Gathering all her reserves of strength, Tessa slowly sat up.

Her head and her stomach protested in tandem and she almost sank back down and gave up.

But she didn't.

Giving up wasn't in her nature.

Even if she wanted to, she couldn't.

So, she clamped her teeth into her bottom lip and waited out the frantic swirling in her head that was echoed in her stomach.

After a few minutes, it settled down; it didn't go completely, but at least it calmed down to a more manageable level, and she was able to swing her legs over the edge of the bed and push herself into a standing position.

She suffered through round two of the spinning sensations but again, with patience, they eventually faded and then she was moving toward the door as fast as she could with a leg that was swollen, extremely painful, and virtually useless.

Tessa didn't let it stop her. Using the wall for leverage, she managed to get to the door and sighed with relief when the handle turned, and it swung open.

She found herself in a hallway, and although it was obvious that he had tried to clean it up, she could see the stain on the floorboards from where the man who had been in her bedroom had died.

She sidestepped that, not bothering to go through any of the rooms up here. They were no doubt all bedrooms and bathrooms, and there wasn't likely to be any phones. If there was one in the house, it would probably be downstairs.

Her whole body was shaking uncontrollably, and she ached to go and lie back down and rest, but she made herself keep going. Somehow, she made it to the staircase, where she was faced with what seemed like an impossible task.

Walking down it.

Thankfully, there was a big sturdy banister and she was able to use it to drag herself from one step to the next.

It was slow going, and by the time her feet touched the floor at the bottom, she had to sink down and rest.

Tessa leaned her head back against the wall and closed her eyes.

She was so out of breath.

It took her a good ten or fifteen minutes before she could draw enough air into her lungs to function.

Getting back up on her feet was harder this time than it had been getting off the bed, but somehow, she managed it. Tessa wasn't even sure how. She thought she was pretty much just operating on autopilot now.

One look at the downstairs had her heart sinking.

Part of her had been hoping that she might be able to flee through a window. The other part of her knew that if there were any chance of her escaping, then he wouldn't have let her have free reign of the house.

But it was still disappointing to see that all of the windows she could see from the bottom of the stairs were boarded up just like the one in her room had been.

Going out a window might be out, but there was still a chance of finding a phone.

Although she didn't want to start walking again, she didn't have a choice. The longer she stayed still doing nothing, the more she felt like she was wasting time.

She had no idea when he was coming back.

She might have hours, or she might have minutes.

She was going to have to make the most of this opportunity and get moving.

The only way she could move was to keep using the wall for support, so Tessa had no choice but to stick to it, and make her way into the next room. This place was enormous; she was never going to be able to search it all. She'd just have to do what she could and hope for the best.

With agonizingly slow progress, she managed to stagger into the next room, which was a sitting room. To save time, she didn't bother circling around it—just scanned it—and when she didn't see a phone she kept going. Next was a study, also without a phone, although there were a stack of papers spread everywhere.

Curiosity got the best of her and she pushed away from the wall and somehow managed to hop, dragging her bad leg behind her, over to the desk.

Her heart stopped when she saw what was there.

Cases.

Hundreds of printouts of case files.

Parker's case files.

She knew that he was killing people that had been victims in cases Parker and Skylar had worked, but she hadn't really grasped the extent of it until she saw all of this.

It looked like every single case her husband had ever worked.

So many people.

So many innocent people who had already suffered so much and now they might be going to suffer all over again.

Her friend Melanie was already dead and Lizzie Landry and Lucas Mianta who had been especially close with Parker and who she had spoken to a couple of times after they met one year at Parker's grave on the anniversary of her husband's death.

He had brought her locks of their hair like she would be impressed with his actions.

But she wasn't.

She was repulsed.

Who else had he killed?

She had lost track of time, it had seemed like he was killing one person a day but she wasn't sure how many days had gone by since he killed Lucas, so she wasn't sure how many other people were dead.

Had he gone after her friends Lila and Eric Abbott? They had been a case of Parker's when their son was killed and their infant daughter abducted. After they got their daughter back, they had all become friends. Eric's brother Charlie was also her friend and psychiatrist.

There was no point in obsessing over the cases any longer. She had to keep moving.

Making it to the other wall, she circled back out of the study and around past the front door. Although she knew it was going to be locked, she tried opening it anyway.

It didn't budge.

Tessa kept going. She was starting to feel like if she stopped moving, she would crash and burn.

Moving was the only thing keeping her on her feet.

She made her way into the kitchen.

It was a mess; there was garbage everywhere, and dirty dishes were piled in the sink. The cupboards all had glass panels and she could see that they were well stocked. It looked like he had been planning this for a while.

Knowing that sickened her.

Then she saw it.

A phone.

Relief almost knocked her over.

She wanted to just go running to it, snatch it up, and call for help but she couldn't.

Her leg was aching so badly, and so were her arms from the pressure of clutching the wall so tightly.

Inch by inch, she got closer.

It felt like a mirage.

The more she moved, the farther away it got.

But she didn't give up and finally, she was there.

Her hands were shaking so badly that when she picked up the phone, she dropped it and it clattered to the floor.

Tears were streaming down her face. She was exhausted. She needed to rest, but more than that, she needed to get help.

Awkwardly, she managed to lower herself down to the floor and got the phone back in her hands.

As she dialed Skylar's number, she prayed the call went through.

* * * * *

9:15 A.M.

Wyatt was in a bad mood today.

Lachlan Mountain wasn't the man they were looking for. He didn't have Tessa, but he had almost killed Mattie.

Five days.

That was all the time they had left to find Tessa.

He had been going through his and Parker's old cases nonstop for the last few days, and so far, nothing had jumped out at him. If it wasn't Lachlan Mountain, then he had no other ideas.

None.

"Maybe we should take another go at Cassandra Stanton's husband," he said, drinking the cold coffee left in his cup.

"He didn't see anything," Jack Xander reminded him.

"Now that a bit of time has passed, he might have remembered something," Wyatt pushed. They had to do something and right now the only person who had seen the killer and lived was Leon Hawk.

They had tried to set a trap for the killer, but even that hadn't worked. Either they had been wrong about who he was going for next or he had realized they were there and bailed.

Since there hadn't been any other murders that matched the MO, it was more likely he had been going to kill Kelita McNamara but had somehow figured out they were there waiting for him and driven on past.

"I don't think he knows anything, Wyatt," Xavier said in that cop voice that he hated. He knew he had used it when dealing with families of victims, or victims themselves, but he didn't want to be handled. He wanted to be a cop on this case because if he was just Tessa's friend then he wasn't going to be any help.

Not that he had been any help so far.

The only lead he had offered had turned out to be nothing.

"We're still going through footage from Kelita's street," Paige reminded him. "Maybe we'll find something on that."

That was true.

They had set up cameras on either side of Kelita's block so they could monitor every car and person that entered in the hope that even if the killer made them and realized it was a trap, they still might get something on him.

"Paige and I are going through the footage. The second we find anything, we'll let you know," Ryan Xander reminded him.

"You should keep going through the files," Jack told him.

"What are you and Xavier going to be doing?" he asked. He didn't want to be left out, and he needed to feel like he was doing something, but he didn't think the answers were in there.

"We're interviewing everyone who was involved in any of your and Parker's cases that also involved Tessa since those seem to be the ones the killer is targeting," Xavier replied.

Those *did* seem to be the cases the killer was targeting.

It was like this was about Parker *and* Tessa.

He wasn't sure what that meant yet, but he knew it meant something. His phone buzzed on the table and he picked it up, only registering the fact that the number was blocked after he pressed answer.

"Hello?" There was no answer. "Hello?" he repeated, frustrated. He didn't have time for this now.

Soft crying sounded in the background.

"Tessa? Tess? Is that you?" Everyone in the room stopped what they were doing and turned to listen in.

"Yes," came the faint reply.

"Oh, thank goodness you're still alive." He felt a weight lift off his chest. "Do you know where you are?"

"No," she cried.

"All right, well, we'll find you, honey, we're coming for you, okay? Just hold on. We'll trace this call and we'll come and get you. I'm going to put you on speakerphone; I'm at the station, the detectives who are looking for you are here with me: Xavier Montague, Paige Hood, and Jack and Ryan Xander."

"Ryan Xander?" Tessa repeated, sounding a little breathless. "Sofia's husband?"

"Yes," Ryan answered. "Sofia told me you two were old friends. Try to remain calm, we're going to find you, Mrs. Bell."

"Tessa," she corrected in a murmur.

"Honey, are you okay?" Wyatt asked her, concerned. She sounded weak and a little disoriented, and since they'd found her blood in the back of the van, they knew she was injured. They just didn't know how badly.

"I got hurt in the crash. I'm really tired." She sounded exhausted.

"Try to hold on, Tessa," he told her. He didn't know how badly she was injured but she didn't sound too good, and he was worried she wasn't going to make it until they could find her.

"I'm scared, Skylar," she whimpered.

"I'm sorry, Tess," he begged. "I'm sorry I didn't get there in time to save you, but I'm coming. I'm going to find you. Okay? Okay, Tess?"

"Okay," she echoed half-heartedly. She didn't believe him.

"I need you to think, Tess." He was panicked and he knew it. The thought of Tessa in the hands of a maniac, again, was utterly terrifying. "Did you see where he took you?"

"No," she whispered.

"Come on, Tess, think," he commanded. "You must have seen something." Wyatt hated feeling this helpless.

"I don't know," she sobbed. "I don't know where I am. I'm sorry, Skylar."

"Tessa?" Ryan interjected calmly. "Did you pass out in the crash?"

"Uh-huh." She continued to cry but responded to Ryan's calm by calming a little herself.

"Okay," Ryan continued, "did you wake up in the car or wherever you are now?"

"In the car," she replied, Ryan's calm voice seemed to soothe Tessa's hysteria.

"All right, could you see anything?" Ryan asked.

"No, he put a blindfold on me," she told him.

"How long were you driving for before you stopped?"

"A long time ... but I think we may have been driving in circles."

There was the smart Tessa Wyatt was used to. Keeping his voice as calm as Ryan's, he asked, "When you stopped and he took you inside, did you see anything?"

"No."

"Can you see anything from where you are?"

"The windows are all boarded up," she replied. Her tears returned. "I'm so scared, Skylar. I didn't know he was so far gone."

He glanced at the others. "Do you know who took you, Tess?"

"It was PJ." Tessa sounded distraught.

Surely, he must have heard her wrong. "PJ?" he repeated.

Back to hysterical. "He's going to kill us, Skylar, me and him. In ten days, on his birthday. That's what he said. He wants to right Parker's wrongs. He wants to kill surviving victims in Parker's old cases because he thinks that he's saving them. You have to warn Lila and Eric. I don't want him hurting them. You should warn Charlie and Savannah, too, in case he goes after them. Skylar, you can't waste time looking for me. Try to find who PJ's going to kill. Save them. Looking for me will just be a distraction," she rambled.

"Don't be ridiculous," he admonished wildly, completely horrified by what he was hearing. "Of course, we're going to look for you."

"Tessa, try to calm down," Jack soothed. "You're going to make yourself sick."

He fought to keep in control for Tessa's sake. "Jack's right, honey, you need to calm down. Are you sure it's PJ?"

She sucked in a shaky breath. "Yes. He killed Melanie ... and Lizzie ... and Lucas. He's going to keep killing, and then in ten days, he's going to kill us both. He blames Parker. He blames Parker for all our problems. Skylar, you can't waste time looking for me ... find those poor people before PJ does."

Jack spoke before he could. "We're going to keep looking for you, Tessa. We're going to find you. And we're going to find your son's intended victims. So there's nothing for you to worry about."

"Do you know who he's going to go after?" Wyatt asked her.

"No."

"Are you sure? Has he said anything that might give you a hint?"

Quiet now, Tessa said, "I don't know, Skylar. I don't know who he's going to go after."

She was sounding worse by the second. She was breathing heavily and she sounded disoriented. "Honey, did you hit your head in the crash?"

"I think so ... I'm having trouble concentrating," she murmured.

"Okay, honey, just rest, just hold on, we're going to find you. I promise you, I am going to find you."

"No, Skylar," she insisted. "PJ's unstable; he blames Parker for everything. You're Parker's best friend … I can't risk him hurting you."

"Don't worry about me; just focus on hanging in there until we find you."

"Don't come after me, Skylar," she pleaded. "I already lost Parker, and now I'm losing PJ. I can't lose you too. I hear him coming." She sounded panicked again. "PJ's back. I have to go. Don't come, Skylar."

"I'm coming, Tessa. Don't hang up the phone, stay with me," he begged. They needed more time if they were going to trace the call.

"I can't. PJ will go ballistic."

There was silence for a long moment and Wyatt thought she was gone when she spoke one last time.

"Skylar, tell Daniel and Winter and Matilda and Casey that I love them. I love you too. You've been a fabulous friend to me."

"Stop," he admonished frantically. "Stop telling me your goodbyes. You can tell everyone you love them once we bring you home."

"524 874 7826. Goodbye, Skylar."

Then she was gone.

Wyatt stood frozen, praying desperately that this wasn't going to be the last time he ever talked to Tessa.

What she had said couldn't be true.

It couldn't be PJ who was doing this.

And yet …

PJ's birthday was the twelfth.

"Well, that was worrying," Xavier said when the phone went dead.

"It's worse than worrying." Wyatt begun to pace. "She sounds awful. She should be in the hospital, not in the clutches of her deranged son."

"We'll find her, Wyatt," Ryan comforted.

"Before he kills her?" He wished someone could assure him of that.

"She's a strong woman," Jack reminded him.

He shook his head. "Emotionally, she still struggles, and physically, she's never fully recovered from what Charlotte Lainie put her through. She never got over her husband's murder. The only thing that kept her going was her son, and now she's lost him too."

"You've found her alive every other time," Paige pointed out.

"Her luck has to run out sometime," he muttered, hoping that wasn't the case.

"What did she mean with the number?" Xavier asked.

He recalled the number she had said to him. Tessa didn't want him coming after her because she was worried PJ would hurt him. She didn't want her son to kill her, but she knew that police resources could only stretch so far. Depending on where PJ had stashed her away, it could take them weeks or months to find her.

And they had a deadline.

PJ was going to commit a murder suicide in just a few days. But Tessa had given him the perfect way to find her. She'd given him the number of someone with unlimited contacts who would move heaven and earth to find her alive.

Isaac Worthington.

* * * * *

9:52 A.M.

Now that she'd said the words to Skylar, it made it seem real.

For the first time since this nightmare began, Tessa couldn't hide from the facts. She couldn't try to block them out; she couldn't pretend that she was wrong and that this was all just some big mistake.

It was real.

Her son was a killer.

Tessa didn't want it to be true.

She wanted to do anything it took to make it not be true.

But she couldn't.

PJ had killed at least four people, probably more.

Not only that, but he had killed people that she cared about. People that she loved. She and Melanie Gardner had been friends since childhood. They'd been through a lot together, and the last few years they had really gotten close. And Lizzie Landry, she'd met through a case of Parker's and had helped the girl deal with her attempted abduction. She had made sure that Lizzie got the help she needed, and she had always made it a point of being available any time Lizzie needed her.

Now they were both dead.

All because PJ hated the father he'd never even met.

How had she not noticed that her son was this dangerous?

Tessa had always thought she was a good judge of character. She usually got a sense of people the second she met them. Reading people had always come so easily, but with PJ she'd been blinded by her love for him.

Obviously, that had been a mistake.

Her son had hired someone to break into her room in the middle of the night, terrifying her before tasing her, tying her up and throwing her in a van. PJ knew that she was hurt. He knew how sick she was, and yet, no matter how many times she had asked him to take her to a doctor, he had refused.

"Mom?"

PJ appeared before her, a concerned look on his face. His face that was the spitting image of his father's. Every time she looked at PJ, she saw Parker.

Maybe that was the problem.

Deep down she knew that there was something off with her

son; she just hadn't wanted to admit it.

If Parker had lived, would PJ have turned out like this or would he be a normal, well-adjusted almost-sixteen-year-old kid?

"Are you okay?" PJ asked as he crouched down in front of her.

She still held the phone. There was no way to hide that she had tried to make a call. She just had to hope that PJ wouldn't be too angry about it.

"You know I'm not okay, honey." She looked up at her son. She remembered the day he was born. She remembered the first time he called her Mama and the day he took his first steps. She remembered his first laugh and his first word. She remembered when he learned to ride a bike without training wheels and when he learned to read.

Every time he reached a new milestone, it made her miss Parker more.

Was it her fault that PJ had turned into … into … this unrecognizable monster?

"You'll be okay," PJ said, but he looked doubtful.

Part of him knew that what he was doing was wrong, but she had already tried every time he had come into the bedroom upstairs to convince him to turn himself in, but he kept refusing, claiming that he was doing this *for* her.

A headache was raging between her temples. Coming downstairs and searching for a phone, then speaking to Skylar had drained whatever small amounts of energy she had left. She wanted to go to sleep, but Skylar had begged her to hold on and she felt like she was letting him down if she didn't do whatever she could to talk PJ into turning himself in.

She knew that Skylar and the other cops were looking for her. She knew that Skylar had been an amazing cop, and she knew that Ryan was as well. She and Sofia had been friends since they were babies, and Ryan and Sofia's daughter, Sophie, had been friends with PJ since they were babies. Sophie was a great kid, a real testament to the parents who had raised her, and she knew that PJ had a crush on her.

"PJ, please," she begged.

"I'm doing this for you, Mom," he pleaded. As if he hadn't noticed before, his gaze dropped to the phone which she still clutched in her hands. "Did you make a call?"

"I don't want you to get hurt," she told him. If she couldn't talk PJ into giving himself up, then he was most likely going to get himself killed. When—most likely *if*—the cops found wherever PJ had them hidden away, then they would shoot him if he didn't let them get her and let them cuff him.

And she knew that he wasn't going to do that.

All PJ cared about was this idea that he had that she was suffering, and he was the only who could save her.

Unfortunately, he wasn't completely wrong.

She was still grieving her husband.

And that had affected her son.

"I'm not going to get hurt." He smiled at her. A creepy smile. Not the smile of the son she loved.

"Sweetheart, you are. I had to call Skylar, I had to tell him that we need help."

"*We* don't need help." PJ looked offended by the notion. "And neither do you. *I'm* helping you."

"I don't need this kind of help. I'm okay, PJ … I don't need you to save me."

"You do," he contradicted. "You're always so sad. You don't like to go out, you cry all the time. It's because of *him*." He spat out that last word.

"That *him* is your father," she reminded him.

"He wasn't my father. I never even met him. He may have been my sperm donor, but that doesn't make him my father."

Where had all this hostility toward Parker come from?

She knew he had never really liked to hear about his father, but she hadn't realized that PJ hated him this much.

"PJ, you know this is wrong. You know that you can't go

around killing people just because you're angry at Parker for not being your dad. He didn't want to die. He didn't want to leave us. He died trying to protect us. Charlotte was never going to leave me alone … she was going to keep coming after me. Your dad died so that we could live." Tessa just wished she'd been able to live a life that honored Parker's sacrifices. She had tried; she had tried to move on. She had tried to learn from her mistakes, and to some extent she had, but she had struggled. She loved Parker and she hated that because of the secrets she had chosen to keep, a wedge had driven them apart and someone had used that to their advantage and Parker had paid the ultimate price.

"That man broke your heart. You asked him to stay with you and he didn't. He chose to abandon us."

Tessa didn't know PJ knew about that.

It was true.

When Parker and Skylar and Daniel had found her, she hadn't been in good shape. Her friend Maisy had already succumbed to an infection, and she was close to death from dehydration. She had begged Parker not to leave her, and he had promised to remain by her side. Only he hadn't. He had gone after Charlotte instead of going to the hospital with her, and Charlotte had killed him.

At first, she'd been angry like PJ was.

If only Parker had been with her, he wouldn't have died. But over time, she had accepted that what he'd done, he'd done out of love. So, she and their baby would be safe. How could she be angry with him for that?

"Sweetheart, you need help. This isn't you; this isn't how I raised you. I taught you to love others, to help people."

"I *am* helping people. All those people from Dad's old cases, they were hurt by him too."

"How?" She wasn't seeing his logic there. Melanie and Lizzie, and Parker's friend Lucas, they had all built great lives for themselves. They had all found happiness. Something she hadn't been able to find. Maybe that was why PJ was killing them. He was angry that Parker had helped them find peace by solving their cases, and yet, she hadn't been able to find that same peace.

"I made sure their deaths were quick," PJ said like that was somehow reassuring. "I love you, Mom. I really do. I'm not doing this to hurt you. I just want to make it so you don't have to cry anymore. I hate when you're sad. I hate seeing your tears. I want to make it so you finally find the peace you've always wanted."

He really believed that.

He believed that she was so sad that she would rather be dead than alive.

She had tried to hide how much she missed Parker from PJ. Not only did she not like to cry in front of people—it made her feel vulnerable and exposed—but she especially didn't like to cry in front of her son, so she only cried when she was alone in her room at night.

But PJ seemed to know.

A horrible thought occurred to her.

Had he been watching her?

Had he snuck into her room when she was too busy crying to notice, or put cameras in there so he could watch her?

No.

She was being crazy.

Her son wasn't evil; he was just sick.

Tessa wanted to argue with him.

She wanted to convince him that this wasn't the way.

She wanted to tell him that maybe some people just weren't destined for peace.

She wanted to keep talking to him until he finally understood that what he was doing was wrong and that he needed help.

But she couldn't.

Her eyes fluttered closed and she slipped into unconsciousness.

* * * * *

10:01 A.M.

He hoped this worked.

Wyatt knew that Tessa was in really bad shape because she hadn't told him that she was fine.

I'm fine.

How many times had he heard those words fall from her lips in the seventeen years he'd known her?

Hundreds.

It was Tessa's favorite line.

Well, it had been back when they first met her.

Back then she hadn't been able to let anyone in; she hadn't trusted them. She had believed that just like every other person in her life, they would eventually betray her. Over time she had become comfortable enough with them that bit by bit she had begun to open up.

But he knew Tessa well enough to know that if she'd been well enough, the first words out of her mouth would have been that she was fine and not to worry about her. That she hadn't said that told just how serious her condition must be.

"Are you sure this Isaac Worthington guy isn't involved in the murders and Tessa abductions?" Jack asked.

"Yes."

"The guy runs a child sex trafficking ring," Xavier said, looking unconvinced.

"My understanding is that ever since he got Rebecca back, he no longer does that. He only ever got involved in it in the first place because the cops couldn't find his daughter. I'm not making excuses for the guy, and I think he still deals in drugs and weapons, but I think he genuinely loves Tessa, and he's saved her life on more than one occasion. He also killed the woman who killed Parker. He knew that Parker made Tessa happy, and he would never go after people from Parker's cases."

"Still, the man is a criminal," Ryan said. "I think he bears looking into."

"It would be a waste of time. Isaac would be an old man by now. I don't think he'd be capable of committing the murders. Besides, we already know who the killer is. It's PJ." Wyatt still didn't want to believe that was true. He had raised that boy like a son. How could he have turned out like this?

"I don't like the idea of bringing a criminal into this, especially one who's done the things that Isaac has," Paige said.

"I don't either. I don't like Isaac, but right now I don't have a better idea. We have five days left."

"Now we know who it is, we might be able to find them without needing Isaac," Xavier said.

"And if we can't, do you want to sit Tessa's family down and tell them that we might have been able to save her, but we didn't?" He was doing this with or without their approval.

He would do anything to bring Tessa home.

The four other cops exchanged glances. Then Jack sighed and said, "Fine, make the call."

His hand was shaking as he dialed the number Tessa had given him.

"Detective Wyatt, what's happened to Tessa?" Isaac's voice came down the line. He sounded different than Wyatt had been expecting. He'd expected some sort of evil, villainous voice, but instead the voice was smooth and almost melodic. He was surprised that Isaac Worthington had known it was him. It wasn't like they'd ever spoken before, and of all the people in the world who could have called him, why would Isaac immediately go to him?

"Tessa is the only one who has this number, even Rebecca doesn't. And when she calls, she always lets the phone ring three times, then hangs up and rings back so I know it's her," Isaac explained, seemingly reading his mind. "And when one of my men went to check on her, he told me there were cop cars all over her estate," Isaac added with a sigh.

"You keep tabs on her." Wyatt wasn't surprised to hear that.

"Of course, although obviously not close enough. What's happened to her?"

"She's been abducted." Fear sliced through him as he thought of what might be happening to Tessa at this second. He didn't know what PJ was capable of, so he didn't know what to expect.

"Who?" Isaac demanded.

He still found this difficult to believe. He had been a father figure to Tessa's son; he couldn't imagine PJ as a psychotic killer. "It was PJ."

He expected Isaac to be as shocked about this as he was, instead the old man simply sighed. "I told her that boy was trouble."

"You've met PJ?" If he was completely honest with himself, Wyatt had thought that something was off with PJ, although not to this extent. Although, unlike Isaac, he hadn't said anything to Tessa. He'd been afraid that Tessa would blame herself because she had been taking medication while pregnant. But Tessa had been suffering from post-traumatic stress disorder even before Parker's death, with the added burden of a kidnapping and her husband's murder, they had all, including Tessa's psychiatrist Charlie Abbott, been concerned about the possibility of her harming herself. Taking her off her medication back then had not been an option. Not that he thought the medication was to blame for this. He didn't know *what* was.

"Of course. I know everything that goes on in her life."

Wyatt didn't like that. If it were up to him, he would sever every connection between Isaac and Tessa. "Are you going to come in and help us find her or not?" he snapped.

"Of course," Isaac said again.

Surprised, Wyatt asked, "You'd really risk your own freedom for Tessa?"

"I love Tessa. I'd do anything for her."

"What about Rebecca? She's your daughter. You come in here and I arrest you, you won't get to see her ever again."

"Rebecca knows I love Tessa like a daughter. Besides, Tessa wouldn't have given you my number if she trusted you to find her yourself."

He got goaded into losing his temper even though he knew that had been Isaac's intent. "If Tessa trusted you so much, she would have told you about Dylan Riley and what he did to her," he said smugly.

"Nice try, Detective." Isaac chuckled. "We both know why Tessa didn't tell me about Dylan Riley and it had nothing to do with her not trusting me."

From the tone of Isaac's voice, he realized something. "It hurt you that she didn't tell you."

"It did," Isaac acknowledged. "I understand she didn't tell me because she knew I would kill him and make sure he suffered, and she would have felt responsible for his death. But she had told me everything else. About her parents and Daniel and Cordelia."

"You knew about Cordelia?"

"Yes. Although if I had known that she was as violent as she was, I'd have put a stop to her. Tessa wouldn't have liked that though. She's so stubborn, and she doesn't like the way I do business. But she knows without a shadow of a doubt that there isn't a single thing I wouldn't do for her."

Of course, Tessa didn't like the way Isaac did business.

Despite everything that she had been through and all the people who'd hurt her, Tessa wasn't bitter. She was scarred, her ability to trust had been decimated, and her sense of self-worth had been distorted, but she never wished ill on anyone. When she had been forced to kill Dylan Riley in self-defense, she'd been traumatized about it for years. It probably still affected her.

As much as he hated Isaac and everything he'd done, all the children he had destroyed to try to save his own, all the families he had broken up just so he could get what he wanted. He had put his own needs above others and gone to the extreme; yet, in a way, Wyatt understood.

What lengths would he go to if it had been Sam or Stacey in Rebecca's position?

He liked to think he would have trusted the authorities to find his child and bring them home, but if they couldn't, would he have become what Isaac had?

That he couldn't answer that made it hard to completely hate Isaac Worthington.

And although he intended to arrest the man, he knew that Isaac wouldn't agree to come in unless he knew he had a foolproof way of walking back out. And since they had no proof other than Tessa, who refused to give a statement, that Isaac Worthington had ever done anything illegal, it wasn't likely he was going to be able to get any charges to stick.

But that Isaac was willing to risk arrest and life in prison spoke in volumes of his love for Tessa. And since he knew that Tessa loved Isaac and trusted him, he forced out the words that wanted to stick in his throat. "Thank you."

He expected a witty retort or a mocking insult; instead, Isaac said, "You're welcome. Oh, and Detective Wyatt, don't bother calling me again. This number will be disconnected as soon as we hang up. I'll be there as quickly as I can."

Unexpected relief flooded through him.

He might not like the way Isaac did things, but Isaac loved Tessa and would stop at nothing to find her. And he had the resources to scour every inch of the city and surrounding countryside until they *did* find her.

For the first time in five days, he actually felt like they had a chance at getting her back.

* * * * *

11:35 A.M.

"You doing okay?" Elisabeth Bennett asked as she rested a hand on Wyatt's shoulder. She knew what a toll this was taking on him. Not only had he been Parker's best friend, but he was Tessa's as well, and he had been her rock over the last fifteen years, and PJ's surrogate father.

Wyatt's head rested in his hands and he gave it a single shake.

She wished there was something she could do to help him.

It was her job. She was a criminal psychologist who had worked with Wyatt and Parker and the police department for decades before retiring last year. She had worked with countless victims, and she always knew what to say and how best to say it.

But not this time.

She was too close.

Too emotionally invested.

She cared about Tessa a lot, and although they hadn't gotten off to a good start thanks to Tessa's dislike of psychiatrists, they had grown close.

The key to getting close to Tessa was to be patient and allow her to get to know you. When she had pushed too hard and tried to help too much, Tessa had just gotten stubborn and refused to let her guard down. Tess had just been hurt too many times and was too scared of it happening again, so she built a wall as high as the sky around herself.

Since Parker's death, Tessa had mellowed a little. She hadn't been as stringent about keeping people out. She had learned the hardest way possible that when you worked so hard to keep people out, sometimes you lost them.

"You want to talk?" she asked as she slipped into the chair beside Wyatt. She remembered being in this same police station, eighteen years ago, asking Tessa if she wanted to talk.

So much had changed since then.

Back then she had been a thirty-eight-year-old new mother

who had recently been attacked and nearly killed by a psychopath she was interviewing. Now the physical and psychological scars had mostly healed, although the thin red line was still visible on her left cheek. Tania was eighteen now and heading off to college in the fall.

"Beth?"

She blinked and saw that Wyatt had lifted his head and was now looking at her, his green eyes crinkled with concern.

"Thinking about Tess?" he asked.

"Yeah. I was thinking about when we first met her. Remember how crazy she drove Parker when she wouldn't tell him who wanted her and her friends dead?" she asked with a wry smile.

"I remember," he said with a small, sad laugh. "He tried everything to get her to talk but once she makes up her mind about something, nothing can change it."

"She is off-the-charts stubborn."

"She and Parker both," Wyatt added.

"Yeah," she agreed, the smile falling from her lips. Tessa's refusals to tell Parker the secrets she was hiding, and his determination to not accept that, had almost ruined their relationship. Before Parker's death, he and Tessa had been estranged, and had only reconciled minutes before she stopped breathing and Parker went off to find Charlotte.

She was glad they'd had those moments together to make peace and lay their problems to rest. Beth couldn't imagine what it would have been like for Tessa to lose her husband if they had still been angry with one another.

They loved each other and they'd both been through so much. They'd deserved a happy ending, and yet, it had been ripped away from them. And now Tessa was losing the only thing she had left of Parker.

Her son.

Beth and her husband had tried for years to get pregnant before finally having Tania. Her daughter was the light of her life.

She loved her more than words could ever express, and she didn't even want to try to imagine what it would be like to find out that her daughter wasn't who she thought she was.

"It's my fault," Wyatt said softly.

"What is?"

"This. All of this." He threw his hands up in the air.

"How do you figure that?" she asked, confused. How was Wyatt responsible for PJ and this plan of his to save his mother by killing her?

"I promised Parker that if anything ever happened to him that I would take care of Tessa. After Parker was shot and I was holding his body, I promised him that Tessa and the baby would always be safe and loved. And I failed."

"You didn't," she said gently. "You have always been there for both of them. You've been the friend to Tessa that she needed, and you've been the only father figure that PJ has ever had."

"Exactly." Wyatt nodded as though she had just proved his point. "I was the only father figure PJ had and looked how he turned out."

"You are an amazing father," she reminded him. "Sam and Stacey are proof of that. I don't know why PJ is the way he is, but I *do* know that it isn't because of you or Tessa."

Tessa had been a loving, caring mother. She had always been there for PJ, and she'd taught him values and morals.

Yet it hadn't been enough.

PJ hadn't turned out anything like his mother or his father.

It wasn't nature that had led PJ to kill people, and it wasn't nurture, it was just one of those things.

She wished she had a better explanation for it, but she didn't.

Until they had Tessa back home safely, the whys didn't matter. Once she was safe, then they could worry about why PJ was the way he was and get him the help he needed.

"I failed Parker, Tessa, and PJ." Wyatt looked like he wasn't going to be convinced otherwise.

As much as Beth wanted to convince him that he wasn't to blame, they didn't have time for her to talk with him and help him see the truth. Right now, finding wherever PJ had locked his mother away had to be their priority; everything else had to wait.

Then once they had her back, and PJ was in a psychiatric hospital where he belonged, then they could all start to process this.

It was going to be hard for all of them.

Just like Wyatt, she had vowed to help Tessa raise PJ; and just like Wyatt, she was wondering how PJ could have been this delusional without any of them knowing. Beth suspected that just like her, Wyatt had known there was something off with PJ but hadn't said anything for fear of upsetting Tessa.

That guilt was going to take a long time to work through.

"So, the infamous Isaac Worthington is coming here?" she asked. She wasn't surprised that Tessa had asked Wyatt to contact Isaac, and she wasn't surprised that the man was dropping everything to come and help her. Despite what he had become, Isaac still possessed the ability to love, and he loved Tessa.

"Yeah. He said he'd be here as soon as he could. Isaac also said that he told Tessa that PJ was trouble. I thought about talking to her a few times about something being not quite right with PJ, but I never did it."

"Me neither," she admitted.

"What did you think was off about him?" Wyatt asked.

"That he never wanted to hear about his father. I would have expected him to want to learn as much as he could about the father he had never met. But every time I talked to him about Parker he just shut down, dismissed me, said that he didn't like to hear about his dad because it was too painful. But he didn't look sad; he looked disinterested."

"He didn't have any photos of Parker in his room," Wyatt said. "Tessa had them everywhere, but there were none in PJ's room."

"Add that to the fact that he was so protective of his mother and we should have seen that something was more than just off. We should have seen that something was wrong." Wyatt might be feeling guilty, but she was the psychiatrist. She was the one trained to see through the lies that criminals told. She was the one who should have noticed and should have sat Tessa down and said that they should have PJ speak with a professional.

"Isaac said that he had met PJ several times. Maybe he knew something that we didn't. Something that might help us find where PJ is hiding out."

Beth hoped so.

Because right now, they were running out of options.

None of them knew where PJ was, and they knew that Tessa was hurt and needed medical attention. Even if they didn't have PJ's self-imposed deadline, they would have been running out of time.

Now their only chance of finding Tessa and her son rested in the hands of someone who was the head of a large criminal organization.

She prayed this worked out.

* * * * *

1:26 P.M.

He strode into the police station.

Once again, it was proven that if you wanted something done right then you had to do it yourself.

Isaac wished he had trusted his instincts and taken care of Tessa's boy himself. Then the kid would have been too scared to ever have tried something like this. He knew that Tessa loved the boy, and she might not have forgiven him for doing it, but at least she would be alive and in one piece.

Every time he had brought the issue of something possibly being wrong with PJ up with Tessa, she brushed him off. She didn't want to see it. She always told him that he was imagining things and PJ was just a sensitive kid who found it too painful to think of the father he had never known.

PJ thought he had everyone fooled.

He certainly had his mother fooled

But you couldn't fool a monster.

Isaac had spent much so long living in the darkness surrounded by pure evil that he could recognize a fellow monster when he saw one.

He had tried to make amends in some small part for the horror he had heaped on unsuspecting children and their families, all in the pursuit of getting his own child back. Once Rebecca was reunited with him, he no longer had to burrow himself deep in the world of sex trafficking. So, he had worked with Tessa to find as many children as they could and buy—or steal—their freedom, returning them anonymously to their families.

Isaac knew he could never undo what he had done, and to be honest, he was okay with that. Spending so long pretending to be a monster had turned him into one. He couldn't change that; it was what it was, but he was glad he and Tessa had been able to save some of those kids.

Now he would do whatever it took to save Tessa.

Even if that meant killing her son.

He headed up the stairs and opened a door to a large conference room. Skylar Wyatt was there, so was Tessa's brother Daniel, sister-in-law Matilda, niece Winter, and the cops he had investigated on the way over here. He never did business with anyone unless he knew everything about them—most importantly, their weaknesses. He was confident that if the need arose, he could take down Xavier Montague, Jack Xander, Paige Hood, and Ryan Xander.

"You really did come." Wyatt sounded surprised.

Isaac just rolled his eyes at the man. He didn't have time for this. This was precisely why the cops were as useless and ineffective as they were. They couldn't think outside the box, and they couldn't step outside the box when the occasion called for it.

"I don't want him here," Daniel snapped.

"You think *they* can find Tessa?" he scoffed. Tessa had inherited all the sense in her family.

"They're the cops," Daniel returned.

"Exactly. They don't know what they're doing, and Tessa knows it. If she thought they would be able to find her, do you think she would have given them my number?"

"She called me first," Wyatt said, like they were children trying to one-up each other.

This was going to be more tedious than he'd thought.

If the stakes weren't so high, he would never be in a police station.

It was a sad state of affairs when he preferred the company of criminals to cops.

At least criminals got things done.

All cops had ever done for him was tell him that they couldn't do anything to find his kidnapped eight-year-old daughter. Say what you want about the route he had chosen, but, at least, it had worked. Rebecca was alive and he had her back. If he'd left it up to the cops, she'd have been lost forever.

"I'm not wasting time bickering with you," he told Detective Wyatt. "If you think you can find Tessa yourself, I'll just leave. I'm sure I'll find her first."

He turned but hadn't gone more than a couple of steps before Detective Montague called out. "Mr. Worthington, don't leave."

Isaac stopped but didn't turn around.

"Let him go," Daniel growled.

"You're the ones who let this happen, so I don't know why you're taking your anger out on me. I'm just here because Tessa wanted my help." He would rather do things his way, but he was trying to play nice for Tessa's sake because he knew that she didn't want her son hurt, and if he did things his way, PJ would most definitely wind up hurt.

"You're blaming us?" Daniel stormed over and Isaac turned slowly to meet him, glowering back at the younger man.

"Well you're the ones who saw PJ every day. Did you ever speak up and tell Tessa that something was wrong with him?" The guilty looks on all of their faces gave him his answer.

They hadn't.

He was the only one who'd been honest with her. Maybe if they had all told her the same thing, Tessa wouldn't have been able to pretend it wasn't so. Then none of this would have happened.

"Look, I don't like any of you and you don't like me; I'm fine with that," he said. "We're here because we all have a common goal. Tessa. I'm willing to set the animosity aside for her. Are you?"

Daniel just glared but then huffed and turned and stalked back over to his wife who slipped an arm around his waist.

He scanned the rest of the faces. As much as they all hated to admit it, Tessa had thrown them together, and they could hardly refuse her request under these circumstances.

"Come and sit," Detective Jack Xander said, gesturing at the table.

Once they were all seated, Detective Hood asked, "Do you know where PJ might be?"

Isaac had thought about that the entire ride here. He had even bounced ideas off his driver, but he hadn't been able to come up with anything. "No. But PJ has access to a tremendous amount of money, so the possibilities are endless."

"PJ has access to money?" Wyatt asked.

"Tessa set up an account for him when he was born and deposited money into it every month." From the look on his face, Wyatt hadn't known anything about that. "It depends on how long PJ has been planning this as to where he would be. If he's been thinking about doing this for long enough, he could be virtually anywhere. I have my men and every single contact that I have looking for him."

He had expected them to protest him using his underworld contacts to look for Tessa, but nobody said anything.

"Who do you think PJ is going to go after next?" Ryan Xander asked.

"He's going after the people who rebuilt their lives."

"What?" Wyatt asked.

"What do you mean, what? Didn't you know how he was choosing his victims?"

"We thought he was going after people who were in cases of mine and Parker's," Wyatt said.

"Yes, but specifically those who had rebuilt their lives. They had all suffered, and yet, they had all managed to move on and find happiness again. Tessa didn't. She never moved on from losing Parker. That's why he's angry with them. They got what his mother didn't. He wants to strip them of their happiness, and then do what he thinks will give Tessa peace by ending her life." How had the cops not got that? What kind of idiots was he working with?

"That makes sense." Paige Hood nodded. "And is just the next logical step from what we were thinking."

"I think he'll go after the Abbotts next," Isaac said thoughtfully. "PJ knows them, and since he knows that Tessa got to a phone and called for help, he's going to be angry. He's going to want to take that anger out on someone but not on his mother. I believe he genuinely doesn't want to hurt her and believes that by killing her he is, in fact, easing her suffering. He's going after the Abbott family next."

He'd had enough of this.

He'd told them what he knew, and now he was leaving.

When he stood, Wyatt stood too. "You're not going anywhere, Isaac."

"Oh, I think I am." He smiled.

"You're under arrest." Wyatt smirked like he had the upper hand.

But no one had the upper hand with him.

He never did anything that he hadn't entirely thought through.

"Eight reasons why I'm walking out of here a free man."

Wyatt arched a brow.

"JP, Katie, Zach, Rosie, Sophie, Ned, Hayley, and Arianna," he beamed.

"What?" Xavier asked, panic brewing in his face, on Jack, Ryan, and Paige's faces as well.

Weaknesses.

Always know the enemies' weaknesses.

In this case, it was their children.

Isaac picked up his phone and opened an app, turning it around for the others to see. "I have my men on all of them. I don't walk out of here in the next fifteen minutes, all those poor children will die."

The smell of defeat was sweet.

Game.

Set.

Match.

* * * * *

2:16 P.M.

PJ wasn't sure if he was making a mistake.

His mother wasn't happy with him.

She didn't understand.

It didn't matter how many times he tried to explain it to her, she just didn't get it.

He thought it was because she was sick.

He couldn't take her to the hospital because if he did, he would never get her back in time for his birthday. Maybe he should go to the pharmacy and get her some antibiotics.

But if he did, he might get caught.

Since his mom had called Wyatt and told him that he was the killer they were looking for and the one who'd organized her abduction, the cops would now be looking for him. He could no longer move about freely. He couldn't go back home to see his family or visit with Sophie or try to find out whatever information he could on the case so he could remain one step ahead.

Now he had to be even more careful.

Given who he was, he didn't think the cops would hurt him. They would do whatever they could to end this peacefully. Which might actually give him the advantage.

He didn't want anyone to get hurt, but if he was backed into a corner, he didn't know what he would do.

As long as he and his mother were able to pass from this life into the next on his birthday, he would be happy. And if anything got in the way of that happening, he would do whatever he had to in order to remove that obstacle. He had already taken the lives of five people, so he couldn't say that killing to make sure he got what he wanted was out of the question.

PJ didn't think of himself as a killer.

Yes, he had ended the lives of a few people, but that didn't make him a killer. Joey Geller had hurt his mother. It was because of him that he'd had to carry her upstairs because she was too sick to walk and tuck her into bed while she tossed in a fitful sleep. The man had deserved to die.

In their own ways, the others had too.

They had all been through horrendous tragedies at the hands of the monsters that walked the street. They had been tossed to the brink of utter despair; they'd been forced to stare their own mortality in the face, they'd had their lives scarred so deeply that they shouldn't have been able to move on.

But somehow, they had.

They had managed to move past what had happened. They

had married. They'd found a purpose for their lives, and they'd found happiness.

And his mother hadn't.

His mother had been stuck in that sinking sand of sorrow ever since her husband had died.

Her husband.

That man had nothing to do with him.

A sperm donor.

That was it.

That was all Parker Bell was—his sperm donor.

The man had single-handedly ruined his mother's life. His mom had fought so hard, always putting everyone else before herself, making sure they were happy and taken care of, protecting them, risking herself for them, even going so far as to willingly sacrifice her very life for them.

She had deserved a happily ever after.

And yet, it had been snatched away from her.

When she should have been celebrating the birth of her firstborn child with her husband, she was instead swamped in a sea of tears grieving his death.

It hadn't had to go that way.

If his mother's husband had just listened to her and done what she'd asked of him, then his mom would have been happy.

Instead, she spent her days locked away in her house because she just couldn't bear to get close to anyone else and lose them just like she'd lost everyone else in her life. She cried at night when she thought she was alone because she didn't want to sleep and meet her husband in her dreams only to have to give him up again as the sun rose.

PJ knew that because he often crept into her room and lay under her bed at night because he liked to be near her.

She was his mother.

The only family he had.

He had an uncle and aunt and cousins, but that was different.

They weren't his mom.

He had come up with the perfect way to finally ease her suffering. He was going to give her what his namesake had not. While Parker had left her alone and ruined inside, he was going to make sure that the two of them were together forever in eternal bliss and peace.

His birthday was still five days away, and he was getting more concerned that his mom wasn't going to make it.

He wanted to do the right thing; he just didn't know what that was anymore.

Should he risk getting her some medication?

Should he just hope that everything would go to plan and she would make it till the twelfth?

Should he move things up and move onto the last stage of the plan early?

PJ didn't know which option to take. He was afraid that if he made the wrong choice, he'd ruin everything. What if by changing the date he had planned to end their lives meant they wouldn't move on to a peaceful place? Or what if he didn't move things up and she died before he was ready and then they wouldn't leave this life together? He was worried that if they didn't die together, they wouldn't be able to spend eternity together, and he didn't want to spend eternity alone. Nor did he want his mom to leave loneliness in this world only to find it in the next.

He needed to clear his mind.

There was only one thing that calmed him at the moment.

Killing.

It was ironic, in a way. He was the son of a decorated police officer who had died in the line of duty, and yet, he had turned into one of the very people his father had spent his life arresting.

The house he was about to enter was one that he had originally intended to leave until last. Of all the cases his father had ever worked, these were the people who had ended up becoming closest with his parents.

Which was precisely why he had decided to move this murder up to today.

He was edgy; his last kill had to be aborted, and now after knowing his mother had ratted him out to the cops, he was angry but had no outlet.

No outlet except for this.

PJ realized with surprise that he actually *needed* this.

If he didn't kill soon, he didn't know what was going to happen.

How had that happened?

How had he gone from simply righting his father's wrongs to actually enjoying killing people?

Was there something wrong with him?

His mother wasn't a violent person and neither had his father been one. Other than losing his father before he was born and growing up with a recluse of a mother, his childhood hadn't been abusive or neglectful or bad in any way. His mother had loved him. She'd been firm but kind, and she had spent time with him. She had made sure that he knew she loved him, and she had encouraged him to have friends when all he wanted was to find a quiet place somewhere in the woods and curl up with a book.

It wasn't nurture and it wasn't nature that had created him; he was just some sort of fluke.

When he was finished here, maybe his mind would have cleared enough that he'd be able to see the path he should take.

Leaving his car in the next block over from the Abbott house, he grabbed the dog from the backseat and snapped on the leash. He had thought that he better have an actual dog with him just in case anyone should notice him. He was going to have to pay even more attention to detail from now on. This time he was going to "accidentally" let the dog off the leash outside the Abbott house, then follow it into the yard.

The Abbotts had almost self-destructed in the aftermath of a carjacking that left their five-year-old son dead and their infant daughter—who had been in the car at the time—abducted. Lila Abbott had sunk into depression and ended up attempting suicide. But somehow, they had managed to rebuild their lives; they got their daughter back and had even gone on to have more children.

It wasn't that PJ had anything personal against them. He didn't hate them or anything. It was just that his father had worked that case, and somehow, they had rebuilt their lives, because of what Parker had done for them. And yet Parker couldn't do anything to help his own wife rebuild her life.

For that, the Abbotts had to die.

* * * * *

2:38 P.M.

This had to work.

It had to.

Anything else was unacceptable.

If something went wrong and PJ didn't turn up where they expected him to, or he was able to slip through their fingers, Wyatt was worried that they wouldn't get another chance.

PJ would panic and might kill himself and his mother earlier than he had originally intended.

"Do you see him?" Wyatt asked.

After they had finished talking with Isaac Worthington—who had manipulated his way out of the police station by showing them footage of Xavier, Jack, Ryan, and Paige's kids and threatening to have them all assassinated if they tried to arrest him—they had set up a plan.

Assuming that Isaac was right and PJ was going to break with his plan to have a go at killing the Abbotts now instead of later, they had cops all over the block. The Abbotts had been safely locked away in a safe house where PJ wouldn't be able to get his hands on them, and hopefully, in just a few short minutes—or hours, tops—they would have PJ in custody and be rushing to get Tessa to the hospital before it was too late.

Wyatt wasn't done with Isaac yet. The man might have weaseled his way out of arrest this time because they had more pressing matters to attend to, but that didn't mean he wouldn't make sure he got another shot at the man.

If they got Tessa back alive.

If they didn't, he wasn't sure that he would be able to face hunting down the elderly criminal and then trying to find enough evidence to keep him in prison. Tessa was the only solid evidence they had, and if she was dead, then all of that died with her. There was circumstantial evidence, and possibly, if he dug long enough and deep enough, he could find something concrete, but he wasn't sure he would have the heart.

"Nothing yet," Jack said.

It took a moment for Wyatt to figure out why Jack had said that, but then he remembered what he'd asked.

He'd asked if anyone had seen anything yet.

He was getting antsy just sitting in the back of the fake florist van waiting.

He hated waiting.

He wanted to be doing something productive and waiting felt like wasting time.

Wyatt picked up his radio and asked for updates from every other team patrolling the block.

As well as removing the Abbott family, they had cleared out the rest of the houses on the block and put cops in them instead. They couldn't afford for PJ to get his hands on a hostage. If he felt backed into a corner, there was no telling what he might do or who he might hurt in his attempts to get away.

No one had reported seeing anyone that might be PJ and he couldn't help but growl in frustration.

If PJ didn't turn up here, he didn't know what he was going to do.

Tessa was running out of time, that he did know.

If they didn't find her soon, he didn't think it was going to matter if they found PJ or not. She would already be dead.

"We can't be sure he's going to come here," Xavier reminded him. "This was always a gamble."

He knew that.

There was no way to know that PJ was going to try to make a kill at all, let alone that it would be the Abbotts.

And yet, somehow, Wyatt knew he was coming here.

It wasn't a matter of if, just of when.

They had interrupted his last murder by being at Kelita's house, and now he needed to kill.

Wyatt believed that it had become a need.

PJ could no longer control it.

He *had* to keep killing until his birthday when he killed his mother and then himself.

He would come here.

They knew he had used a dog ruse in the past because he had left behind—either intentionally or unintentionally—the dog lead at Lucas Mianta's house, so they were paying particular attention to anyone who had a dog or was walking around with a leash looking for a dog.

"Maybe you should have waited at the station," Jack said, giving him one of those doubtful looks he was starting to hate.

He wasn't going to fall apart.

He had been a cop for almost two decades before he retired to spend more time with Tessa and his family.

He wasn't some amateur wanting to play at being a cop.

He knew what he was doing, and he was well and truly able to keep his emotions under control and do what had to be done.

"You think PJ is going to listen to you?" Wyatt said. "He doesn't even know you. You try to talk him down and he's going to freak out and do something stupid. If he gets himself killed, we're never going to find Tessa. She'll die alone." He couldn't allow that to happen.

Not under any circumstances.

Being alone was Tessa's greatest fear because all throughout her life she had been left alone after the people she cared about her left.

"We've done this before," Xavier said wryly. "We'll be able to talk PJ down."

"No." He shook his head adamantly. "I know PJ. He's not like most teenagers. He's not like most people. I have to do this. I have to be here. He knows me; I'm the one who's most likely to be able to talk him down without anyone getting hurt." As far as he was concerned, this wasn't up for discussion. He *was* going to stay here until they got PJ.

Jack and Xavier exchanged glances, then Xavier reluctantly nodded. "Okay. But I still think you're too invested in this. Parker was your partner and best friend, you and Tessa have been friends for years, you've been PJ's surrogate father. I don't know that you trying to talk him down is going to work any better than Jack or me trying."

"Trust me," Wyatt said. "I have a *much* better chance of getting everyone to walk out of this alive than anyone else."

"We might have something."

The words came through the earphone he was wearing, and he just about jumped out of his seat to see what it was. "Is it PJ?" he demanded.

"Could be," the voice replied.

"What do you see?" Jack asked.

"Looks to be a young man walking a golden retriever."

"What does he look like?"

"Curly blond hair."

It was PJ.

"It's him," he announced.

"How can you be so sure?" Xavier asked.

"Because Tessa has blonde curly hair, and he wants to think of himself as her son and not Parker's. Where is he?"

"He's coming down from the next block."

"Did you see where he came from? Was he walking or did he get out of a car?" Wyatt asked.

"He got out of a car."

This was it.

Wyatt didn't wait to discuss it with the others; he just opened the door at the back of the van and climbed out. He scanned the street and then spotted him.

PJ was about halfway down the next block. He had a leash in one hand and the retriever was intently smelling the bottom of a fence post like it was the most enticing fragrance on the planet.

So far, PJ hadn't spotted them, and he didn't seem to know that he was walking into a trap. There were two dozen cops posted in houses, front yards, and cars all the way up and down this block.

He took a couple of steps toward PJ, aware that every single cop was monitoring his every move but hanging back waiting to see how this played out.

The pressure was enormous.

One wrong move and PJ, Tessa, cops, and innocent bystanders could wind up hurt or worse.

He took one step closer, and suddenly PJ looked right in his direction.

Despite the distance, Wyatt knew that PJ had seen him.

For a second, neither of them moved.

Then PJ released the dog and ran.

Wyatt took off after him, as did several cops.

"PJ, wait!" he screamed as he ran. "I just want to help you."

PJ didn't stop. He ran into the road and right up to a car that was stopped at a red light. He pulled a gun from his pocket and used it to carjack the driver.

It wasn't until he saw the fifteen-year-old kid he thought of as a son use a gun to steal someone's car, traumatizing them in the process, that all of this really sank in.

It became horrifyingly real.

PJ was a danger to Tessa, himself, and anyone who got in his way. He had to be stopped by any means necessary.

Tires screeched as PJ took off in the car. Three police cars took off after him, including the van he'd been sitting in just moments before.

A minute later, he heard the sound of a car crashing.

* * * * *

7:53 P.M.

"How are you feeling?"

"I think I caught whatever Arianna Hood had," Daisy Xander groaned.

Her husband, Dr. Mark Xander, pressed the back of his hand to her forehead. His cool touch felt wonderful on her burning hot skin, and she wanted to grab his hand and keep it there.

"You definitely have a fever," Mark said as he perched on the edge of the bed beside her. "Here, drink some water."

He held out a bottle of water, but she curled her nose up at it in disgust.

She knew that she had to keep hydrated but the thought of putting anything in her stomach was extremely unappealing.

"You need to drink something," Mark said when she didn't make any move to take the water.

"I can't … my stomach is all swirly."

"Just a little," her husband insisted. "If you don't, I'll set up an IV."

Daisy raised a suspicious brow. She didn't think that he actually had anything here at their house to set up an IV, but she wouldn't be surprised if he'd brought something back with him from the hospital since he knew that she'd been feeling sick this morning.

Because she wasn't sure whether he was bluffing or not, Daisy took the bottle and tried to unscrew the cap. Her hands were shaking, and after letting her make several attempts herself, Mark took the bottle and opened it for her.

She took a couple of tiny sips then handed the bottle back. "That's all I can drink."

"That's better than nothing." Mark nodded approvingly. "Are you cold?"

"No, I'm boiling hot."

"I'd turn the AC up, but if you have a fever, you're probably going to start getting chills soon. Are you comfortable? Do you need another pillow?"

"Maybe," she said, snuggling down into the mattress. She hadn't really done anything but lay on the couch all day, but she was still tired. Every muscle in her body was achy, and a dull headache drummed at her temples.

"Here you go." Mark grabbed a spare pillow from the top of the closet and slipped an arm around her shoulders, held her up while he fluffed up the pillow, then eased her back against them, and tucked the covers up around her.

Daisy couldn't help but smile.

This was nice, having her husband fuss over her. It almost made being sick worth it.

Five years ago, she'd almost thrown away their marriage and their family to keep her family's secrets. She hadn't wanted to, but it was the only way she could ensure that her husband and their four children stayed safe.

Although she had done it because she hadn't been able to see another option, and when the truth had come out anyway Mark had understood, there had still been damaged to their relationship. Trust had been broken and it had taken time and effort on both of their parts to rebuild it.

But now, things were even better than they'd been before because now there were no more secrets hanging over her head.

"What are you smiling about?" Mark asked, as he stretched out beside her and wrapped his arm around her, drawing her close. His body heat made her even hotter, but she didn't care. She loved being in her husband's arms.

"I just love you, and it's sweet when you take care of me," she said, nestling her head on his shoulder.

"Love you too." Mark pressed a kiss to her temple. "Why don't you close your eyes and try to sleep."

"You don't have to stay with me," she told him. He may as well go downstairs and enjoy time with the kids, if they were here. Brian was twenty-one now, Eve and Elise were eighteen, Tony was fifteen, and her nephew Blaze who lived with them was also eighteen. Hanging around the house on a summer evening with their parents wasn't really high on their priority list anymore.

"This is exactly where I want to be." Mark smiled.

Daisy smiled back and then snuggled closer. She was sleepy; maybe she'd just close her eyes for a little while, and tomorrow she'd wake up feeling better. Ari had been down with this bug for a couple of days, so she hoped she could get over it quicker than that if she just got enough sleep.

And kept herself hydrated. She smiled to herself.

She closed her eyes and was just drifting off when she heard footsteps and voices.

Both she and Mark turned to the door as all five of their kids came bursting in. Eve was carrying a tray with a bowl of what looked like homemade soup, a couple of slices of the homemade bread that she made every couple of days, a small vase of flowers, and a glass of sparkling water. The kids must have made the bread and soup themselves, because today was bread making day, and she just hadn't felt up to making it so there wasn't any in the house.

"Hey Mom," Elise beamed. "We know you're not feeling well,

so we made you a special dinner."

"I think Mom is—"

"It's perfect," she interrupted before Mark could tell the kids she was too nauseous to eat. If her kids had gone to this much trouble to try to cheer her up and make her feel better, she wasn't going to say no. She'd just eat a little, then set it aside.

Mark helped her prop herself up on the pillows, and Eve set the tray down on her lap. "We made your bread for you since you weren't feeling well enough to make it today," Eve said.

She ate a couple spoonfuls of the soup. Despite her nausea, the hot liquid tasted amazing.

When had her kids gotten to be such good cooks?

Whenever she tried to get them to help cook meals, it was always such a production with whining and complaining.

"This is delicious," she said.

"We followed your recipe," Tony said. "The one you used to make for us whenever we were sick. It always made us feel better, so we thought it would help you."

Her kids were so thoughtful.

She loved them so much.

But they were growing up. Brian was following in his father's footsteps to become a doctor. He had just finished his bachelor's degree and was ready to enter medical school. Eve and Elise would be college sophomores in the fall, Eve wanted to become a cop like her grandfather and uncles, and Elise wanted to become a teacher. Blaze wasn't sure what he wanted to do with his life yet, but he, too, would be a sophomore this year. The four of them were only home for the summer, and before long, they wouldn't even do that.

They'd be gone.

Even her baby was going to be sixteen in a couple of weeks and was starting his junior year of high school next month. Another two years, and he'd be out of the house and off to college, too, and it would just be Mark and her.

She loved her husband and she wanted to grow old with him at her side, but it was so quiet around here these days. She missed the days where their lives had one big hectic, exhausting mess, constantly shuffling kids to and from school and activities, while juggling jobs, family, friends, and housework. Back then, all she had wished for was a full night's sleep and a couple of days lounging on the sand at the beach. Now, she would trade the peace and quiet just to get those days back.

"Mom?" Brian asked. "You okay?"

"Fine, just wondering what plans you guys had for tonight."

"None," Blaze answered for all of them. "We thought we'd hang out here with you and Uncle Mark tonight."

"Is this because I'm sick?" Daisy asked. "Because you really don't have to. I'm sure there are other things you'd rather be doing."

"Nope," Brian said, sitting down on the bed. "We really want to just hang out together tonight. Like we used to when we were all kids."

"You want to hang out with your mom and dad when you could be out with your friends?" Mark looked doubtful.

"We do," Elise said as she too joined them on the bed.

"We can watch movies." Eve sat down beside her twin sister.

"I think Mom needs to get some rest," Mark said.

"No, I'd rather do this." Sleep wasn't going anywhere, but time with her kids was too precious to give up.

"Okay, then," Mark said.

The seven of them piled onto the bed together, the kids poking and giggling at one another like they used to when they were younger. They hadn't spent time together like this, watching movies in their king size bed, since Brian had been Tony's age.

Daisy yawned. Her eyes wanted to close, but she fought it.

She didn't want to miss a second of time with her family. She cherished moments like this because there wouldn't be many more of them. Soon the kids would have families of their own and there would never be another night like this.

Content, Daisy couldn't wipe the smile off her face as she laid her head back on her husband's shoulder. She simultaneously felt awful and like the happiest woman on the planet.

AUGUST 8TH

She was going to go for it.

Sophie had been thinking about it ever since she and PJ had kissed the other day. She hadn't been able to think of anything else.

That kiss.

For three days, she had obsessed over it. Replaying everything that had happened over in her mind and wondering whether she had been wrong when she'd said she wasn't ready.

She was afraid.

But afraid didn't necessarily mean not ready.

Who wouldn't be a little afraid about the possibility of starting a new relationship after how her last one had ended?

That was completely normal.

So, really, there was nothing to stop her from going for it.

Once she was over this hurdle, maybe everything would fall into place. She was afraid of putting her trust in someone again in case they turned out to be another deranged killer and she got hurt.

But that wasn't going to happen.

What were the chances that of the only two guys she had ever liked, they would both be killers?

Besides, she knew PJ. They had known each other their entire lives. He wouldn't have been able to hide something that sinister from her for all these years.

And anyway, what else could she do?

The kiss had infected her brain. She hadn't been able to

concentrate on anything else and she'd even dreamed about it.

Only, in her dreams, she and PJ had done a lot more than just kiss.

A *whole* lot more.

Now *that* she wasn't ready to do, but Sophie thought she could do kissing and dating. And she knew that PJ would move as slowly as she needed him to.

And there wasn't any rush.

If what she had felt when PJ kissed her was real and was going to develop into something like her parents had, then they had the rest of their lives to spend together.

It was exciting, embarking on a new journey, especially after the year she'd had. This time twelve months ago, she'd felt so lost, she no longer knew who she was and what her place in the world was. She had been angry at her parents for keeping her true parentage from her, and she was scared because she didn't know if the DNA of her biological parents was going to shape who she was.

Now she knew who she was, and she knew that her parents loved her. She no longer worried that because her biological parents hadn't been good people that she was going to turn out bad too. She knew that the home her parents had given her and the example they'd set could override any bad genes she had inherited.

And now, on top of that, she might have found love.

Real love.

Sophie couldn't wipe the grin off her face as she spotted PJ up ahead.

He looked so good standing in the sunshine.

His black hair caught the sunlight and sparkled like those black diamonds her mother kept in the safe at home. Although most of her mom's possessions had been destroyed in the fire at her family's estate, there were a few things that had survived because they were kept in a safety deposit box at a local bank. Her mom's family—hers too although she had never met any of them—had been extremely wealthy, and her mom had some gorgeous jewelry that one day would be hers.

Sophie had always loved the black diamonds best of all.

Maybe it was because part of her had always known that she and PJ were destined to be together.

As if sensing her coming, he turned toward her.

Just as his hair sparkled like black diamonds in the sunlight, his eyes glowed like gold.

Black diamonds and gold.

It was almost like PJ was too good to be true.

And yet, he was true.

Because he was standing there smiling at her like she was the most amazing thing in the world to him.

"Hey." She smiled shyly when she reached their special spot.

"Hey, yourself." He smiled back, just as shyly.

Sophie loved that they were both as nervous around each other as they were. It made it feel more real. Like they both knew that whatever was between them was so special that they had to nurture it so it grew into something beautiful.

"I'm glad you called," she said when she reached him.

"So am I." He arched a dark brow, silently asking for permission to kiss her.

She nodded, and he stooped to brush his lips across hers.

She wanted more.

One little kiss wasn't enough.

"I know a place we can go, hang out together for a while," PJ said.

"Okay," she agreed readily. Her parents thought she was hanging out with Haylcy today, but she knew her best friend would cover for her. She and PJ could spend the whole day together. Kissing factored quite prominently in those plans.

He reached out and took her hand, leading her through the woods. She had no idea where they were going, but she didn't care. The woods were so beautiful with the chirping birds and the dappled sunlight.

She'd love to live out here.

That would probably suit PJ. He had always lived out on a large country estate, and given his personality, she couldn't see him ever wanting to live in the middle of a busy, heavily populated city.

"So, where are we going?" she asked.

"I have a place out here. It's kind of a secret," PJ replied.

"I won't tell anyone," she promised.

"I know you won't. There isn't anyone else I would trust to know about this place. Not even my mom knew that I had it. I bought it with money from my account. I got a good deal because it needed quite a bit of work done on it, but I did it myself. It was nice doing something with my hands."

"Is this it?" she asked as they came upon a large brick house nestled deep in the woods.

"Yep." PJ beamed proudly.

"It's not finished, I take it," she said, gesturing at the boarded-up windows.

"Sort of," he agreed, tugging her onward.

"Wow, you've done a great job." She admired the house as they got closer. It was huge—three stories high—and she saw at least ten windows on either side of the front door. "It must have taken you ages to do all of this. What condition was it in when you bought it?"

"It had been partially destroyed in a fire; there was just something about it that appealed to me. It spoke to my soul. I know that sounds kind of stupid—"

"No, it doesn't," she assured him. "It doesn't at all."

"I've had it for almost eighteen months. It's been hard keeping it a secret. I wanted to tell you before now but then you were going through a rough time last year and it just didn't seem like the right time to bring it up. Then you were dating that guy, and then you and your friend Hayley were, you know, and it still didn't feel like the right time. But now ..."

"Now what?" she asked as they stood on the large porch.

"Now I know for sure that I want to spend the rest of my life with you," he said, his head dipping to claim her mouth.

This kiss was anything but a gentle brushing of his lips against her.

This kiss was like he was starving, and she was the only food in the world.

Sophie wrapped her hands around PJ's neck and dragged him closer, pressing her body against his and deepening the kiss. Kissing PJ was nothing like kissing Dominick. She thought she had been in love with Dom, but now, she wasn't so sure. This felt so different.

This was something on a whole other level.

"You want to take this inside?" she asked, when they paused to drag in ragged breaths.

"Do you?" PJ asked, his chest heaving, his eyes glittering with heated desire.

"Oh yeah." She gave a sly smile. She might not be ready for sex, but there were plenty of other things they could do with the whole day to themselves.

PJ picked her up and she wrapped her legs around his waist, as she claimed his mouth again. He fumbled with the door but managed to unlock it and open it, then carried her inside. It was dark in here with the boarded-up windows, and as she glanced around, she was surprised to see that everything looked finished.

Did you put the windows in last when you were renovating a house?

Sophie had no idea, and as PJ's hands found their way under her tank top, she didn't really care.

They didn't stop kissing as he carried her up a flight of stairs, and then another, then down a couple of hallways before flinging open a door and depositing her on a bed.

She expected him to join her, but he just stood there staring down at her instead.

"I'm so glad you wanted to come here," he said. "I wasn't sure you would."

"Of course, I would, you know how important you are to me," she said, resisting the urge to fling herself at him. Her whole body was aching for PJ to touch her.

"I know." His smile changed, morphing into something she couldn't quite read. "But to know that you want to stay here with me forever. You don't know what that means to me."

Forever?

She liked PJ and she thought that they might be able to fall in love one day, but not today.

They were only fifteen. They had a lot of growing up to do before they were ready to make a lifelong commitment to one another.

Maybe they shouldn't have come here.

She really liked PJ and she didn't want to give him the wrong idea and hurt him.

"PJ, maybe we should go home," she said, sitting up.

"We are home," he said, looking puzzled.

"I know that you want us to live here together when we're older and we get married, but for today, I think we should just go back to our homes."

"We are home," PJ repeated. "And we aren't going anywhere. I just have to go and check on my mother, then I'll be back."

Check on his mother?

Tessa was here?

If Tessa was here, then that meant that PJ was the kidnapper.

She should have made a run for it.

She should have tried to stop him.

She should have tried to kill him if she had to.

Instead, Sophie sat in dumfounded shock as PJ walked out the bedroom door, closed it behind him, and she heard the unmistakable sound of him locking it.

Something was wrong with her.

She had fallen for Dominick Tremaine, and he had turned out to be a psychopathic killer. Now she'd fallen for PJ, and he was a psychopathic killer too.

* * * * *

9:02 A.M.

It was hard not to feel like this was helpless.

Four days.

In four days, PJ would turn sixteen and murder his mother and then commit suicide.

So far, everything they had done to try to stop him had failed.

Twice, they'd correctly predicted which prior victim of crime he was targeting next. Twice, he'd been within yards of the cops, and yet, twice he had slipped through their fingers.

In his mind, Wyatt was already mentally preparing to sit Daniel down and tell him that his sister was dead. It would be the third hardest thing he would ever do in his life. The first had been telling his wife that their three-year-old daughter had died thanks to a criminal with a grudge against him who had stolen their car with little Serena inside. The second was having to tell Tessa, who had just regained consciousness after almost dying, that her husband had been killed.

He was tired of telling people he loved that they had lost other people he loved.

He was tired of criminals and their messed-up reasons for justifying taking another human life.

He was tired of murder.

He was tired of death.

Wyatt glanced up as the door opened and Ryan Xander stepped into the room.

"She and the baby made it," Ryan announced as they all looked at him expectantly.

Wyatt let out the breath he had been holding as relief rolled through him. At least that was one person who had survived. One less death to deal with.

"We're going to have to wait to interview her, but we already know its PJ," Ryan continued.

"He's becoming reckless," Paige said.

"He left behind a witness that can ID him this time," Jack added.

"Because he knows we know it's him," Wyatt said. "He doesn't have to worry about hiding his identity anymore. Plus, he's close. Very close to getting what he wants. Four more days, and this will be over."

"He doesn't seem to care as much about those he deems not part of his plan anymore," Xavier said. "He set up the woman he carjacked and deliberately crashed that car into the wall to give himself a chance at escaping."

Anyone who would risk their own life just for a chance at getting away was dangerous.

PJ was a risk to anyone he came into contact with.

With Melanie Gardner he had timed things so she was home alone. With Lizzie Landry he'd made sure he killed her while everyone else in her family was otherwise occupied. Although Cassandra Stanton's husband had been there at the time of her murder, PJ had made sure that the man was left virtually uninjured.

"I don't think we can expect him to leave family members alive if he gets a chance to kill whomever else is on his list," he said.

The others nodded their agreement.

"And we know to expect him to come disguised," Paige said.

Which would make him harder to spot and give him an opportunity to use another distraction to escape just as he had yesterday afternoon. After using a gun to carjack a nearby car that just happened to be in the wrong place at the wrong time, PJ had forced the eight-month pregnant woman to drive her car into a wall. He had then dragged her body into the passenger seat and put the blonde wig on her, so when they arrived on the scene, they had wasted valuable minutes ordering PJ—who had already escaped by climbing down into the sewer system under the streets—to exit the car.

By the time they approached slowly and cautiously, knowing PJ had a gun and suspecting he wouldn't be shy about using it, the woman and her unborn child had both been in bad shape. Thankfully, they had both survived, but PJ was still in the wind.

"He hasn't been home?" Ryan asked.

"No. He didn't come home last night. He knows that Tessa called us, and he knows that we know it's him. There's no way he'll risk coming back home. Besides, there's nothing there for him; he already has what he wants."

Tessa.

That was what PJ wanted.

That had always been all PJ wanted.

Wyatt had always felt that PJ's relationship with his mother was a little unusual. He was so protective of her, even from family. He was jealous when Tessa spent too much time with her nieces and nephews, or with him and Casey and their family, or with Daniel and Matilda.

Tessa didn't seem to notice that there was anything off with PJ, and he had always just assumed that not having a father had just made PJ more possessive of the only parent he *did* have.

Now he knew it went deeper than that.

He saw Parker as the person who had destroyed Tessa and he saw himself as her savior.

Which would be fine if his idea of saving his mother meant encouraging her not to be so isolated, or to try dating again so she might meet someone else with whom to fall in love.

But PJ *wanted* her isolated.

He *wanted* her all to himself.

He *wanted* to be the only person in her life.

Now he was and Wyatt was terrified about what PJ was doing to his mother. Had he been angry that Tessa had called him and tried to turn him in? Had he hurt her? At the very least they knew that PJ had not gotten Tessa the medical care she needed after the accident.

"Since Isaac Worthington told us about the bank account that Tessa set up for PJ," Paige said, unable to hide her angry glare as she said the name of the man who had threatened her children to force their hand and let him leave, "Ryan and I looked into it."

"What did you find?" Jack asked.

"PJ made a large withdrawal around eighteen months ago," Ryan replied.

"How large?" Xavier asked.

"Over two million dollars," Paige told them.

"Two *million* dollars?" Jack echoed.

"Two million," Ryan nodded.

"Tessa didn't mention anything like this to you?" Paige asked him.

Wyatt shook his head. "But she didn't even tell me that she had set up an account for PJ."

"What would he want with that kind of money?" Jack asked.

"A house," Wyatt said. "He bought a house. He's been planning this for a year and a half."

That was frightening to think about. He saw PJ almost every day. They had meals together or discussed things PJ had been studying with his tutor. PJ played with his grandkids when they came to visit and had even babysat them on more than one occasion.

All that time, he'd been plotting this murderous scheme.

And none of them had seen it.

"Tessa must have noticed that amount of money missing from his account," Ryan said. "Wouldn't she have asked him what he did with it?"

"I'm sure she would have, but whatever lie he came up with she would have bought. He was the only link she had to Parker. She spoiled him rotten. Anything he wanted, he got. She would have done anything to make him happy. PJ had her completely wrapped around his little finger."

"He didn't tell her it was a house though," Jack said thoughtfully. "Because when she called, she didn't know where she was. If she knew PJ had bought a house, and she knew that he was the one who had kidnapped her, then she would have surmised that was where he had taken her and told you the address."

That made sense.

What didn't make sense was how PJ had turned into this monster who had lived in plain sight right under their noses the whole time he was planning this. "Right now, all I care about is finding him before it's too late," he said.

"His phone is off, so we have no way to trace it," Paige said. "Our best bet is to continue gathering the information we need to deduce who he's going to target next, set traps, and hope that sooner or later we catch him. We've been right twice now; we just keep trying to play things too big. Next time, we need to keep police presence to a minimum. One or two cops inside the house as decoys, and maybe your psychiatrist friend Elisabeth Bennett."

"No," he protested immediately. "I should be the one to talk him down."

"I think you're too close to him," Xavier said. "But he knows Elisabeth, and she knows how to deal with criminals. I think she's the one who has the best chance at being able to talk reason into PJ."

As much as he hated to do it, he had to check his ego at the door on this one.

This wasn't about him.

It was about PJ and Tessa.

And making sure that they both made it home alive.

PJ had always responded well to Beth. She was smart and intuitive, and in some ways like what Tessa could have been, if she hadn't suffered so much trauma in her life.

If anyone could talk PJ into turning himself in and telling them where Tessa was, he had to agree that it was Beth.

* * * * *

12:10 P.M.

"What time do you have to be back at work?"

"I don't," Ryan answered his wife's question.

"Oh?" Sofia turned from the counter where she was assembling an array of sandwich fillings. "I thought you guys were still looking for Tessa."

"We are," he assured her. He knew that Sofia was worried about her friend because she'd had bad dreams last night. He could always tell when she was having nightmares because she thrashed a lot in her sleep. As a child, Sofia had sleepwalked when she was upset or nervous, and that had carried into adulthood, although now, she just kicked and tossed and turned rather than sleepwalking.

"Not that I'm not thrilled to have your company since I'm working from home today, but why exactly do you not have to be back at work when you're working such a high-profile case?" Sofia asked as she grabbed a loaf of bread from the freezer.

"I'm working from home too. At the moment, all we can do with this case is keep trying to get ahead of PJ and hope that we can catch him in a trap. Since we think he's been stalking his victims to get a sense of their routines, we're just making phone calls to pretty much anyone involved in any cases Parker and Wyatt worked. Hopefully, some of them might remember someone following them or hanging around, which will help us narrow down who he might be going after next," he explained.

"Do you think she's still alive? I know she was hurt in the abduction, and you said she wasn't sounding too good when she called." Sofia looked up at him, her silvery-gray eyes anxious.

Ryan fought the urge to tell her what he knew she wanted to hear. But that wasn't helpful. All of Tessa's family and friends had to be prepared for the worst. "I don't know. I hope she is, but we're running out of time to find her. It's only four days until PJ said he was going to kill her, so even if she *is* still alive, she doesn't have long left."

"I don't think she's in very good shape if she's alive," Sofia said as she began to build a sandwich.

"Why not?"

"Because it's not like Tessa to not have found a way to escape. She always has a plan. She managed to escape from a child sex trafficking ring; how could she not find a way to get away from her fifteen-year-old son? The only reason she wouldn't is if she *couldn't*."

He couldn't argue with that logic. He knew about Tessa and what she had managed to deal with in her life. He just wished he'd had a chance to know her like Sofia did. "Why didn't you ever introduce me to her?"

"Anytime I asked, she didn't want to. She would always say, 'maybe later.' She didn't like to meet new people. She just wanted to keep to herself, raise her son, and live quietly and peacefully."

"Did you ever meet Parker?"

"No. Tessa and I kind of drifted apart as we got older. Her grandparents died, and then there was no real connection left. Then after she lost her husband, I went to the funeral and we kind of reconnected. I really would have told you about her, but she asked me not to and I had to respect her wishes."

He was about to ask another question when his phone beeped. He picked it up and saw a message from Sophie. Sofia picked her phone up, too, and he assumed she had messaged both of them.

"Sophie needs us to go pick her up," he said, standing up and pushing his chair back into the kitchen table.

"She hurt herself," Sofia began to quickly pack up the food to return to the fridge.

"She also said she was fine," he reminded his wife.

"Should we call an ambulance?" Sofia asked as she grabbed her bag and headed for the car.

"I don't think so." He laughed as he followed her. "She said that she just rolled her ankle and doesn't want to walk back to the road, then ride her bike all the way back."

"What were she and Hayley doing out there in the woods anyway?" she asked as they got into the car and he started the engine.

"I think she and Hayley enjoy the quiet," Ryan said. "You know, after what happened last winter."

He didn't think he would ever get over that.

Learning his daughter was missing was the most horrific moment of his life.

Learning that she had been abducted because of him was even worse.

Every second of those days were seared into his mind.

As was the image of his unconscious daughter being dumped on the side of the road when he and Paige traded themselves for their girls.

"It wasn't your fault," Sofia said softly.

She had said that more times than he could count over the last six months.

But her saying it didn't change the facts.

It *was* his fault.

Sophie and Hayley were kidnapped because of a grudge against him and Paige.

Your child being hurt because of you wasn't something you got over.

Ever.

"I know," he told his wife, because he knew it was what she wanted to hear.

"You know that Sophie doesn't blame you, and I don't blame you; you have to find a way to stop blaming yourself."

Sofia was right.

He knew that.

He just didn't think it was an achievable goal.

They both lapsed into silence as they drove out to the woods just outside the city.

It was beautiful out here. He could see why Sophie and Hayley liked it. Over the summer, the girls had gone out here most days. When they hadn't been hanging around either their house or the Hoods'.

Ryan understood that right now it was easier for the girls to spend time together than with their other friends because of what they'd gone through. Sophie had even turned down the idea of a big sweet sixteen party, saying she wanted a quiet day with family and close friends. He just hoped that the two of them weren't going to isolate themselves too much. They were both so young and they had their whole lives ahead of them. While he knew they would never get over what they'd been through, and it would forever shape them, he hoped they wouldn't let it hold them back from getting whatever they wanted to out of life.

He never thought he would ever say this about his teenage daughter, but he hoped that she would start dating again once school started back up. He wanted her to ease herself back into normal life, and for an almost-sixteen-year-old girl, a big part of that was dating.

"I think this is where she said to park." Sofia suddenly announced, gesturing to a small side road just up ahead.

Ryan pulled the car in and they both climbed out. "There's her bike," he said, pointing to where Sophie's blue bike leaned against a nearby tree.

"There's only one bike," Sofia said.

She was right.

One bike.

Two girls.

Immediately, he was on edge.

"I want you to get back in the car and lock the doors," he told his wife.

"Oh no." Sofia shook her head, sending her red ponytail whipping around her head. "You're not leaving me behind. I'm safer with you than alone in the car if something is wrong. Besides, Sophie is here somewhere; that *is* her bike."

"Maybe the girls had a fight," he suggested as he pulled out his gun and ushered Sofia behind him. "Hayley might have left already and then Sophie tripped and hurt herself. Or maybe Hayley was never here. Maybe Sophie just needed some time on her own to think."

"I don't think the girls would fight, they never fight, and even if they did Hayley would never leave Sophie out here alone. Maybe it wasn't Sophie who sent us those text messages," Sofia said.

That had occurred to him as well.

"Keep your eyes open for anything that looks out of place," he said as they headed off the road and into the woods.

"You really think someone might have hurt her?" Sofia sounded terrified.

He was barely holding it together, but knowing that his daughter needed him was forcing him to remain calm. "I don't know. Maybe she really did just hurt her ankle and didn't want to ride her bike the hour it would take her to get home."

"But you don't think so."

No, he didn't.

His gut was telling him something was wrong.

After a couple of decades as a cop, he had learned to trust his instincts. They weren't usually wrong.

Ignoring Sofia's question, he called out as they walked,

"Sophie? It's Dad ... are you here?"

According to the text they had received, Sophie was only a quarter of a mile from the road where they had parked.

"Sophie?" he called again when he got no answer. If she was here, then she should have heard them.

"Ryan, what if she tried to get back to the road and she fell and hurt herself worse?" Sofia whispered from behind him.

As much as he hoped his daughter wasn't seriously injured, that was actually the better scenario right now.

They walked a few steps more and then he spotted it.

A dozen yards or so ahead of them, partially obscured by a tree.

It looked like a body.

A teenage girl's body.

From the sharp gasp, he knew that Sofia had seen it too.

He started running toward the body without clearing the area.

That was a mistake.

He was halfway there when a sharp burst of fire exploded in his back and he dropped to the ground. A second later, he heard the thump of Sofia's body joining him.

His body jerked in a series of painful jolts, then the world faded away.

* * * * *

6:30 P.M.

Laura turned the car into her brother-in-law and sister-in-law's driveway.

There were no other cars parked there.

That immediately seemed odd.

When she and Sofia had made plans for her and Jack to have Ned last night, then Sofia and Ryan to have her son Zach tonight, they'd made six-thirty as the drop-off time and it was six-thirty on the dot.

She was one of those people who was obsessive about time. When she had spent ten years alone in her apartment never talking to or seeing another person, it had been her routine that had kept her sane. Sofia knew that and wouldn't have popped out right before she was about to arrive.

And where would she go anyway?

Sofia had said she would be working at home today. She should be here.

"Mom?" Her twelve-year-old son Zach leaned forward and poked his head between the driver's and passenger's seats. "Is something wrong?"

Laura blinked and pasted on a smile. She was being ridiculous—seeing problems where there weren't any.

When you had encountered monsters, it was hard not to see them lurking about in the shadows, and sometimes in the sunlight too.

But this time, she really did think she was imagining things. What could possibly have happened to Sofia while she was working at home?

"Nothing is wrong," she told her son. With his blond hair and bright blue eyes, Zach was the spitting image of his father. He also had his dad's keen analytical mind and ability to read people. When he was older, he would no doubt follow his dad into the police force. Her ten-year-old daughter was her own mini me. Rosie was sensitive and intuitive and very attuned to people's feelings. She was spending the night with her best friend Arianna Hood, and she and Jack were supposed to be having a night together, just the two of them. Ever since Jack had mentioned the possibility of having more kids, she hadn't been able to get it out of her head.

"Are you sure?" Zach asked, looking like he didn't quite believe her.

"Positive. Grab your bags," she told the boys as she turned off the engine and opened her door.

Zach and her twelve-year-old nephew Ned clambered out, babbling animatedly about some video game they had been obsessed with all summer. If she hadn't ordered the boys outside to swim in the pool and made them come and eat meals at the table, they would have spent the entire time holed up in Zach's room staring at a screen.

The boys beat her to the door, and Ned pulled out his key and let them both in. Laura followed them, assuring herself that Sofia was inside and that maybe the car was just at the garage being serviced. Or maybe they had finally gotten rid of the Ping-Pong table that had been in their garage ever since it was broken two Christmases ago. Sofia had been asking Ryan to take it to the dump ever since, but so far, he hadn't gotten around to it. Maybe he finally had.

Laura smiled as she remembered that Christmas. The entire family had gathered here late morning and spent the rest of the day together laughing and talking and eating and exchanging gifts. The kids had started a game of hide-and-seek, and the guys had decided to join in. Only by "join in," they meant hide and then jump out and scare the kids.

It had worked.

Her brother-in-law Mark's younger son Tony, who had been fourteen at the time, had gotten such a fright that he had fallen over right into the Ping-Pong table, cracking his head open and breaking his elbow.

They'd spent Christmas night in the ER.

"Sofia?" she called out as she walked inside. She could hear the boys' voices upstairs. No doubt they were getting ready to settle in for more video game playing.

There was no answer, and as she walked through the downstairs, she found it empty.

She had been right.

Sofia wasn't here.

If her friend had needed to pop out and run an errand, she would have called or texted.

The uneasy feeling in her stomach that had started the second she pulled into the driveway and found it empty, started to grow.

Laura pulled out her phone and dialed her husband's number. "Jack, is Ryan with you?" she asked as soon as he answered.

"No, he was working from home this afternoon. Why?"

"I'm here now, dropping off Zach and Ned, and he's not here. Neither is Sofia. Something is wrong."

"We don't know that," Jack reminded her. "Had anyone broken in?"

"No, Ned used his key to get in."

"Does it look like anyone has been in there? Are there any signs of a struggle? Any blood?"

"No, no signs of a struggle and no blood," she replied.

"Car there?"

"No, it's gone."

"Then they probably just went out to run an errand," Jack said, but she could hear the glimmer of doubt in his voice.

"Why would they do that when they knew I was coming by to drop off the boys?"

"What time were you supposed to drop them off?"

"Six thirty."

"Well it's only six thirty-five. Give it a few minutes, and maybe call Sofia. I'll call Ryan and then call you back in five minutes."

"Yeah, okay," she agreed. It was as good a plan as any. And maybe something last minute really had popped up and Sofia and Ryan would be back any minute.

"Love you," Jack said.

"Love you too," she echoed then disconnected the call. Laura dialed Sofia's number and waited.

And waited … and waited.

While the phone rang, she looked around the kitchen. There were plates and glasses on the counter; it looked like Sofia had started getting ready for lunch and had been interrupted before she ate with something important enough for her not to put everything away.

When a full two minutes had passed and the call hadn't been answered, she hung up and dialed Paige instead. Paige's daughter Ari was Rosie's best friend, and her older daughter was best friends with Sofia and Ryan's daughter, Sophie. Maybe Paige knew what was going on.

"Laura? What's up?" Paige asked.

"Do you know where Sofia and Ryan are?" she asked.

"No. Ryan wanted to work at home this afternoon, so I thought I may as well too. I haven't spoken to Sofia since yesterday. What's going on?" Paige was sounding all cop like now.

"I'm here at their house to drop off Zach and Ned and neither of them are here. Is Hayley with Sophie?"

"Hayley is here. She said that as far as she knew Sophie was spending the day with a friend, and she wanted to hang out here at the house with her sister. Rosie and Ari are upstairs playing, but Hayley is just in the other room, want me to ask her if she knows anything or if she's heard from Sophie?"

"If you don't mind."

"I'll be right back."

While she waited for Paige to check with her daughter, Laura went and stood at the window, staring out.

What was going on?

This made no sense.

Where would Sofia and Ryan go when they knew she was bringing their son home?

Why wouldn't they have called to let her know something had come up? If they needed to take care of something, she would have kept Ned even if she and Jack had had plans.

There were two plates and two glasses out. That implied that they had left around lunchtime. If they'd been getting ready for dinner before they left, there would have been five plates and glasses. Where had they been all this time?

Could they have crashed their car somewhere and been rushed to the hospital?

No, even if they were unconscious, they would have had ID on them, and the family would have been notified.

Had someone done something to them?

But who? And why?

"Laura?" Paige came back on the phone.

"Does Hayley know anything?"

"She said she hasn't heard from Sophie all day. I'm coming over. Elias will stay with the girls."

"Okay, see you soon," she said. She felt better knowing that Paige was coming. If something criminal was going on here, she wanted the cops involved.

Just as she hung up, her phone rang. It was Jack. "Did you get on to Ryan?"

"No, did you get on to Sofia?"

"No. I called Paige and she said Hayley didn't have plans with Sophie today and doesn't know where they might be. Something is wrong, Jack. I can feel it. Something happened to them … I just don't know what."

"I'm on my way there."

Jack hung up before she could respond, and Laura turned from the window to survey the room. She wished it could give her some answers.

It was like Ryan and Sofia had just gotten in the car, driven off, and disappeared. But they hadn't driven into a black hole. They had to be somewhere.

But where?

* * * * *

8:37 P.M.

"Are you okay?" Ryan grabbed her the second the door closed behind them.

Allowing his arms, wrapped tightly around her, to calm her terror, Sofia whispered against his chest, "I'm okay."

When they had been searching for Sophie in the woods, they had been tased. She must have passed out, and when she'd woken up, she had been tied up in the trunk of a car, her body draped on top of Ryan's. They had been in there for hours, and her cramped muscles still hadn't recovered. A few minutes ago, they had been dragged out of the trunk at gunpoint and ordered to walk through a house to this room, where they had just been locked inside.

"That was PJ Bell," Ryan said, even though she knew that already.

If PJ had taken them to the same place where he had taken his mother, then Tessa could be here. And from the way Ryan had described her earlier phone call, she hadn't been doing too well. The phone call had been well over twenty-four hours ago. Who knows what condition her friend was in now. The look Ryan gave her let her know that he was thinking the same thing she was.

He released her and scanned the room they were in as he spun around. It had been set up as a living room and they were the only two people in it. A door sat in the far wall, and both she and Ryan headed for it. Ryan gestured for her to stay behind him. Through the door was a bedroom. A figure lay unmoving on the enormous canopy bed in the center of the room.

Ryan ran to the person, Sofia hot on his heels. They both let out muttered curses when they saw that the person in the bed was indeed Tessa Bell. Ryan pressed his fingers against Tessa's neck, while Sofia took in her friend's condition. Tessa's face was bruised, a mottled mix of purple, black, and blue. There were two deep-looking gashes—one in the middle of her forehead while the other ran along her left cheekbone. PJ had washed away the blood and attempted to hold the gashes together with small strips of tape, but it looked like both of the cuts were infected. Tessa was so still that Sofia was afraid they were too late.

"She's still alive." Ryan's voice broke through her terrified haze. "Sofia? Are you hearing me? She's alive. Tessa is still alive."

She nodded shakily and joined Ryan on the bed. "How bad is she?"

Ryan said nothing, but the look he shot her said enough. He pulled down the blankets covering Tessa, revealing a tatty and blood-soaked bandage on Tessa's arm, and another on her leg. More bruises peeked from the shoulder of her tank top, and now that the blankets were gone, Sofia could see that Tessa's breathing was shallow and way too fast.

"Broken ribs?" she asked Ryan as he lightly rested his hand on Tessa's chest.

"I think so, but I can't be sure," he replied.

Beneath his touch, Tessa winced, her eyes struggling open, dazed and panicked. Her arms lifted as though to fight off an attacker, and Sofia wondered just what PJ Bell had done to his mother.

"Hey, it's all right, Tessa," Ryan soothed, gently grasping her shoulders. "It's Ryan Xander and Sofia."

"Is Skylar here?" she asked hopefully, letting her eyes fall closed again.

"No, I'm sorry, honey." Sofia took her hand.

"Then PJ took you." She sounded distressed. "Did he hurt you?"

"No, we're fine," she assured her friend, glancing at Ryan as he lifted Tessa's wrist to take her pulse. She raised a questioning brow at him, and he gave a slight shake of his head. Trying not to let her concern show, she sat on the bed beside her friend. Tessa's condition was serious, but they had no way of getting her the medical assistance that she desperately needed.

"I'm sorry," Tessa murmured.

"It's not your fault," Sofia said firmly.

"I think I lost too much blood." Tessa's eyes fluttered back open as Ryan pressed the back of his hand to her cheek.

"Yeah, I think you did too," Ryan agreed grimly, turning his attention to unwinding the bandage on Tessa's leg so he could examine the wound.

"It's infected." Tessa watched Ryan. "My arm too. Maisy died from an infection."

Sofia squeezed Tessa's hand tightly. She'd heard the story of how Tessa's friend had died in her arms while they were both held captive by the woman who killed Tessa's husband. "You're not going to die, Tessa. Ryan and I won't let you."

"Is there a bathroom?" Ryan stood.

"Through there." Tessa raised a trembling hand to point to another door.

"Okay, I'm going to go get some water and a cloth and clean these."

"Who else has PJ killed?" Tessa asked once Ryan was gone.

Sofia wanted to keep Tessa calm, so she didn't want to answer any questions about PJ's crimes. "Don't worry about that now."

"I need to know," Tessa begged.

"Know what?" Ryan returned, meager medical supplies in hand.

"I need to know who else my son has killed. I know he killed Melanie Gardner and Lizzie Landry, and Parker's friend Lucas Mianta. But I need to know who else," Tessa pleaded.

"You don't need to know that," Sofia insisted.

"Here, take these. It's only Tylenol, but it should take the edge off your pain." Ryan tipped some painkillers into Tessa's hand, slid an arm behind her shoulders and helped her sit, then held a glass of water to her lips. When she had swallowed the pills, he eased her back down against the mattress. "Sorry, this is going to hurt."

"Squeeze as hard as you need to," Sofia kept hold of Tessa's other hand.

"Ryan? Please tell me." Tessa turned her blue eyes to Ryan.

For a moment, he didn't say anything, just ripped at Tessa's sweatpants to make a bigger hole so he could better see the deep, jagged cut. "He's killed four people so far," he said at last as he began to wash the wound.

"Ryan," Sofia admonished. "We need to keep her calm."

"Right now, I want to keep her distracted," Ryan murmured, gesturing at Tessa, who had scrunched up her face in pain as Ryan cleaned out her infected cut. "Cassandra Stanton was the fourth. We were able to interrupt his last two attempts."

"Cassandra?" Tessa echoed, tears seeping from the corners of her closed eyes. "She was doing so well. She'd just gotten married; she was so happy. Why would he do that to her?"

"I'm sorry, Tess." Sofia tried to comfort her, but Tessa wasn't listening.

"Did Skylar tell the Abbotts to leave?" she asked.

"Yes, they're safe, Tess. Try not to worry about them." Ryan wrapped a clean bandage tightly around her leg. He moved on to her arm, then asked, "Do you think there's any way you can talk PJ into taking you to a hospital?"

"No," she cried quietly. "PJ wants to kill me. He thinks that he's saving me. Maybe I can convince him to let you two go. He's mad at Parker. You two have nothing to do with Parker, so he might agree to it."

"Do you know if he has Sophie here?" Ryan asked the question they had both been wondering. PJ had texted them from Sophie's phone, so it made sense their daughter was here somewhere, especially since she knew that PJ had a crush on Sophie.

"Sophie?" Tessa looked horrified. "Did PJ kidnap her too? I knew he liked her, but I don't know why he would bring her here. He wants to kill himself and me on his birthday."

Birthday.

August twelfth wasn't only PJ's birthday.

It was Sophie's too.

"Do you think he wants to kill Sophie too?" she asked, terrified by the prospect. Her daughter had already been through so much, and now, once again, she'd been abducted by someone she trusted.

"I don't think he would hurt her, but then again I didn't think he would do all of this either."

"Where was the phone you used to call us?" Ryan asked.

"Downstairs," Tessa replied, her voice gone faint. "He left the door open because he wanted me to feel at home here, but I doubt he'll do that now that you two are here."

"Do you think you can convince him to at least bring you some antibiotics?" Ryan asked.

"Maybe." Tessa's voice dropped to a mere whisper.

"Good," Ryan said as he set her arm back down. "If we can get you on antibiotics, we should be able to get you well enough to last until the others find us."

"I'm so cold." Tessa was shivering. "I can't stop shaking."

"You're in shock, honey," Ryan reminded her, pulling the covers back up and tucking her in.

"I'll talk to PJ again." She continued to speak even though she looked half unconscious by now. "I'll try to make him see reason. I'll try to convince him that he needs help. I'll try …"

"Tessa, rest now, save your strength," Ryan soothed.

She and Ryan settled on either side of Tessa to try and help keep her warm, and in less than a minute, Tessa had passed out into a fitful slumber.

"Ryan," Sofia half-whimpered.

He reached over and took her hand. "It'll be okay," Ryan assured her.

"You can't know that." She was so afraid, afraid for Tessa, afraid for Sophie, afraid for herself and Ryan, afraid for PJ's other victims. "Do you really think Tessa can last until the others find us?" *If* they found them.

He took a deep breath and released it slowly. "Maybe," Ryan

replied. "She lost a lot of blood; her wounds are already infected. I wouldn't be surprised if the infection was already in her bloodstream. If PJ brings some antibiotics, she can probably last a little longer. Hopefully long enough for us to get her proper medical help."

For a moment, Sofia let fear and panic and despair swamp her, but then she resolutely pushed it away. "How are we going to get Tessa, our daughter, and ourselves out of here?"

AUGUST 9TH

5:45 A.M.

Hayley pressed redial on her phone.

Just as it had every other time she'd done it in the last twelve hours, it went straight to voicemail.

Where was Sophie?

Why wasn't she answering her phone?

Had something happened to her?

Was she with her mom and dad?

Ryan and Sofia were missing too. It was like the three of them had just vanished into thin air.

Only people didn't really do that.

When they vanished, it was because someone had *made* them vanish.

So, who had made Sophie and her parents vanish?

She wished she knew something helpful that she could contribute, but all she knew was that Sophie had texted her early yesterday morning to say that she was hanging out with PJ to try to cheer him up. Hayley had thought that was great. She had taken it to mean that Sophie was going to go for it with PJ, and she had been so proud of her friend for being brave enough to move on.

Hayley had been kind of glad to spend the day at home. As much as she loved hanging out with her best friend, she hadn't really spent much time with Arianna all summer. She knew her little sister looked up to her, and she knew Arianna still felt like she should have done something to prevent her and Sophie being abducted last winter. So, she had been grateful to have some time with her sister, just the two of them, before Ari's best friend Rosie came over. She had been planning on texting Sophie straight after dinner to find out how things had gone with PJ. Instead, Laura had called them to ask if she knew anything about where Ryan and Sofia were.

She hated that this was happening again.

Her friend had been through enough, and now she was forced to endure another ordeal.

Maybe whoever had taken PJ's mom had done something to him and Sophie?

But why go after her parents too?

It had been almost twelve hours now since Laura had realized something was wrong and no one had heard from Sophie, Sofia, or Ryan.

That meant something had definitely happened.

Ryan and Sofia wouldn't just go off somewhere and leave their twelve-year-old son behind. She had known them ever since she was five years old, and she knew what great people and what great parents they were.

If it was the same person who had taken PJ's mother, why would he go after Sophie and her family? Maybe it was an accident? Maybe Sophie was just with PJ when the kidnapper came for him?

She wished she knew more than just these vague questions and speculations.

Hayley hit redial again.

Again, there was no answer.

"Sophie, where are you?" she muttered under her breath.

"You doing okay?"

She looked up in surprise as someone stood above her. She was at the police station. When her mom had come down here, she had insisted on coming along. Sophie was her best friend; she couldn't just sit around at home while she was missing. She had spent the night here, hovering about, not wanting to get in the way but not wanting to leave in case someone figured out what was going on.

At least one member of the Xander family had been here at all times. They would check in with her, make sure she was doing okay, but mostly they left her alone, understanding that she needed to attempt to process what was going on.

Now Brian Xander stood in front of her.

She didn't know what to say and she knew her cheeks were probably a bright flaming shade of red.

This was so embarrassing.

Did he know that she had a huge crush on him?

Other than Sophie and her mom, she hadn't told anyone, but she had a feeling that what she felt for him was written all over her face.

Why did he have to be so much older than her?

He was twenty-one and was about to start medical school. He didn't have time for a fifteen-year-old high school junior.

So why did she always get this ridiculous gooey feeling in her stomach whenever he was around her?

Why couldn't her feelings get in touch with her brain and realize that nothing was ever going to happen between them?

To him, she was just a kid.

Nothing more than the best friend of one of his cousins.

Sure, their families hung out pretty regularly, and sometimes they spent holidays together, and they had even gone on vacation together more than once.

But that was it.

Nothing more.

Nothing.

She had to let go of this stupid crush before she did something to make a complete and utter fool out of herself.

Last Christmas, she almost had.

Their families always did a secret Santa thing where all their names went into a box and they all picked one out. She had gotten Brian's name, and she had obsessed for a full month about what she was going to get for him that wouldn't make her look childish or stupid or reveal her gigantic crush. And the gifts had to cost under ten dollars because it was about putting thought into it and not about spending a lot of money. But what could you get for someone you were hopelessly in love with for only ten dollars?

In the end, she'd finally settled on the game Operation since Brian wanted to be a surgeon like his dad. He had seemed to like it, but he was probably just being polite since all their families had been there and he wouldn't have wanted to hurt her feelings.

"Hayley?" Brian looked concerned as he sat down beside her, drawing her attention out of her own head and back to him. "I know you're worried about Sophie, but your mom, and my uncle Jack and Xavier, they're doing everything they can to find her."

Sophie.

Right.

Her best friend who had gone missing.

How had she forgotten about that even for a second?

She didn't know what to say, and her throat had closed up probably making speech impossible anyway, so she just nodded.

"Can I get you anything? Have you eaten?" Brian asked.

Hayley shook her head.

"Okay, well, if you need anything, just ask. And if you need to talk, I'm right here." Brian reached for her hand and squeezed.

He was touching her.

And he was being so sweet.

Why couldn't she do something other than just stare at him and move her head?

"Th-thank you," she managed to force out.

Brian smiled and then released her hand and walked off farther down the hall, pulling out his phone.

Hayley groaned at herself.

She was so stupid.

She blinked back tears as she hit redial on her phone again and then stood and went in search of her mother.

They were all in a conference room—her mom and Jack and Xavier, and some retired cop whose name she thought was Wyatt. They were chattering away; there were stacks of paper everywhere and dozens of case files spread all over the table.

No one noticed her entering the room, and her attention was drawn to a huge board taking up most of the adjacent wall.

It seemed to be some sort of timeline, with photos, dates and times, and notes scrawled all over it.

PJ's photo was on there and she assumed it was just because his mother was missing or maybe it was because he was gone too. She wasn't sure why, but her feet started to walk toward the board. When she was close, she saw the word "suspect" scrawled underneath the photo.

Suspect?

It was PJ?

He was the one who had kidnapped his own mother?

He was the one who had taken Sophie?

"Hayley? Are you okay, sweetheart? You shouldn't be in here." Her mom's arm came around her shoulder and turned her away from the board.

She had to tell them what she knew.

That PJ liked Sophie and that she liked him back and that she had been going to spend the day with him before she had disappeared.

But her mouth opened, and no sound came out.

"Honey, you look pale. What's wrong?" her mom asked.

Jack pulled over a chair and guided her into it.

That was good.

If she didn't sit, she thought her legs might give out.

"Sweetheart, what's wrong?" Her mom brushed her hair off her cheek and tucked it behind her ear.

"I-I know where they are," she said, her voice coming out all strange.

"What do you mean?" Jack asked.

"Where who are?" Xavier asked.

"PJ. He's the one you're looking for, right?" She looked up to find all four pairs of eyes fixed on her.

"Why would you know where he is?" her mom asked.

"He and Sophie, they have a special place in the woods where they meet to hang out. They're friends. He likes her and she likes—well she *liked* him too."

"You've been there? Tell us where it is," the man she thought was the retired cop practically screamed at her, and she shrank away from him.

"Calm down, Wyatt," her mom warned. "Yelling at her isn't going to help. Honey, can you tell us where this special place is?"

Hayley shook her head.

"But you said—" Wyatt started.

"I can't tell you how to get there," she interrupted, "but I can show you."

"No," her mom said immediately. "You're not going anywhere near that kid."

"This could be the only way we're going to find them," Wyatt argued. "And Tessa doesn't have much time left. For all we know, your friends don't either."

"I'm not taking my fifteen-year-old daughter to where some psychotic kid is holed up with his mother, who he plans to kill," her mom said.

But this wasn't up to her mother.

Hayley rarely did anything against either of her parents' wishes, but this was different. This could save lives. She wasn't going to sit here safe at the police station while her best friend was in danger.

"I'll take you there," she said firmly.

*   *   *   *   *

6:08 A.M.

"She's getting worse."

Tessa heard the words, but they floated above her.

Kind of like clouds floating slowly across the sky.

She had always liked clouds.

They moved at such a leisurely, relaxed pace.

She liked how they changed personality.

They could go from soft, sweet, white fluffy little things, barely more than wisps, to dark, dangerous masses of gray and black that looked like they wanted to kill you.

It was kind of like life.

It could go from all innocent and nice one moment to throwing you into the depths of despair and heaping trouble on you to see how much it took to crush you.

She'd had more trouble heaped on her than most people ever did.

A father who abandoned them, a mother with drug and alcohol problems, grandparents too disinterested to care, an abduction that led to her best friend's death and her having to take a life to escape, an obsessive stalker who would stop at nothing short of owning her, and that was all before she hit the age of eighteen.

Parker had been the only good thing to ever happen to her.

But she had destroyed him.

Just like she had destroyed everything else she touched.

She had warned Parker not to get involved with her. She had warned him that it would only lead to his death.

Everyone who got involved with her in any way wound up dead.

And she always survived.

Survived to live, coated so thickly in guilt that just functioning was more than she could bear.

Two and a half years together.

That was all she and Parker had had.

But when he had left her, he left behind a piece of himself.

His son.

Their son.

Their beautiful, smart son, who every time she looked at him, she had seen his father.

Maybe that was where things had gone wrong.

Maybe she shouldn't have seen Parker in PJ.

Parker was strong and kind, and he risked his life to save people. He had certainly saved her, in more ways than one. Parker cared about people. He always tried to see the good in them even when it didn't seem like they had any.

But by looking at her son and seeing her husband, she hadn't seen PJ for who he really was.

She had brushed off Isaac's concerns that something wasn't right with PJ. She thought he was just jealous because she was raising her son while he had been deprived of raising his daughter.

She should have listened to him.

If she had, maybe all of this wouldn't have happened.

She didn't care about herself. If PJ was going to kill her, at least, in death, she would be reunited with the one and only love of her life.

But PJ had killed so many people.

Melanie Gardner, who had been her friend in school, who had suffered at the hands of her obsessive stalker for no other reason than that they were friends. Lizzie Gardner, who she had helped and supported as she dealt with nearly being abducted just because a lunatic killer wanted some attention. Cassandra Stanton, who had been hurt by the very same people who had hurt her and Ellie when they were children, but who had fought back and was stronger than Tessa had ever been and embraced being happy while she had hidden away from life.

They were all dead now.

And yet, that wasn't enough to satisfy PJ's murderous cravings.

Now, he had his hands on fifteen-year-old Sophie Xander. She had known the girl since she was a baby and she liked the teenager. The girl had also been through a lot, and yet, there was a spark inside her that couldn't be extinguished.

Tessa prayed that if Sophie made it out of this alive, she would hold on to that spark. That she would let it lead her out of the darkness and back into the light. That it would be enough to help her overcome whatever life threw at her. That it would help her find happiness.

Her friend Sofia and Sofia's husband were here too.

Even though they and their daughter had been kidnapped because of her son, they were trying to help her.

They shouldn't bother.

She wished that she could go back and live her life over again.

If she could, she would take what Parker had taught her and use it. She would learn from her mistakes instead of stubbornly forging down the same path hoping for a different outcome.

That was the very definition of insanity.

"Here, Tess, drink a little water." Ryan's arm slipped around her shoulders and he eased her off the bed.

"I can't," she murmured.

"You need to keep up your strength," he protested and held the glass to her lips.

To satisfy him, she took a few sips, then just as he was laying her back down, she heard the door open.

"I have a gun," PJ announced.

A gun.

The son she had known hated guns. She had always thought it was because a gun had taken his father from them, but apparently, she had been wrong about that too.

Tessa struggled to sit up, but Ryan held her down. "Stay here," he said, moving so he was in between PJ and her and Sofia.

She hated that.

She had never let anyone try to protect her before, and she wasn't going to start on her deathbed.

Pushing aside Sofia's well-meaning hands, she managed to push herself up and swing her legs over the bed, ignoring Ryan's frustrated growl.

"PJ, put that away," she told her son.

"I can't, Mom, I'm sorry," he said, and did actually look apologetic.

"You have to stop this," she told him.

"I can't."

"You can. You mean you won't," she corrected.

"Okay." He nodded. "I won't."

"Because you think you're saving me?"

"I *am* going to save you," he said.

She wasn't going to argue about that right now. Maybe in a way, he was actually right. Despite a drug and shock-induced attempt to end her own life when Skylar had first told her about Parker's death, she had never attempted suicide. But that hadn't stopped a part of her from wanting to die and find her husband in whatever lay beyond this life.

She lived out her life the best she could, and she had been the best mother she could, but she hadn't done a very good job of either. And the thought of death and no more guilt and suffering certainly held its appeal.

But Sophie, Sofia, and Ryan had done nothing to deserve this. They wanted their lives and she would do whatever she could to make sure they kept them.

"What about them?" she asked, as she somehow found the strength to clamber to her feet. Ryan immediately moved to stand at her side, hooking an arm around her waist to steady her and keep her on her feet. "They haven't done anything to hurt you, and they don't have anything to do with Parker. Let them go … you never should have brought them here."

"I did it for Sophie," he said, a faraway look in his eyes as he said her name. Tessa knew he had a crush on her, but she wasn't sure if he intended to kill her, too, or if he had just brought her here to spend the last few days of his life with her.

"You shouldn't have brought her here," she admonished her son.

"I know." He looked guilty, and she hoped that meant because he didn't plan on harming her.

"But we kissed, and she said that she liked me, and I thought that maybe …"

"Maybe what?" Sofia asked.

"I don't know," PJ said. "I don't know what I thought. But after we kissed, I couldn't get her out of my head. And even though she said she wasn't ready, I knew she felt the same spark between us that I did. And then the next thing I knew I had just brought her here. And then I felt bad. Because she loves you …" PJ gestured at Ryan and Sofia. "… and I know she would have missed you, so I thought I should bring you here too."

"This is a mistake, PJ, and you know it," Tessa said, swaying even as Ryan held her up.

"You need to get your mom some antibiotics," Ryan told PJ.

"I can't. She called Wyatt, so now they know it's me. I can't go anywhere; if I do, then they'll arrest me or kill me."

Given what PJ had done, the cops would more than likely shoot him unless he surrendered quietly, and she wasn't sure that was something he would do.

"Please, PJ, think about this," she begged. "Think about what you're doing. Think about who you're hurting. You say you love Sophie and yet you've hurt her by bringing her here. You know what she's been through. Just please think about it. Think about letting Sophie and her parents go home. Then it will be just the two of us. Just like you wanted. Just like you always wanted. Do the right thing, please."

She had intended to say more, but unconsciousness crashed down on her like a large wave in the ocean, and it washed her away with it.

* * * * *

6:46 A.M.

His head felt like it was going to explode.

He didn't know what to do.

PJ had been convinced that he was doing the right thing, but now he wasn't so sure.

Maybe he *had* been just taking out his anger on people that his so-called hero of a father had saved. Maybe that had been wrong. He *supposed* it wasn't their fault that it had been his father who had worked their cases. And he *supposed* it wasn't their fault that they had been able to move on with their lives and find happiness.

Perhaps he had been a little unfair.

He didn't know.

He wasn't sure.

He wished there was someone who could tell him what he should do next.

PJ felt like he had painted himself into a corner and now he didn't know how to get out.

His mom had said that this wasn't the way to get what he wanted. She said that he was making a mistake.

What if she was right?

What if in ending her life he wasn't ending her pain?

What if he was causing her *more* pain?

He didn't want to.

He wanted to take all of her suffering away so she could finally be at peace.

He wanted to do the same for himself.

He was tired of being angry.

That was the only emotion he had ever really experienced. He had never really felt sad; he didn't miss his father. How could he? He'd never even met him. And he had never really been happy. How could he be when his mother lived in constant pain?

Anger.

That was what his life had been.

He was angry that his father had died and left him and his mom all alone. He was angry that his mom had been hurt again. He was angry that he was missing out on the life he should have had.

He was so angry.

Except …

Except when he was with Sophie.

When he was with her, he felt that heavy layer of anger that he always carried around lift. It didn't completely go away, but it got lighter. What would it be like if he could be with her all the time?

He thought his life would finally be better.

Finally be good.

But he couldn't end his mom's life and not his own. And even if he *did* decide not to kill himself and his mother, he wasn't sure his mother would make it anyway. And then, how would he live with himself knowing that because of him, she had died? He couldn't take her to the hospital even if he wanted to because the cops were looking for him. PJ knew how much Wyatt loved Tessa, and he knew the man would do whatever it took to catch him.

And he really wasn't sure that the part of his plan that was to end his and his mom's suffering was wrong.

The part about Sophie and her parents, though. Maybe his mom was right. Maybe bringing them here had been a mistake.

Tentatively, he unlocked the door to the room he had put Sophie in and edged it open.

The second he did, a screeching figure flung itself at him.

He wasn't prepared, and they both went flying backward, crashing into the wall in the hall.

The second they hit the wall, Sophie took off.

She was fast, but he was faster, and he grabbed her before she had made it more than a couple of feet.

His body slammed into hers and they both fell to the floor, Sophie grunting in pain as his weight came down on top of her.

"I don't want to hurt you," he said as he wrapped his arm around her waist and dragged her up with him. She kicked and swung her fists at him as he carried her back to her room. "Stop it."

"I want to go home!" she screamed. "Why are you doing this to me? You said you loved me. You said you thought we could have a future together … is this what you meant? That you wanted to keep me here as your prisoner?"

"You're not my prisoner," he protested, struggling to keep his hold on her.

"You're keeping me here against my will, locked up in a room. That makes me your prisoner."

He guessed he could see her logic there, and he really didn't want to argue with her. "I don't want to hurt you," he said again.

"You *are* hurting me. Just like Dom did. All he could see was that he wanted revenge. He didn't care who he hurt, he didn't care what he had to do, he didn't care that the people who he wanted revenge on had never even done anything to hurt him. And you are doing the same thing. You're making the same mistakes that he did. You know what Dom did to me and now you're doing exactly the same thing. You took my feelings for you and used them against me. I hate you," she said and finally went limp in his arms.

PJ didn't know what to say.

The only person in his life who made him feel something good, and now he had ruined it.

Just like his father had ruined things and hurt his mother. Now he had done the same thing with the woman he loved.

He released his hold on her and she dropped to the floor, lying in a heap where she landed.

"I'm sorry," he said, but she didn't reply.

His mom was right.

He shouldn't have done this.

He shouldn't have brought Sophie here, and he shouldn't have brought her parents here either.

He should let them go.

He would.

He wouldn't hurt Sophie further by killing her or her parents.

His mother was right about that. It was wrong to hurt people who hadn't done anything wrong.

On his birthday, he was still going to do what he had planned all along. He was going to give him and his mother the peace they sought, but right before he ended things, he would call someone and tell them where Sophie and her parents were.

"I'm sorry, Sophie," he said again.

She still wouldn't answer him. Wouldn't even lift her head to look at him, but he could hear her crying softly.

With his heart hurting, he left the room and locked the door behind him. He hated doing it, but he couldn't see any other options. He couldn't let her go. There were still three days to his birthday and Sophie knew the way here. If he took her and her parents and dropped them off back at their house, she would just lead the cops right back here.

His head was spinning.

He couldn't think clearly.

There were too many worries and doubts and concerns spinning about in there.

Why was life so hard?

Why couldn't everything just run smoothly?

He was smart. He had made the potassium chloride that he had used to put his victims to sleep himself. He could have done anything. The sky was the limit. He could have invented a cure for cancer or found a way to live on Mars or anything else, but instead, he was going to kill himself on his sixteenth birthday because he couldn't stand to live any longer.

He was going to have to do something.

His birthday was three days away. He couldn't just sit here knowing that Sophie was here, locked in a room, hating him.

He needed to get out.

He needed to be anywhere but here for a while.

He knew what he needed.

He needed to kill.

It had become the only thing that calmed him. It was his drug. He was addicted.

That's what he'd do.

He knew it was probably wrong, but he didn't have a choice. Staying here was unacceptable. If he could get out, make another kill, get the thrill of taking a life running through his veins, maybe it would clear his head. Then he would be able to come back here and figure out a plan for getting through the next few days.

PJ went to his room and grabbed his kill kit and a disguise. Since Wyatt and the cops were looking for him, this wasn't going to be easy. He was going to have to go off script, since they seemed to be able to figure out his next moves, and he really didn't want to have to carjack some random stranger and go traipsing through the sewers like last time.

With his disguise on and his bag in his hand, he headed out into the warm morning. The sky was a gorgeous bright blue; the sun was a huge yellow ball; everything was getting that washed-out greenish brown look of a long, hot summer. It was like the season was echoing life.

The end of his life was coming, and he was surprisingly calm and content about it.

* * * * *

7:04 A.M.

"I think I might be able to get out through the ceiling," Ryan said as he stared up at it.

Sofia followed his gaze. "Really?"

"If we can stack the armchair on the desk, then the desk chair on top of that, I should be able to reach the ceiling. Then I just need to break through it, which shouldn't be too hard. Once I'm in the room above this, I'll be able to get access to the rest of the house."

"How are you going to get through our door?" Sofia asked. "It's locked, and we already know you can't knock it down."

"Maybe I can find the keys, or I can find something to break it down with, or worst-case scenario, I'll go and get help then come back for you." He didn't want to leave Sofia, Sophie, or Tessa behind. He didn't think PJ would really hurt Sofia or Sophie, and he wasn't even sure the teenager would follow through on his threats to kill his mother and himself, but *still*, leaving them behind felt wrong.

"We'll be fine," Sofia said, as though she could read his mind. Which, she usually did. Fifteen years of marriage did that to you.

"I know you will." He pulled her closer and kissed her deeply, like for some reason his brain thought it could be the last time he would ever get to do it.

But that was ridiculous.

There was no denying that PJ Bell was a killer, but the kid was more messed up than anything. He needed psychiatric help, and if Ryan could just get out of here, he could make sure the teenager got it.

"We'll be fine," Sofia said again when he'd finished kissing her.

"Are you going to be okay with her?" he nodded at the bed where Tessa lay with her eyes closed.

Ryan thought she was asleep—or passed out—but Tessa murmured, "We'll be fine."

"Okay, okay." He laughed.

Sofia helped him drag the armchair over to the desk and then up onto it. While she grabbed the large heavy lamp that was on the nightstand, he climbed up on the desk, then lifted up the desk chair and added it to the armchair.

"Here you go," Sofia said as she handed him the lamp.

It should do the trick.

Ryan pulled out the light globe and passed it down to Sofia, then slammed the lampstand up into the ceiling.

Just as he had hoped, it went straight through the thin plaster, and within a couple of minutes he had made a hole big enough for him to climb through.

"Don't say it," Sofia warned.

"Say what?" he asked with an innocent smirk. "If PJ comes back, try to keep him talking. I'll get you two out if I can and then I'll search for Sophie."

"Okay," Sofia agreed. "Just be careful."

"I will."

Squeezing up through the hole he'd made in the ceiling, Ryan climbed up into another bedroom. It was large, and mostly empty save for a wrought iron bed. The door to this room was unlocked and he ran through it and out into a hall. The house was large with lots of corridors and it took him at least a minute to wind his way through them to get to the staircase. He headed down it carefully. They'd heard a car drive off, but that didn't mean that PJ hadn't come back. The kid might not be evil, but he was scared and confused and unbalanced and that made him even more dangerous because he was unpredictable.

He didn't really think the chances of finding the keys were particularly high, but when he ran down the hall to the room where Sofia and Tessa were waiting for him, he saw them hanging on a hook on the wall beside the door. Gotta love teenage boys and their laziness. Ned would be thirteen soon, and he was already well and truly heading into teenage mode.

Ryan grabbed the key, unlocked the door, and beamed at Sofia who was waiting for him. "Should have tried this twelve hours ago," he said as he gave her a quick kiss.

"Better late than never." Sofia smiled.

"We better hurry; I don't know when PJ will be back, and she really needs a doctor," he said as he scooped Tessa out of the bed and into his arms.

"Let's stop by the kitchen," Sofia said as she closed the door behind them and relocked it. "Since he took your gun, we don't have any weapons, and we know he has more than one gun, since he has yours and the one you said he had the other day when he carjacked that woman."

"Good idea," he said as they headed down the hall. A knife wasn't going to beat a gun, but it was better than nothing.

They made it down the first flight of stairs and were about to go down the second flight to the first floor when he heard voices.

Sofia obviously heard them, too, because she froze, but then her eyes grew wide. "Is that Jack's voice?"

It *did* sound like his brother.

Could they have managed to track down PJ's house?

Cautiously, he looked around the corner, and saw Jack, Xavier, Paige, Hayley, Skylar Wyatt and his wife Casey. What were Hayley and Casey doing here?

"Jack," he said and stepped out into view.

The others all came running up the stairs and Wyatt immediately grabbed Tessa.

"Is she still alive?" Wyatt demanded.

"Barely. How did you find us?"

"Hayley had been to Sophie and PJ's special meeting place in the woods. And since Isaac had told us about the bank account, and we knew he had taken large amounts of money from it, we assumed he'd bought a place up here," Jack explained.

"Where is PJ?" Xavier asked.

"Not here; he left about thirty minutes ago," he replied.

"We must have just missed him." Wyatt looked annoyed.

"Hayley, you should go lock yourself in the car now," Paige told her daughter.

"I'm not going on my own," Hayley protested.

"Sofia will go with you," Ryan said.

"Hey," his wife protested, glaring at him.

"We still have to find Sophie, and PJ could be back at any second," he told Sofia.

"Fine." Sofia glared at him, then softened and kissed his cheek. "Be careful, and bring our little girl safely out of this place. Come on, Hayley."

Hayley gave her mother a quick kiss, then she and Sofia disappeared.

"I'll check out Tessa, then we'll go join them in the car," Casey Wyatt, a doctor, said.

"Paige and I will look for Sophie," he said.

"Jack and I will make sure there aren't any other victims here," Xavier said.

They were about to split up when they heard a car pulling up.

"PJ. Take Tessa," Wyatt said, handing the barely conscious woman off to Jack. "You guys get Sophie, and make sure no one else is here. I'll try to talk PJ into being reasonable. You hang in there," he told Tessa.

Ryan hoped that Wyatt was able to talk the unpredictable teen down before he did something they would all regret.

* * * * *

7:27 A.M.

"Get Tessa out of here. Casey too," he whispered to Jack Xander.

Leaving Jack to get his wife and Tessa someplace safe, Wyatt stalked to the top of the stairs. PJ was down on the first floor in the foyer, shoving keys into his pocket.

"Enough, PJ," he said.

The teen looked up in surprise. "What are you doing here?"

"Putting an end to this."

260

"How did you find me?"

"I spoke with Isaac," he said. He wasn't going to bring Paige Hood's fifteen-year-old daughter into this. If PJ didn't know the kid was here, that was for the best. He didn't want to get the girl messed up in this anymore than she already was.

"Isaac was jealous of my relationship with Mom. He wanted to keep her all to himself." PJ pouted.

He had never seen PJ behave so immaturely before. He had always thought of Tessa's son as an old man in a kid's body. Seeing this side of him was disconcerting. You could reason with an adult, but PJ was behaving like a spoiled preschooler. That was much harder to deal with.

"This isn't about Isaac," he said. "This is about you. This is about you doing all of this." He waved his hand at the house.

"Just leave, Wyatt." PJ took a step toward him and pulled out a gun. "I don't want to hurt you. I'm not angry with you, and I have no problem with you. You tried to step in and be a father to me, I appreciate that. And you tried to be there for my mom. I appreciate that too. So, just walk away."

"I can't, PJ. I won't. I can't let you hurt your mom because you don't want to live but you don't want to leave her alive. That's what this is about, isn't it? It's about you, not your mom. *You* don't want to live anymore, you're angry at your dad for getting killed, and you're angry at your mom because she couldn't get over her grief. You think that you're better off dead than alive. But you can't face the thought of abandoning your mom just like Parker did, so you have to kill her too. But you don't, PJ. You need help, not death."

"I don't need help," PJ growled, sounding every bit the petulant child he was acting like.

"You know you shouldn't be doing this. You know that you need help. Your anger is eating you up alive. The only way you can get any relief from it now is to kill."

"H-how did you know that?"

"Because I've seen this before. People can't deal with their emotions; they get overwhelmed by them, and the only way they can get out from under it is to lash out. Take that anger and use it against someone else." Unfortunately, Wyatt wasn't lying. He had seen more criminals than he could count who had unresolved anger that they took out on innocent people.

But Tessa wasn't going to be one of those people.

He didn't want to, but if it came down to a choice between PJ and Tessa, he would kill PJ if it was the only way to protect her.

"I don't want to hurt you, PJ. So put the gun down and surrender. We'll take your mom to a hospital and get her the help she needs. And then we'll get you some help."

"I don't need help." PJ's face grew so dark it was unrecognizable. He was nothing like his father. "And you are not taking my mother anywhere."

"She needs a hospital."

"*I* know what she needs. And I won't let you take her. I don't want to hurt you. I want you to just walk away. This doesn't concern you. This is about my family, not yours."

"You and Tessa *are* my family. Parker was too."

"I don't want to hear his name." PJ waved the gun about wildly. "He wasn't my father. He was just my sperm donor. Mom is the only family I have, and I won't let you get in between us. Either you leave now, or I'll have to kill you."

* * * * *

7:47 A.M.

"Put me down," Tessa insisted, trying to get out of Jack Xander's arms.

"Honey, we need to get you out of here; you need to be in a hospital," Casey said, brushing at her hair.

She didn't want to say it out loud because she didn't want to upset her friends, but it was already too late.

A hospital wasn't going to help her.

She was dying.

PJ had gotten his wish.

She was going to die.

And he had been the one to cause it, albeit indirectly.

"He's going to kill Skylar," she said, still struggling to get free, but Jack had tightened his grip on her.

"Wyatt will talk him down," Casey soothed.

"No, he won't."

Tessa was sure of that.

She should have seen it. What Skylar had said was true. PJ was angry at her and Parker. Parker because he had died, and her because she couldn't get over it.

All of this was her fault.

She was the reason that all of those people had died, but she wasn't going to let her son take any more lives.

"Please, Jack." She turned her attention to the cop. Casey was her best friend, and there was no way she could convince her friend to let her walk into danger in her current condition, but she had never met Jack Xander. There was no emotional connection between them, she was much more likely to convince him to let her go. "He's my son, I can't let him kill anyone else."

"I don't know," Jack said, exchanging glances with his partner Xavier Montague. "I'm not sure you can even stand up. I don't know how you think you're going to be able to talk your son into putting the gun down and surrendering peacefully."

The same way she had done every difficult thing life had thrown at her.

"Because I have to," she replied simply.

"Tessa," Casey warned. "I made Wyatt bring me with him because we knew you were in bad shape, and I'm a doctor. Tess, honey ..." Casey took her hand. "... you're in worse shape than we thought. You need to go to the hospital. Now."

263

"I know," she said. That wasn't new information. But she *was* dying, and this might be the last thing she could do for someone else.

Besides, these were her wrongs to right.

She was the reason that PJ was like this.

She had been too wrapped up in grief to be the mother that he needed. She had spoiled him too much, made him think that he was the center of the world. She had buried her head in the sand when it came to his problems because she wanted to believe that her son didn't just look like his father, but that he was just like Parker.

But PJ was nothing like his father.

How could their son be like this?

Whatever the reasons, now she had to do something to stop him before this got any more out of hand than it already was.

"The only way we're all walking out of this alive, is if I can get him to put the gun down," she said firmly.

"All right," Jack reluctantly agreed. "You stay close to Wyatt. Xavier and I will check the house and make sure it's empty. Casey, you should go out to the car and stay with Sofia and Hayley."

"I'm staying here," Casey said, a scowl on her face.

Jack slowly lowered her legs and her feet touched the floor. Her body was so weak she honestly wasn't sure that she could physically do this, but she was going to have to find a way. Her legs wobbled wildly, and Jack kept an arm around her waist until she was steady enough to at least remain upright.

"Good luck," he whispered, then he and Xavier disappeared.

Tessa took a couple of steps and was pleased when she managed to stay on her feet.

"You and Tessa *are* my family. Parker was too," Skylar said.

"I don't want to hear his name." PJ was waving his gun about wildly. "He wasn't my father. He was just my sperm donor. Mom is the only family I have, and I won't let you get in between us. Either you leave now, or I'll have to kill you."

"No, you won't, PJ," she said, stepping out from the relative safety of the hall to the top of the staircase. She could feel Skylar's fear and annoyance that she hadn't already been taken out of here, but she had never relied on anyone to save her before and she wasn't going to start now.

"Mom," PJ looked surprised. "You're not in your room."

"No, I'm not." She took a step closer, so she was right on the edge of the stairs. In her condition, she probably wasn't strong enough to make it down them, so she better not try. "If you were angry with me, why didn't you ever say anything?"

"You were always sad. I didn't want to make it worse," he said, dropping his gaze to the floor.

"But I'm your mother. I would have done anything for you." That was true. There wasn't anything she wouldn't do for her son. She wasn't sure how she would have gotten over Parker, but if PJ had needed her to do it, she would have found a way.

"Don't you see, Mom?" He was looking up at her again. "The one thing I needed you to do, you couldn't. I know you loved him; I know that you still love him; I know that you couldn't get over him if you tried."

"I'm sorry."

"I don't want you to be sorry. I might have been angry that you were still grieving, but mostly, I was jealous. I always felt like you loved him more than me. I always felt like you just loved me because I was all you had left of him."

"That's not true, sweetheart. I loved your dad, even when I made mistakes and didn't always make the best decisions. I loved him more than life itself. I love you like that as well. You're not just a piece of Parker. I love you for you because you're my son." Tears were streaming down her cheeks. She had messed up her relationship with Parker and ended up losing him and then she had messed up her relationship with their son as well.

"Really?" PJ looked hopeful. "You really love me just for me?"

"Of course, baby. I wish you had told me all of this sooner."

"Me too."

The floor was starting to sway beneath her.

She really needed to lie down.

But she thought she was close to getting PJ to surrender.

Maybe if he did and she got to the hospital quickly enough there might still be a chance for her.

Especially since she had so much to live for.

Her son needed her.

She would do whatever it took to make sure he served his sentence in a psychiatric facility where he could get the help he needed, and she would be there for him every step of the way. She would make sure that he never again felt that she didn't really love him.

"Please put your gun down, honey. Please let Skylar put cuffs on you and take you to the station. Please don't make this any worse than it already is. I don't want to lose you, PJ. I lost your dad and you're all I have. I need you."

"You need me?" PJ asked. He was wavering, she could tell.

"Of course, I do. Please, PJ, please just put …"

A door slammed somewhere in the large house.

The explosion of the gun going off seemed to reverberate through her.

The shifting pain in her chest told her where the bullet had gone.

"Mom, I'm so sorry."

She heard the words, but they were far away.

Very far away.

She crumpled, but her landing was soft as Skylar caught her and laid her out on the floor.

"Casey!" he screamed, looking over his shoulder.

Something was shoved against the hole in her chest and she winced at the resulting pain.

"Tess, just hang on!" Skylar screamed at her.

The chances of her surviving even before she'd been shot were slim, but now she knew that she was dying.

She was cold.

The icy cold of death's fingers curled around her and dragged her along with it, back to its dark dungeon.

"Tess, just keep breathing, you'll be fine, we're getting help," Casey babbled beside her.

"Tess."

Was that Parker?

She looked around and saw him standing over Skylar's shoulder.

He was smiling at her and he held out his hand.

She reached out to take it.

She'd missed him so much.

Fingers pressed to her neck as Casey felt her pulse. She could feel them but then the sensation began to fade.

All sensation was fading.

"Come on, Tessa, fight," Skylar begged her, as he dragged her into his arms.

She was tired of fighting.

She didn't want to do it anymore.

She just wanted to rest and be with her husband again.

"Tessa ..." Casey sobbed.

As much as she hated leaving her friends behind, and the son who needed her, she lifted her hand and took hold of Parker's.

He led her out of this life and into what lay beyond.

* * * * *

8:14 A.M.

"Think she can talk him into giving up?"

Ryan looked at his partner, "I really don't know. I think if anyone can convince PJ to turn himself in, it's his mother."

"You're okay, right?" Paige asked—the third time she had

asked him that in the last ten minutes.

"Fine," he assured her. "PJ didn't hurt us. He tricked us into coming out here by texting us from Sophie's phone and pretending to be her. He tased us and then tied us up and put us in the trunk of a car for a few hours. Then he brought us in here at gunpoint and left us in the room with Tessa."

"It doesn't look like he was planning on having more houseguests," Paige said as they opened the next door and found another empty room. "We know the room he had Tessa in was set up for someone, and I'm guessing he has a room here. That means he didn't initially intend to have anyone else here."

"The impression I got from him was that bringing Sophie here was spur of the moment. I think if he had planned to have her here all along, he would have done it sooner—not waited until this close to when he intended to commit suicide."

"Hayley said that PJ and Sophie had been dancing around their feelings, and that PJ had finally kissed her. She said that Sophie felt like it was too soon after Dom for her to start dating again, but then she was having second thoughts. I'm guessing the kiss was more of a goodbye thing, but then when Sophie showed an interest in wanting more, PJ decided to bring her here."

"PJ doesn't know what he's doing anymore. Everything spun out of control, and I think he wants out, but he doesn't know how to get out. Killing has become his crutch. It was the only thing he had control over. If he feels like he's being backed into a corner, he could resort to that crutch."

Ryan opened the next door and found it empty as well. He knew Sophie had to be around here somewhere, but there had to be at least thirty bedrooms spread over two floors. It was taking too long to find her. PJ could lose it at any second and start shooting. He wanted his fifteen-year-old daughter far away from here before that happened.

"This door is locked," Paige said, rattling the handle of the next door.

Chances were, it was the one where Sophie was being kept.

"Keys," Paige smiled, lifting them off a hook beside the door.

"Teenage boys." Ryan shook his head as he took the set of keys and slid them into the lock.

The second he opened the door, something flew at him.

He wasn't expecting it and the force of the smaller body crashing into his sent them both crashing backward into the wall.

"Sophie, it's me. It's Dad," he said, as Paige helped him drag his daughter off him.

"Daddy?" Sophie froze and brushed her wild red hair out of her face so she could see him.

"Are you all right, baby?" he asked, looking her over, searching for any signs that she had been injured.

"I'm fine," Sophie half sobbed as she threw herself into his arms.

Ryan held his daughter close and breathed out a sigh of relief. Sofia was safe and out of the house, Sophie was okay, and as soon as he reassured his thumping heart that she really was all right, he would send her off to join Sofia and Hayley. If Tessa could talk her son into doing the right thing, they would all make it out of this alive, with the possible exception of Tessa, who was closer to death than he had ever seen anyone get while still actually being alive.

Reluctantly, he pulled Sophie—who had plastered herself against him—off his chest and held her at arm's length. "I'm so proud of you, you hear me?" She'd gone through more in the last six months than most adults did in an entire lifetime. He hoped that this didn't set her back, but he suspected that it would. "I need you to go with Paige now, okay? She's going to take you to your mom, and Hayley. Then she's going to stay with you until backup arrives." He raised a brow at Paige to see if she was okay with that, she nodded that she was.

They were so close to ending this.

Once PJ was in custody, it would all be over.

Then he heard the gunshot.

* * * * *

8:28 A.M.

"Did you hear that?" Xavier froze.

"Sounds like a gunshot," Jack said. "I knew I shouldn't have let Tessa try to talk PJ down."

"Who do you think he shot?" he asked as they both drew their weapons and headed back to the staircase. This place was a maze of corridors, like PJ had done it on purpose to confuse anyone should they stumble upon this place, which would give himself time to flee.

"Tessa," Jack said without hesitation.

"Is she even strong enough to talk to PJ?" When they'd left Tessa with Wyatt and Casey, she'd barely been able to stand. How did she think she was going to be able to hold a conversation where she had to convince a killer with a gun to turn himself in?

"I don't know if she's strong enough or not, but she's certainly determined enough."

They rounded a corner and almost walked straight into Ryan. "Did you find Sophie?" he asked.

"Yes, she and Paige are heading outside to wait with Sofia and Hayley. Did you hear a gunshot?"

"We did," Jack nodded grimly.

"Hey, over there." Ryan suddenly pointed to something behind them.

It was PJ.

"PJ, stop," Ryan stepped toward him.

"I didn't mean to," PJ sobbed. "It was an accident."

"I'm sure it was," Ryan soothed.

"I'm not going to prison," the teenager screamed and took off the way he'd come.

"I'll go after him; you two go check on Tessa," Xavier said, already running off after the kid.

They weaved through a couple more corridors, then burst out through a side door.

PJ paused and for a second, Xavier thought that he had realized he was never getting away, but then the world exploded, and he was thrown to the ground.

Sometime later, he woke up.

His ears were ringing.

The smell of smoke permeated his nostrils.

Groggily, Xavier dragged himself to his feet.

The mansion that he'd just left was on fire.

An explosion.

PJ had rigged the house to explode if he got caught.

Jack, Ryan, Paige, Sophie, Wyatt, Casey, and Tessa were still in there.

That realization snapped him out of his daze, and as he was about to head into the burning building, he heard footsteps. Xavier whipped around, but it wasn't PJ who appeared from the trees. It was Sofia and Hayley. He saw blood on both of them, but they were both moving, so he assumed neither of them was too badly injured.

"Is my mom in there?" Hayley asked, wiping at the blood trickling down her cheek.

"Ryan and Sophie?" Sofia asked.

"All in there. Are you two okay?"

"The car was knocked over by the blast, but we're both all right," Sofia told him. "We have to find the others."

"Did you see PJ?" Xavier assumed the teenager had fled, but there was no way to be sure. He could still be around here somewhere.

"No," Sofia said. "But assuming he did this," she waved her hand at the building, "to get away, then he's long gone."

"You two stay out here," he ordered.

"No," Sofia said firmly, that determined look in her gray eyes saying she had already made up her mind. Hayley looked just as determined.

"All right, we all go in, but we stick together." He knew it wasn't safe in there, but their friends and family were inside, and they couldn't just do nothing. Help was coming, but he didn't know when it would be here, and the others might not have very long left.

If they were even still alive.

Since Hayley's mother and Sofia's husband and daughter were in there, he didn't want to say that out loud, but the house had exploded. It was now on fire and parts of it had fallen down. There was a very real possibility that one or more people weren't making it out of there alive.

"Stay behind me," he said as he wrenched open the door he and PJ had left through, and all three of them stepped inside.

It was like stepping into hell.

Flames danced about, and parts of the walls lay in piles of rubble. There was thick smoke, and because all of the windows were boarded up, it was so dark you could hardly see where you were going. The explosion had obviously knocked out the electricity.

Xavier pulled out a flashlight and the three of them started their search.

He headed back toward the staircase because that was the last time they had all been together, and he knew that at least Wyatt, Casey, and Tessa were probably still there.

"Is that a light?" Hayley asked, suddenly pointing up ahead.

"I think it is," he said, then called out, "hello?"

"Xavier?" came the reply.

"Mom," Hayley said and started running forward.

Xavier tried to grab her. They had to move slowly, try to find a safe path through the debris, and running could be dangerous, but Hayley was too quick.

"Sophie was with Paige," he told Sofia, and she took off at a slow run toward the other light. With a sigh, he followed.

"Hayley, what are you doing in here?" Paige asked as Hayley threw herself into her mother's arms.

"Looking for you," Hayley sobbed.

"You have to get out of here," Paige told her daughter.

"Ryan is still in here," Sofia said as she wrapped her arms around Sophie.

Paige and Sophie were also both streaked with blood and dirt. Sophie was limping, and Paige had one arm braced around her ribs. They were hurt but it didn't appear to be anything life threatening.

"You should all go outside. I'll look for the others," he announced.

"I'm not leaving without Ryan," Sofia countered.

"Neither am I," Paige added.

"You're hurt," he told Paige, nodding at her chest. "And the girls shouldn't be in here. The four of you go back down there, get outside, and wait for help. It shouldn't be far away. I'll keep looking."

"All right." Paige sighed. "Be careful, this place could come down at any minute."

Exactly.

That's why he needed to get the girls and their mothers out. If Paige wasn't hurt, he could have used her help, but if she had broken ribs, they could puncture a lung.

It was safer for him to go alone.

He watched to make sure they were on their way before he headed farther into the belly of the beast.

It was hard to know where he was going. Everything looked the same in the hazy red glow, but he thought he was making progress. He thought things were starting to look familiar and when he rounded the next corner, he came into the foyer.

Part of the ceiling at the top of the stairs had collapsed.

That was right where they had left Tessa, Wyatt, and Casey. Had the three of them managed to get out? At least one of them was probably shot, and Tessa had already been in bad shape.

"Wyatt?" he called out as he took the stairs three at a time.

"Go away," came the hoarse reply.

Xavier reached the top, and even in the bad light, he could see the blood.

A lot of blood.

From that alone, he knew that someone was dead.

"Tessa?" he asked, crouching down beside the man who was holding two people in his arms.

"PJ shot her," Wyatt said softly. "She died before the explosion."

There was more blood than what had come from just one person. "Casey?"

"When the ceiling collapsed, she was hit in the head. I think she died instantly," came the dull reply.

A double blow.

Wyatt had lost his wife and the woman he thought of as a younger sister in one go.

Xavier knew the man was suffering, but they had to keep moving. Jack and Ryan could still be in here; they could be injured and in need of help.

"We have to go," he said.

"I can't." Wyatt finally looked up.

"You have to. This place is going to come down around us."

"I don't care."

"Jack and Ryan are still in here somewhere. They have families, young kids, we need to find them."

Wyatt was wavering, as much as he hated the idea of leaving Tessa and Casey behind, he knew that they were gone. There was nothing that could be done for them, but Jack and Ryan could still be alive.

Ever so gently, Wyatt laid Casey and Tessa's bodies down and staggered to his feet. He was covered in blood, but Xavier suspected none of it was his own.

"We have to hurry," he urged. He had a bad feeling.

The flames were closing in, claiming more and more of the house, and right behind them he heard a crash as another wall crumbled.

As soon as Wyatt was on his feet, they took off. Earlier, he and Jack had met up with Ryan on the second floor. He'd followed PJ down a small flight of stairs near the door they had exited through, and when he'd come back in, he'd stayed on the ground floor. Maybe Jack and Ryan were still up here. That made sense since they were coming back to where they had last seen Wyatt, Casey, and Tessa.

They had been walking for about three or four minutes when he saw them.

Jack lay on the floor. Ryan was on his knees beside him, with his hands pressed to his brother's abdomen where a piece of wood was embedded.

"Ryan," he called out as he and Wyatt jogged over.

"He's lost a lot of blood." Ryan's terrified blue eyes shone an eerie orangey red in the fire's glow. "We have to get him out. Now."

"Moving him could kill him," Xavier said.

"Leaving him here *will* kill him," Ryan countered.

"Here." Wyatt thrust a long plank of wood at them that at one time had been a door to one of the many bedrooms he and Jack had searched earlier looking for any other victims.

They could use it as a stretcher, carry Jack out without risking moving the wood and causing more internal damage. "Did you tie that around the wood to keep it steady?" he asked Ryan.

"I did. I rolled up my shirt, circled it around the wood, then used Jack's shirt to secure it."

With as much care as they could, they rolled Jack on his side, then lowered him back down onto the door. Then they picked it up and began to carry him out.

PJ had killed Tessa.

The explosion had killed Casey Wyatt.

Xavier prayed it hadn't killed Jack as well.

AUGUST 10TH

10:59 A.M.

"Anything?" Paige asked as the door opened and Xavier walked into the room. She and Ryan were at the station finishing up paperwork after what had happened yesterday at PJ Bell's house.

She wanted to get it over and done with as quickly as possible so she could get home.

Hayley had nightmares about the explosion last night. Her daughter didn't usually suffer from bad dreams, even after everything she'd been through as a small child, and after being abducted and held prisoner six months ago. She rarely had them. That she was having them now let Paige know just how much her daughter was suffering.

Paige didn't think she could do this anymore.

She used to love her job, even after she had her kids, even after she had been tortured by her obsessive and murderous stalker. None of that had changed how she felt about being a cop.

But now something was different.

Now, she didn't get that same feeling.

Now, when she came to work, she felt like she was just going through the motions.

She had lost her passion.

Last night, after they had put Hayley and Arianna to bed, she and Elias had talked about it. He was fine with her retiring from the force and doing something else. She could go to work full time at the center for abused women and children that she helped run with Sofia, Laura, and Annabelle, or she could do something else. She wasn't sure yet. All she knew was that she couldn't keep doing this.

"Paige?" Xavier sat down beside her, and she realized that she had asked a question and then forgotten to listen to the answer.

She hadn't really gotten much sleep last night. Between her talk with her husband, Hayley's nightmares, and the fact that her broken ribs made lying in any position painful and uncomfortable, she wasn't able to sleep.

Not just lying down. Sitting down wasn't comfortable either. She shifted in her chair, wincing as the movement jostled her chest.

She knew she was lucky to have walked out of that explosion with just a couple of broken ribs and some bumps and scratches from when she had been thrown against a wall.

They had all been lucky.

Sofia and Hayley had nothing more than cuts and bruises from the car being knocked over. Sophie had a sprained ankle from being knocked down. Ryan had some bruising and a nasty gash to his arm from the debris that cascaded down when the bomb went off. And Xavier also had nothing more than bumps and scratches.

Things could have been so much worse, but they'd lucked out.

All of them except Casey Wyatt.

And Jack.

Casey had been killed instantly when debris landed on her head, and Jack was currently in the ICU fighting for his life after making it through lifesaving surgery yesterday morning.

Whether he would live, none of them knew yet.

PJ Bell deserved to be punished for everything that he'd done. He had murdered Melanie Gardner, Lizzie Landry, Lucas Mianta, and Cassandra Stanton. He had killed his own mother, and inadvertently, Casey Wyatt. He deserved to spend the rest of his life in prison.

But whether he would, no one knew that yet either.

"Paige, you okay?"

"I'm fine," she assured Xavier, "just sore and tired. And yes, once we're finished up here, I'll go home and get some rest. So, do we know anything yet?'

"No." Xavier shook his head, looking both disappointed and angry.

They were all angry about how things had gone down.

They had been so close.

According to Wyatt, Tessa had all but talked PJ into putting down his gun and surrendering peacefully when a loud noise somewhere in the house—most likely Sophie charging at Ryan when they had unlocked the door to her room, sending both of them crashing into the wall—had spooked him and he'd fired the gun, shooting his mother in the chest. Tessa had bled out in minutes and died in Wyatt's arm.

If he hadn't been spooked, they'd have him in custody already and no one else would have died.

"Nothing?" Ryan asked.

"Nothing," Xavier echoed.

"Have they been through the whole house yet?" Paige asked.

"Preliminary search of the house turned up nothing," Xavier replied. "They still have to go back through once the house is made structurally safe, but we know he wasn't in there when the bomb went off, so I don't think they're going to find anything." Although every inch of the house would be searched in case PJ had gone back inside to look for his mother and been killed as the building collapsed. None of them really expected his body to be discovered there.

"Which means he's still out there somewhere," Ryan said, his gaze moving to the window as though the man he sought was just outside.

She knew what her partner was worried about.

Sophie.

PJ believed he was in love with Sophie, and with his mother now dead, they couldn't be sure that he wouldn't go after her, try to get her back.

"I don't think he'd be stupid enough to make a move on Sophie," Xavier said to Ryan, apparently also suspecting what was worrying him.

"I hope he isn't," Ryan said, but didn't look convinced.

"Where would he go?" she wondered aloud. "His mother is dead, and I don't think he would try to go back home. He knows Wyatt would arrest him, and he has to know that the rest of his family would turn him in too. He wouldn't try to track down Isaac Worthington because he would have to know that the man is likely to kill him for killing Tessa. He doesn't have any friends, so he can't hide out with them. As far as we know, he doesn't own any other property, so he's not hiding out there. The kid is rich. He grew up in a mansion, on a huge estate, where whatever he wanted, he got. I can't see him being able to live rough until he figures out a plan. So, where would he go?"

"For all we know, he had another hideout already planned, in case the house became compromised," Ryan said. Her partner had the same tone in his voice she knew was in her own. A tone of weariness. And not just weariness from the fast pace of the case they'd been working and the events of the day before, but a weariness of needing a change in his life.

She wondered whether he was having the same thoughts as she was about possibly leaving the force.

Paige had to admit it would be easier to leave if Ryan left too. They had been partners for almost two decades now and it was hard to imagine not working side by side every day.

"I don't know where he's hiding out, but I think I know where he'll be tomorrow," Xavier said thoughtfully.

"Where?" Ryan asked.

"The funeral," Xavier replied.

"His mother's funeral," she said, catching on. Xavier was right. If there was one thing that PJ wouldn't be able to resist doing— even if he knew in doing it, he was taking a big risk—it would be saying goodbye to his mother at Tessa's funeral, which would be held tomorrow morning.

"I don't think Wyatt or Tessa's family would have a problem with us staking out the funeral," Ryan said. "They want PJ caught as much as we do, only probably for different reasons."

Paige didn't think Daniel, Wyatt, Winter, and the rest of Tessa's family had different reasons for wanting PJ caught, just mixed reasons. They wanted him caught because of what he had done to Tessa and all those other people, but they also loved him.

You couldn't turn off those feelings just because someone did something you didn't like, or even if they did something you hated.

PJ's family still loved him, and they were no doubt afraid for him, alone and scared and on the run. They would know that PJ might never stop killing, and that if he didn't surrender quietly when he was eventually found, that he would be shot and killed. They would know that the safest place for PJ was in police custody. Then he would be able to get the help that he obviously needed.

"You two may as well head home and try to rest. I'll organize surveillance for the funeral and set everything up," Xavier offered.

As appealing as that sounded, and whatever decisions she was going to end up making about her future, right now she was a cop. And a cop who always saw through every case she was assigned to the very end.

They weren't at the end of this case yet.

They wouldn't be until PJ Bell was safely in custody.

She would stay, help Xavier set up things for the funeral tomorrow, and then she'd head home and spend some time with her family. Hopefully she and Hayley would be tired enough to both sleep well tonight.

"I'll organize getting the church rigged with cameras. Why don't you organize a team to be there during the funeral," she said to Xavier, pulling the bottle of pain pills from her bag, unscrewing the top and tipping a couple into her hand.

"You sure you're up to it?" Xavier asked.

Paige swallowed the pills and a couple of mouthfuls of water from her water bottle. "Positive."

* * * * *

8:07 P.M.

Her eyes burned.

That was the only thing she felt.

Other than abject terror.

Laura sat at her husband's bedside in ICU and stared at Jack's face.

It was as if her mind thought if she stared at him long enough and hard enough, that she could will him to wake up.

Family and friends kept popping in and out of the small ICU cubicle to check on her. She knew they were worried about Jack, and about her, but they were ruining her concentration. She wanted to focus on her husband and nothing else.

She didn't care that she was dressed in the same clothes she'd put on over thirty-six hours ago, or that she hadn't been home in forty-eight hours. She didn't care that she hadn't eaten or slept since she realized that Ryan and Sofia had disappeared.

She didn't care about herself right now.

All she cared about was Jack.

The last two days were nothing but a blur.

Arriving at Ryan and Sofia's house and learning they were missing. Spending the night at the precinct as Jack and Paige and Xavier tried to figure out what had happened.

Then came the phone call.

The one that said that Jack had been hurt and to head straight to the hospital to meet him.

She didn't remember who drove her to the hospital.

By the time they arrived here, Jack had already been rushed into surgery and she had been forced to sit in the waiting room and pray he would survive.

As soon as she had been told he'd made it through surgery and was allowed to see him in the intensive care unit, she had refused to leave.

Zach and Rosie had been in to see him once, but she didn't want the kids seeing their dad like this. Jack was so big and strong, and if he didn't survive, she wanted them to remember him like that. Not like this.

She wanted Jack to quit his job.

Laura knew it wasn't fair. She knew that he loved being a cop and that, in reality, this was only the third time in his two-decade long stint as a police officer that he'd been hurt in the line of duty.

The first time was before their lives had intersected again and they'd gotten back together. He'd been young then, less experienced, more concerned with catching bad guys than in coming home safely. He'd still had that air of immortality that only youth possessed. Jack, and his partner Rose—who had been killed almost fifteen years ago by the man who wanted to destroy her, the same man who had inadvertently brought her and Jack back together, the same Rose who her daughter was named after—had been chasing some junkie who had carjacked a father and his two young children into an alley. The guy had hidden, waited until they passed him, then smashed Jack over the head with a plank of wood. He'd spent the next few days in the hospital recovering from the injuries.

The second time her husband had been hurt on the job was ten years ago. She had been pregnant with Rosie. They had been having dinner with Ryan, and Sofia who had been sick with the flu for days had collapsed. At the hospital, she'd met a teenage girl with a wild story of being kidnapped and held captive. While investigating whether or not the girl's story was true, Jack and Ryan had been in the house in question when it exploded.

Explosions.

This was the second time her husband had been injured in one.

Last time he had been knocked out, but other than a few bruises and some scrapes, he'd been okay.

This time ...

She didn't even want to think it.

Even the possibility that Jack wasn't going to wake up was too terrifying to consider.

What would she do without him?

How would she raise their twelve- and ten-year-olds on her own?

Why hadn't she told him one last time that she loved him?

When Hayley had said she could lead them to where PJ and Sophie would meet up, everything had happened so quickly. Jack, Xavier, Ryan, Paige, Skylar and Casey Wyatt, and Hayley had all rushed off. She had offered to come along to see if she had better luck talking to PJ, because sometimes it was easier to talk to a stranger than someone you knew, but Jack had said it was too dangerous.

They had exchanged a hurried goodbye and he'd been off.

That was it.

That could be the last time she ever got to talk to her husband.

Jack had been an amazing husband. He had been so supportive as she battled her agoraphobia. He had never once gotten annoyed with her about it, even when she was annoyed with herself. He always told her that he was proud of her, which could sound condescending from the wrong person, but with him it was sincere. He knew how much she'd been through and how hard it had been for her to overcome it, and he was proud of her for not giving up.

Laura was terrified that without Jack's support she would slip back into old ways. That she would lock herself, and her children, away from the world and hide, because hiding was sometimes easier than facing what you were afraid of.

She reached out a trembling hand but stopped just short of taking Jack's.

It was almost like she was afraid to touch him.

That somehow her overly tired and stressed-out mind had decided that staring at him could will him to wake up, but touching him would push him over the edge and into death.

She needed to hold her kids and cry and draw strength from them, but she didn't want to scare them. When they had been here earlier, she'd been as positive as she could be, and she knew that the rest of the family would also rally around them and make sure they remained hopeful.

Very slowly, she lowered her hand until it touched Jack.

The second she made contact, the curtain enclosing the cubicle was pulled back and she jerked her hand away as it flew to her mouth.

"Sorry, didn't mean to startle you," her brother-in-law Mark said.

"It's okay," she said, dragging in a shaky breath. Her nerves were frayed, and she was balancing precariously on the edge of sanity. One little push and she was pretty sure she would fall apart.

"How are you doing?" Mark asked as he walked over to the bed and looked his brother over.

"How is *Jack* doing?" she asked pointedly. Why was Mark worrying about her? She wasn't the one who'd had a fifteen-inch chunk of wood removed from her abdomen. She wasn't the one who'd lost almost thirty percent of her blood volume and barely made it through surgery. She wasn't the one fighting for her life.

"He's the same. Not any better, but not any worse. Now, how are *you*?" he asked just as pointedly.

"Fine," she said, brushing off his concern. She didn't want to be fussed over. It made her uncomfortable, and it made her feel like they were already preparing for the worst and were ready to try to help her through it.

"Laura," Mark started in his doctor voice, the one that grated on her already flimsy nerves, "you haven't had anything to eat or drink in forty-eight hours. You haven't slept. You haven't left this room in over a day. You have to take care of yourself or you're going to end up needing a hospital bed too."

"I'm not hungry," she said, and meant it. The thought of food made her stomach churn.

"I'm not surprised," Mark said. "You're past hungry, you're exhausted." He came and stood beside her, looking down at her with brotherly concern.

She loved Jack's family.

After she had first started attempting to deal with her agoraphobia after ten years locked away in her apartment, it had been Jack's family, not her own, she had been more comfortable with. It was spending time with them that had helped her learn to be around people again.

How would she feel around them if Jack died?

Laura knew that they would always be her family. They were Zach and Rosie's grandparents and aunts and uncles, and cousins, but if Jack was dead, then technically, they wouldn't be her in-laws anymore. They would still love her. Jack's death wouldn't change their feelings for her, but things would never be the same.

"I'm worried about you, Laura," Mark told her. "You're going to crash soon if you don't do something about it. Jack is heavily sedated; he's not going to wake up for hours. Let's go down to the doctors' lounge, you can eat a sandwich, drink some water, take a nap, then come straight back here."

"But he'll know I'm not here," she protested.

"I'll stay with him."

"I don't know," she wavered.

"Okay, then I'll make it easy for you. You need to leave. ICU visiting hours are over. You're only here anyway because I work here; otherwise, they would have sent you home already. You agree to go to the lounge for a couple of hours and I won't make you go home and come back tomorrow morning."

"You're blackmailing me," she muttered.

"I know," Mark replied cheerfully.

Despite her fears, she couldn't help but chuckle. "Two hours?"

"Two hours," he agreed.

"All right," she reluctantly agreed.

Laura stood and immediately felt herself falling toward unconsciousness.

The last thing she remembered was Mark screaming for help as she fell into his waiting arms.

AUGUST 11TH

9:56 A.M.

He would search every corner of the world if he had to.

He would never give up.

He would find PJ Bell if it was the last thing he ever did.

Wyatt would never stop thinking of PJ as a son, but Tessa was the little sister he'd never had, and he wouldn't stand for anyone hurting her. He would find PJ and he would drag the kid kicking and screaming to prison.

And if PJ left him no choice, then he would kill him.

The only thing he wouldn't allow was PJ to get away.

That just couldn't happen.

Unfortunately for PJ, he had nothing else to live for now.

His wife was dead, Tessa was dead, his kids were adults with their own kids, partners, and lives.

He had nothing left.

There was nothing tying him down.

He would go to whatever lengths it took to end this.

After that, he didn't know what he would do, but he wasn't ready to think that far ahead yet.

Right now, he had to focus on finding PJ.

If he let all the other emotions that were brimming just beneath the surface come trickling in, he wouldn't be able to do what had to be done.

Right now, though, he shouldn't be thinking of PJ.

It was Tessa's funeral. He should be focused on saying goodbye to his friend. But he knew that PJ would likely be turning up here, probably in a disguise, probably hanging around the edges, maybe only coming to the cemetery where Tessa would be buried beside her husband, but PJ would be here somewhere.

Knowing that made it hard to concentrate.

He was sitting beside Daniel at the front of the church. The minister was speaking, and then there would be the eulogies, but all he could do was keep scanning the mourners, searching for anyone that looked out of place.

Despite the fact that she kept to herself and virtually lived like a recluse, a lot of people had shown up for the service. Aside from family, there were friends of Parker's who had grown close to Tessa after his death. There were Tessa's friends from school—all who were left anyway. There were a few people from the companies Tessa owned. There were some other victims of crimes that Tessa had become close with while trying to help them. There was even Sofia Xander and her daughter Sophie, who, despite what PJ had done to them, had come to say goodbye, knowing that PJ very well may be here.

And there were the cops.

At least a dozen of them were sitting dispersed amongst the mourners, analyzing each person to see whether they could be PJ. Wyatt had wanted to check IDs of everyone who entered the church, but Xavier Montague—who was heading the case now that Jack Xander was fighting for his life in the hospital—had said that would be too upsetting. They had come to a compromise. Anyone Wyatt couldn't identify, one of the cops would approach and get a name, and another cop would run that person through the system. If they turned out to be a legitimate person, they would move on.

The problem with that was that Tessa knew how to create a foolproof new identity that could withstand the closest of scrutiny. She'd done it before, and if she knew how to do it, then there was the very real possibility that PJ did too.

So far, Wyatt hadn't seen anyone here that he didn't know. If PJ was going to try to attend the funeral, it was much more likely he'd do it at the cemetery where he could better hide. He wasn't stupid. He'd have to know that the cops would be looking for him here and expecting him to come.

Someone nudged him in the ribs and Wyatt turned to see Daniel glaring at him.

"Stop wriggling," Daniel whispered.

"Sorry," he whispered back. He knew how hard this was for Daniel and Matilda and their kids, and Winter and her family, and his kids and their families too. Knowing that they had lived with and spent time with PJ and not seen the anger inside him haunted all of them.

This could have been avoided if someone had just noticed it.

Or been strong enough to talk to Tessa about their concerns.

If he had known that PJ was this angry and this dangerous, he would have told Tessa, even if it had upset her and she had blamed herself.

"I don't think he's going to come," Daniel whispered.

Since he believed it was actually likely that PJ might show up and that the funeral or the burial service could wind up turning into a shootout, or at the very least, PJ would cause a scene, he had sat the whole family down this morning and explained to them that there would be several cops in attendance. They had all been understandably distressed. This was supposed to be a chance for them to say goodbye to someone they loved, and no one wanted to see the funeral turn into a circus.

But PJ wasn't thinking about that.

He was only thinking about himself and what he wanted.

Which was why all of this had happened.

If PJ had just told his mother that he felt like she loved his father more than him, Tessa would have done whatever it took to make sure her son understood that she loved him and his father equally.

His phone buzzed in his pocket.

He should leave it.

He was at a funeral.

He needed to say goodbye to Tessa because she was gone, and she wasn't coming back. If he didn't say goodbye, he wouldn't get closure. In just a couple of days, he would be back in this same church saying goodbye to his wife.

If it was important, then whoever was calling would leave a message.

With a sigh he slid off the pew, ignoring Daniel's irritated glare and the questioning glances of both his family and the cops in the church. Walking quietly through the church's back door, out into the small yard, he pulled out his phone.

According to the screen, it was an unknown number calling him.

PJ?

Had he realized he needed help and decided to reach out?

"Hello?" he answered the phone.

"I know where he is. Do you want me to take care of it or do you want to?" a voice said without preamble.

Not PJ, it was Isaac Worthington.

And it seemed he had managed to find out where PJ was hiding out.

Wyatt knew what Isaac meant by take care of it. If he left Isaac to handle PJ, then he would kill him. Isaac had no emotional attachment to PJ. He had no emotional attachment to anyone other than his daughter Rebecca and Tessa. He tolerated anyone who brought Tessa happiness, but he would kill anyone who hurt her.

And not quickly.

He was angry with PJ for what he'd done, but he didn't want the kid dead—at his own hand or someone else's. He wanted him safely locked away where he couldn't hurt anyone else, and where he could get the help he so obviously needed.

He knew it must have been hard for Isaac to call him and give him the opportunity to take care of PJ. And that he was no doubt only doing it because he knew it was what Tessa would have wanted.

"Tell me where he is and I'll handle it," he told Isaac.

* * * * *

12:03 P.M.

This was not how he wanted things to turn out.

He hadn't meant for the gun to go off.

It had just been an accident.

He'd been startled.

Something had crashed somewhere inside the house and he had thought it was the cops coming for him.

PJ had thought that they were going to wrestle him to the ground, snap handcuffs on him, then toss him in a police car and drag him off to prison.

He'd panicked.

That was it.

Panic.

But in that one moment of panic, he had done the one thing he had been convinced he wanted to do, up until the very second he did it.

He had killed his mother.

It was what he had planned all along, albeit a couple of days early.

The moment the bullet pierced her chest, he had felt physical pain, like the bullet had hit him too.

He had wanted to go to her, to hold her, to tell her he was sorry, to beg for her forgiveness, to beg her to live, but he couldn't.

He wanted to take it back, but he couldn't do that either.

All he had been able to do was run.

Anything else was just going to get him caught and thrown in jail, where he would never be allowed out.

So, that's what he'd done.

He had run.

But they had followed.

Again, he had panicked and activated the fail-safe.

In the event that something went wrong and he'd had no choice but to abandon the plan, he had rigged the house with explosives. With Detective Xavier Montague close on his heels, he had only just managed to get out of the house so he could set off the bomb.

He hadn't realized there were so many people inside at the time. He knew that Wyatt was there, and he'd seen Casey, too, but he hadn't known that Xavier Montague was there until the man had been chasing him. Ryan and Sofia Xander must have gotten out of their room at the same time Tessa had, because Ryan, as well as Jack Xander, had been with Xavier. When he'd gotten out of the house, he'd seen Sofia and Hayley Hood staggering from a car that was lying on its side toward the house.

Setting the bomb off knowing that his beloved Sophie was almost definitely inside the house had been awful.

But what choice did he have?

It was kill or be killed.

Activating the bomb was the only thing he could do.

He had been gone before more cops and fire trucks and ambulances arrived at the estate, but he had hacked the hospital's system—just like he had hacked into the police department's system to get information on his father's old cases—to make sure that no one had died. According to what he had seen, everyone but Casey had been treated at the hospital, and that only Jack Xander was in critical condition.

Casey was dead.

He felt bad about that, he really did, but he couldn't change anything.

He couldn't bring her back, just like he couldn't bring back his mother.

Now that he had said goodbye, he had to decide what he was going to do next.

PJ knew that Wyatt and the cops had expected him to show up at his mother's funeral today, but he wasn't stupid. He knew that they were expecting that. He knew that they were waiting for him.

In a lot of ways, he was his parents' son. He had his father's sensible, practical side, and his mother's intuition and innate ability to predict what people were going to do.

It was what had helped him avoid being caught twice already and what had led him to not attend the funeral today. He had found his own way to say goodbye, something that the cops would never expect him to do.

Instead of trying to sneak into the funeral in a disguise or hide out at the graveyard, he had gone a different route.

He had found out which funeral home had his mother's body. Then he had chosen the mortician who looked most like him who worked there, broken into the young man's house, knocked him out, tied him up, and then impersonated him. It had been surprisingly easy. No one had suspected anything. He had shown up at the morgue, found his mom's body, said his apologies and his goodbyes, then snuck back out.

With his mother dead and the cops looking for him, there was nothing tying him to this place. He could move somewhere far away from here, or he could end his own life tomorrow like he had initially planned to.

PJ wasn't sure yet.

One thing he did know was that he couldn't hang around at the mortician's house for much longer. The longer he stayed, the greater the chances that he would be found out. He hadn't killed the young man, he'd just kept him drugged up. When he left, the guy would eventually wake up and no doubt run straight to the cops to tell them about the kid who had broken in, knocked him out, and kept him drugged. The cops wouldn't necessarily link him to the crime; at least, not at first. But once they realized how the mortician was related to his mother, then they would no doubt conclude it had been him.

He wished he knew what he should do next.

Part of him believed he should die. After all, he had taken several lives including his own mother's. And he was afraid that if he lived, he would never be free of the compulsion to kill. He wasn't strong enough to resist its pull on him, and he knew that eventually, no matter how hard he attempted to control it, he would kill more people.

Tomorrow he would be sixteen. He should celebrate his birthday the way he had intended. It was the safest option.

Should he hide out here until then?

Should he get in his car and just drive?

Should he find somewhere else to hide?

Or should he just end his life now?

PJ fiddled with the gun in his hands.

One little bullet and it would all be over.

Lift the gun, put it in his mouth, pull the trigger.

It was so simple.

It would be a quick death, probably quicker than he deserved, given what he had done.

He lifted the gun up and stared at it.

"Don't, PJ."

The voice startled him, and he jumped up and spun around.

Wyatt.

Somehow Wyatt had found him and was standing in the living room door.

"How did you …?" He trailed off, realizing the answer even as he was asking the question. "Isaac." It was the only thing that made sense. Even if he had decided to live, he doubted Isaac would have allowed him to. The man loved his mother and would have slaughtered anyone who dared hurt her.

"Smart plan," Wyatt said. "Impersonating the mortician so you could say your goodbyes to your mom. We didn't think of that. We weren't looking for you there. If it hadn't been for Isaac, you'd have gotten away with it."

He didn't care.

He deserved to die.

Whether it be by his own hand or Wyatt's or even Isaac's, he didn't care.

He had killed his mother.

The only person in the world who really loved him.

All these years, he had been wrong.

He'd thought that she would trade him for his father. He thought that the only thing she loved about him was his resemblance to his namesake. He'd thought that she didn't want him. That she didn't love him.

But he had been wrong.

So many years wasted in anger.

He wished he could take them back.

He wished that he could start over, but life didn't work that way.

"It's not too late, PJ," Wyatt said.

That was a lie.

They both knew that it was.

"I don't want to talk," he said. He was too tired to talk. He was too tired to do anything. He was tired of being tired. He was tired of being.

"We don't have to talk. I can take you someplace where you can rest. We can find a way to make things better."

More lies.

He was sick of lies.

He was sick of everything.

He didn't want to be here anymore.

He didn't like this world.

What lay beyond it?

He wished there was a way to find out.

When he was dead, would he find his parents? Would they finally be a family? Would they finally be happy?

PJ wanted to find out.

"Don't do it, PJ," Wyatt warned. "I don't want to hurt you, and I don't want to see you hurt yourself. Put the gun down and come with me. Whatever happens, you're not alone. You have me and Daniel, Matilda and Winter, and the rest of the family. We're all here for you."

How could his family want to be around for him after what he'd done?

It was just another lie.

He was done with lies.

He lifted the gun, pointed it at Wyatt, and the shot came almost immediately.

Death was instantaneous.

AUGUST 12ᵀᴴ

One second, he was lost in oblivion.

The next, he was lying in a hospital bed.

Jack's eyes snapped open, and despite the burning pain in his stomach, the first thing he noticed was Laura.

His wife was sitting in a chair beside his bed. She held his hand, but she was staring blankly into space.

He didn't have to imagine what she had gone through worrying that he wasn't going to make it. Five years ago, she had been nearly killed by a husband determined to get back his wife and daughter who'd fled for their lives. He had sat beside her as she lay in a bed in ICU, fighting for her life. Ironically, she had been stabbed in the stomach in pretty much the same location where he had been impaled by a piece of debris in the explosion.

It was odd. He knew he'd been unconscious for a period of time, and he knew he'd been in an out of consciousness after the explosion, but what he did remember was crystal clear.

He remembered the pain of the piece of wood embedding itself in his stomach. He remembered his brother performing first aid. He remembered being carried through the burning building. He remembered the fear of dying and leaving his wife and children alone. He remembered the pain; he remembered the smell of the smoke, the way it burned his eyes, its heat, the sound of the walls crumbling around them.

And he knew his wife had sat at his side the entire time he'd been here.

Jack opened his mouth, but when he tried to talk, he found his throat was dry, and all that came out was a croak.

The noise startled her, and she jumped a mile.

Something was wrong.

He could feel it rolling off her.

With him?

Was he more seriously hurt than he felt? Other than a dull throbbing pain radiating from his stomach, he felt okay.

"You're awake." Laura bounded to her feet when she turned and saw his eyes were open. "Mark," she called out, her voice a little too shrill.

Something was definitely wrong.

Barely a moment passed before the curtain was ripped back and his youngest brother appeared. Mark had probably been right outside, hovering, hoping that he'd wake up soon.

"I'm fine," he croaked, forcing the words out of his dry throat.

"Drink this." Mark held a straw to his lips, and he took a couple of sips. The cool liquid soothed his burning throat and immediately refreshed him.

"I'm fine," he said again, stronger this time.

Mark gave him an appraising once-over then nodded. "You will be. You were lucky. Laura, how are you feeling?"

Panic filled his wife's face and she shook her head at his brother in an almost frantic manner.

He'd been right, something *was* wrong. "Laura, are you all right?"

"Fine, fine," she said vigorously.

Too vigorously.

She was hiding something from him.

Mark had agreed that he was doing well, and he'd asked how Laura was doing, so this was about her, not him. Maybe his brother was just concerned that Laura had refused to take care of herself while he'd been out of it. That sounded like his wife, but he sensed this went deeper than that.

"What's wrong?" he asked, glaring from his wife to his brother and back again. He didn't want to be coddled or lied to.

"Laura fainted," Mark said, shooting Laura a pointed scowl like they had already discussed this but had opposing opinions on sharing this information with him.

Laura frowned back. "It was nothing," she said quickly.

Since he knew he wasn't going to get anything out of his wife, he turned his attention to his brother. "What's wrong with her?" he asked, panic slicing through him. What could have happened in the last couple of days? Surely, he hadn't been out any longer than that.

Could he?

"I'll let you two talk," Mark said with another pointed glance. "Then I'll come in and check you over properly." His brother's face softened, and the fear he'd felt shone in his blue eyes. "I'm really glad you're okay, Jack."

When they were alone, he studied his wife. She was jittery and he could see her trembling; her gaze kept jumping around the room, looking at anything but him.

What was going on?

What could his wife be scared to tell him?

"Come sit here," he said, patting the bed beside him.

"I don't want to hurt you," Laura said, her gaze lingering on him no longer than a couple of seconds before it darted away again.

"I don't care, come here," he said in a voice that bordered on ordering. He couldn't help it; he was scared. His pain and discomfort had faded into the background. He needed to know what was going on with his wife.

Laura moved slowly, but she came to perch on the side of the bed. Jack thought he was going to have to drag out of her whatever was going on, but she blurted out, "You got what you wanted."

What he wanted?

He had no idea what she was talking about.

His head was a little fuzzy from all the drugs he'd been given. Maybe that was why he didn't know what she meant.

"What I wanted?" he echoed.

"The other night," she said, twisting her hands in her lap.

Then it clicked.

He could feel his eyes grow wide. "Are you pregnant?"

"Yes," she said, shuddering, sending tears trickling down her cheeks. "I know it's not likely for someone my age to get pregnant so quickly and so easily, but I fainted and Mark ran tests. I'm pregnant."

Pregnant.

They were having another baby.

A huge grin spread over his face. That news was the best medicine in the world. Better than any drugs the hospital could give him.

"Why would you be scared to tell me that?" he asked, unable to wipe the grin off his face.

"I was scared thinking I might have to raise two kids on my own and deal with a difficult pregnancy, then the birth, and raising a baby by myself. And I'm so scared ..."

She trailed off, but he knew what she'd been going to say.

What she *wanted* to say but was too scared to.

Laura was afraid that his job was going to get him killed.

He had always wanted to be a cop. For as long as he could remember, he had known that he was going to follow his father and his grandfather into the police force. There would have been a time, probably even just a couple of months ago, where the idea of being anything but a detective would never have even crossed his mind.

Now, he reached for his wife's hands. "I'm going to retire."

"I can't ask you to do that," she said, squeezing his hands. "You love your job."

"But not more than I love you and our family," he said, his mind already made up. They would need to talk about it later, discuss the details. He would have to decide what else he was going to do, but he knew that his decision was best for himself and his family.

"I love you so much." Laura leaned over and lightly touched her lips to his.

The door burst open and Zach and Rosie came rushing in.

"Daddy," Rosie said, stopping just short of throwing herself at the bed. "Uncle Mark said you were awake, are you okay?"

"I'm going to be fine, princess," he told his daughter. He was sore and he was tired, but he felt great. They were having a baby. He couldn't believe it. Although he had wanted one, he hadn't ever really thought it would happen, given their ages. But it had. In nine months, they would be back in the hospital having baby number three.

Laura caught his eye and he nodded. It was going to be a risky pregnancy and there was a chance the baby wouldn't make it and even if it did that there could be issues, but Zach was twelve, and Rosie going on eleven. The kids were old enough to be a part of this journey.

"We have something to tell you two," Laura told their kids.

"Is something wrong with Dad?" Zach asked.

"No, honey. Dad really is going to be okay."

When both kids looked at him for confirmation, he nodded. "Come and sit down." He patted the bed on the other side of him from where Laura was sitting.

"So, what's going on?" Zach asked when he and his sister sat down.

"Well," Laura said, the first smile he'd seen since he'd woken up slowly spread across her face. Now that she knew that he was going to retire and that he was going to be okay, the reality that they were having a baby was no doubt sinking in. "I'm pregnant."

* * * * *

3:05 P.M.

They all needed this.

The whole family hanging out together, celebrating Sophie's sixteenth birthday. Well, almost the whole family since Jack was still in the hospital and Laura was with him, but his parents were here, and Mark and his family, Paige and her family, Xavier and his family.

Ryan didn't know how many more days like this they'd have. His parents were getting older, and his mom's health had been shaky lately. But today wasn't the time to worry about that. Today was just about enjoying and celebrating family.

Family.

That was the most important thing in the world.

It was what life was all about.

He was so thankful that, while Tessa Bell's family had been decimated, she was dead, her son was dead, and of her two best friends one was dead and the other had been forced to kill her son, his family had survived. Wyatt had somehow managed to figure out where PJ was, Ryan had no doubt it was because Isaac Worthington had tracked the kid, and when Wyatt went to confront him and convince him to turn himself in, PJ had pulled a gun on him.

Although they had found the killer and he was dead now, the case felt like a failure. They hadn't saved Tessa. They hadn't saved Melanie Gardner, Elizabeth Landry, Lucas Mianta, and Cassandra Stanton. They had saved Kelita McNamara and the Abbott family, as well as the other three people who had been on PJ's list, assuming he intended to kill someone every day until his birthday where he committed murder suicide, so that was some small victory.

Today was supposed to have been PJ Bell's sixteenth birthday as well as Sophie's. He had died just one day short of reaching it. Ryan hoped that wherever PJ was now, he had finally found the peace he so desperately sought. And hopefully, Tessa had been reunited with her husband in death.

The Bell family was suffering while his was celebrating. It didn't seem fair, but oftentimes life wasn't fair. You had to make the most of what you had while you had it because you never knew when it could be gone.

Which was why he had come to a decision.

"Just tell her," Sofia said sidling up to him.

His gaze found Paige, who was talking and laughing with Daisy. "I'm not sure I can," he said.

"She'll understand," Sofia said.

Ryan was sure his wife was right. Paige would understand his decision, but that didn't make telling her any easier.

"You can't put it off forever," Sofia reminded him. "You can't even put it off for long. You have to tell her."

How did you tell the person who had been a part of your life every day for almost twenty years, who you trusted to have your back in any and all situations, who was your best friend and not just your partner, that it was over? That you were leaving the job you loved because that love had dulled until it wasn't the bright and shiny thing it had once been.

"You should do it now, get it over with, but it's up to you," Sofia told him then walked across the room and started talking to his parents.

She was right.

He should just do it.

Get it over with.

With a deep breath, Ryan headed for Paige. She saw him coming and immediately, apprehension crossed her face. It was like what he was going to tell her was written all over his face and she knew what he was going to say even before he said anything.

"Can we talk?" he asked when he got to her.

"Sure." Paige nodded.

They left Daisy and walked to a quiet corner of the living room at his parents' house. The kids were all outside in the pool, while the adults had all remained inside, out of the persistent heat. He liked summer, but the unrelenting heat this year was making him look forward to fall.

"What's up?" Paige asked.

He may as well just say it. "Sofia and I talked, and we decided that it's time for me to leave the police force. I spoke to Skylar Wyatt about working with him at his security firm. The hours are more conducive to spending more time at home, and it's safer. They mostly do some bodyguard work, security at functions, that kind of thing. Wyatt offered to let me take over the business. With everything that's happened, he says he doesn't know what he's going to do, but he knows it's not keep working. I never thought it would, but the idea of less pressure is kind of appealing. And with everything Sophie has been through, I feel like she needs more time with Sofia and me. With our crazy hours, it's hard to give her that."

A huge smile broke out on Paige's face.

Not the reaction he'd been expecting.

"Umm, okay," he said, feeling a little offended that Paige was apparently pleased with the idea of getting a new partner.

"I'm so relieved you said it first," Paige told him.

"First?"

"I've been feeling the same way. I spoke to Elias the night of the explosion and told him that I wanted to retire. And last night I talked to Wyatt too. He told me the same thing. So, it looks like we're still going to be partners, only this time business partners," she said, her grin growing bigger.

Relief washed over him.

He'd been so worried about hurting Paige's feelings and the whole time it looked like she had been worried about the exact same thing.

"I'm so excited," Paige said.

"So am I," Ryan said. Things were going to work out even

better than he'd been expecting. Working with Paige on this new venture would be so much better than working on it on his own, and he already knew the two of them worked well together.

"Come here, partner," he said, giving Paige a hug.

More time with his family and starting a new business venture with his best friend, Ryan didn't think life could get better than this.

* * * * *

5:55 P.M.

"Did you do it?" Xavier asked Annabelle when he found her in the kitchen, tidying up the mess the kids had left behind so that Mr. and Mrs. Xander wouldn't have to do it. He'd been looking for her all over the house, but he should have known she would be in here where she could be alone.

When they had first met, Annabelle hadn't really had any friends. Although he had tried to fit her into his circle of friends, it had never worked. Even when he had transferred to work out of this precinct, and he had made new friends, she hadn't been able to connect with them. It had taken her a long time to gain enough self-confidence to let people into her life.

Today, though, he knew that wasn't the problem.

She was just nervous.

They both were.

"No, I didn't," Annabelle replied.

"Go do it," he said, nudging her with his shoulder toward the downstairs bathroom.

"It's probably too soon," she protested.

"You're a week late," he reminded her.

"I just don't want you to get your hopes up. It could be nothing." From the look in her white eyes—which were actually a very pale blue, but appeared white—he knew that she was worried about *both* of them getting their hopes up.

Xavier wrapped his arms around her and drew her against his chest. "If it never happens again for us, I'm fine with that," he told her, and he meant it. He wanted another kid, but whether they got pregnant or they adopted he didn't care.

"All right, I'll take the test," she said, picking up her bag and heading into the bathroom.

He waited nervously outside the door and the second he heard the flush of the toilet, he went in. They had taken enough pregnancy tests over the last few years that he knew it took a couple of minutes to get the results.

"I got a call from the department," he said as Annabelle washed her hands.

"Oh, yeah?"

"They offered me a promotion to lieutenant," he announced.

"They did?" Annabelle spun around and beamed at him. She knew that he had been hoping to get that job.

"It'll mean more paperwork and less field work, but I think at this point in my career and my life, I'm good with that."

"Did you take the job?"

"I did."

"I'm so happy for you." Annabelle threw her arms around his neck and hugged him hard. He loved that she was much more demonstrative now than when they'd first gotten together. He'd had to work to earn her trust, and there had been a few bumps along the way from both their sides, but now their marriage was rock solid.

"Check the test," he murmured into her hair. He had a good feeling about this.

Slowly, Annabelle let go of him and picked up the stick.

Immediately, her gaze flew to his. "It's positive."

"Positive?" He hardly dared to believe it.

"We're having a baby." She giggled, once again throwing herself into his arms. "Let's go tell everyone."

"You don't want to wait a few weeks, until you're farther along?"

"Uh-uh," she shook her head, already grabbing his hand and dragging him out of the bathroom, down the hall, and back into the living room where everyone looked over as they burst through the door. "We're pregnant," Annabelle announced without preamble, holding up the test.

A chorus of congratulations sounded around the room, and Mark Xander laughed. "Perfect timing, Laura is pregnant too."

"That's even better," Annabelle practically squealed. Their twins were a few years younger than the rest of their friends' kids, so he knew Annabelle would be thrilled that their baby would be the same age as Jack and Laura's.

As everyone came over to hug and congratulate them some more, Xavier found his gaze fixed on his wife's glowing face.

Fifteen years ago, he walked into a house in the middle of the night, expecting to find an entire family slaughtered. Instead, he'd found Annabelle—unconscious, but alive—and that had started the greatest journey his life had ever taken.

Now he was happily married, with five-year-old twins about to start their journey at school, and a new baby on the way who would soon be starting the biggest journey of all.

Life.

It wasn't always easy. More times than not it was a bumpy path full of obstacles. But when you fought through those obstacles and never gave up, you ended up with more than you could ever have hoped for.

Nothing stayed the same forever.

Change was inevitable.

It was scary. It was exhilarating. It was what made life worth living.

It's been said that "time heals all wounds."

In his experience, this was both true and untrue.

Wounds from past traumas never really healed. They left

behind scars, but those scars made you into the person you were. They showed your strength. They showed your perseverance. They showed your determination. They showed your resilience, and they showed your capacity for love and faith and hope.

He and his wife and his friends had been through a lot. They had all suffered, and they'd all grown from what they had been through into the people they were today.

Xavier thought scars were the most beautiful part of a person's journey through life.

Jane has loved reading and writing since she can remember. She writes dark and disturbing crime/mystery/suspense with some romance thrown in because, well, who doesn't love romance?! She has several series including the complete Detective Parker Bell series, the Count to Ten series, the Christmas Romantic Suspense series, and the Flashes of Fate series of novelettes.

When she's not writing Jane loves to read, bake, go to the beach, ski, horse ride, and watch Disney movies. She has a black belt in Taekwondo, a 200+ collection of teddy bears, and her favorite color is pink. She has the world's two most sweet and pretty Dalmatians, Ivory and Pearl. Oh, and she also enjoys spending time with family and friends!

To connect and keep up to date please visit any of the following

Amazon – http://www.amazon.com/author/janeblythe
BookBub – https://www.bookbub.com/authors/jane-blythe
Email – mailto:janeblytheauthor@gmail.com
Facebook – http://www.facebook.com/janeblytheauthor
Goodreads – http://www.goodreads.com/author/show/6574160.Jane_Blythe
Instagram – http://www.instagram.com/jane_blythe_author
Reader Group – http://www.facebook.com/groups/janeskillersweethearts
Twitter – http://www.twitter.com/jblytheauthor
Website – http://www.janeblythe.com.au

sic enim dilexit Deus mundum ut Filium suum unigenitum daret ut omnis qui credit in eum habeat vitam aeternam

www.ingramcontent.com/pod-product-compliance
Lightning Source LLC
Chambersburg PA
CBHW031549240626
47153CB00002B/441